PENGUIN BOOKS
PE

Susan Moody was
lived in Paris and th
returning to Englan
vious novels are *Pe*
ful, Penny Royal an
the current Chairman of the Crime
and is on the Executive Committee of the International
Association of Crime Writers.

PENNY PINCHING

Susan Moody

PENGUIN BOOKS

For Jonathon Bertsch

PENGUIN BOOKS

Published by the Penguin Group
27 Wrights Lane, London W8 5TZ, England
Viking Penguin Inc., 40 West 23rd Street, New York, New York 10010, USA
Penguin Books Australia Ltd, Ringwood, Victoria, Australia
Penguin Books Canada Ltd, 2801 John Street, Markham, Ontario, Canada L3R 1B4
Penguin Books (NZ) Ltd, 182–190 Wairau Road, Auckland 10, New Zealand

Penguin Books Ltd, Registered Offices: Harmondsworth, Middlesex, England

First published in Great Britain by Michael Joseph 1989
Published in Penguin Books 1990
1 3 5 7 9 10 8 6 4 2

Printed and bound in Great Britain by
Richard Clay Ltd, Bungay, Suffolk

1

She was tall.

She was black.

She was beautiful.

And she was very dead.

It wasn't necessary to touch her to know. It was obvious that the stuff all over her white-beaded corn-row braids was blood. And brains. Lots of them. Even Albert Einstein didn't have that many spare grey cells.

Barnaby gagged. Inside his chest, some major organ was looking for the way out into the open air. His heart, probably, desperately trying to recover from the shock. When he'd walked over to the window, coffee-cup in hand, he'd anticipated a panoramic view of the ocean off Big Sur. He'd expected to see whitecaps out there in the blue. A glimpse of seals or sea-otters. A guillemot or two. Maybe even the grey whales on their way down to warmer waters. It was the right time of year.

What he'd got was a thick sea-mist.

And the girl lying out there on the deck.

In death, she still had one of the sexiest bodies he'd ever seen. She lay on her back, tumbled between the redwood barrels of plants: camellias, bird-of-paradise, trailing ivy. She was wearing the bottom half of a high-cut white bikini which triangled into the cleft of her thighs. A twist of black hair showed above the top of it, where the dark flesh of her stomach disappeared beneath the white Lycra. Her nipples pointed up into the mist. One hand lay pressed up against the bricks of the built-in barbecue. The other lay across her breast, fingers splayed in an obscene parody of sexual invitation. There was a big gold ring on one of them. Her mouth smiled.

That really bothered him. Someone she knew, liked, had held her close, then slammed something hard and heavy down on her head, splitting open her skull so the contents leaked out. He gagged again. He could taste the shrimps soused in garlic sauce that they'd eaten the night before. He put his hand over his mouth; otherwise he'd have thrown up. Death wasn't a condition he was familiar with. He remembered Grandfather Midas, waxy-yellow in a satin-lined coffin. White candles cutting into the cold air of the funeral parlour. White flowers, lilies and carnations. The black workers standing round, singing something soft and sad in their buttered-toffee voices. But that had been long ago and was buried deep. There was a smudge of sand on one of her long long legs.

'Oh my God,' he said. 'Penny.'

He could feel the shakes beginning at the back of his knees.

'Penny,' he said again.

Her toenails were painted silver. Even in the opaque lemon light, he could see the green flecks in it. He had bought the nail varnish only last week, at Gumps in San Francisco. The contents had writhed like heavy smoke when he shook it, the sparks of green tinsel floating up from the depths to shimmer against the glass. Just a fun present. One of those little tokens to show Penny he never stopped thinking of her. That he loved her.

'Penny.' His voice was no louder this time. She was indubitably dead. She wouldn't be disturbed however much noise he made. Yet noise still seemed out of place. A desecration.

He knew he couldn't go on standing here for the rest of the day, peering out into the murky opalescence. Action would have to be taken. Police called. And undertakers. Funeral homes. Or would the cops deal with that?

If there was one thing he was wary of, it was cops. He'd had too many brushes with them in the past. Too many reasons why they might want him to help them with their enquiries. Especially if what they were enquiring into was the whereabouts of any one of a number of high-class collectables. Silver. Gold. Bank-notes. Stuff like that. Or jewels.

Though, he reminded himself, the local Police Department was hardly likely to tab him as an old lag. Not on first viewing. There was the Etonian accent, for a start. At home in London, it was as good as a platinum American Express card, even though out here on the West Coast they weren't usually able to differentiate between it and something from the East End. Sometimes, in fact, he was asked if he was Australian, for God's sake. Which didn't alter the fact that he would be the first to fall under suspicion. The man on the spot always was. And standing there in Dr Benjamin Wanawake's California beach house, if ever there was a spot, Barnaby was aware that he was on it. Nor did he doubt that the LAPD, or whatever PD it was here, would probe into his past in the course of their investigations. They'd liaise with their English counterparts. Scotland Yard. Thus uncovering his not-terribly hidden past. Although he went to school at Eton, it was in Parkhurst Prison, Isle of Wight, that he received his education. Not that he regretted the stretch he'd been sent down for. The main trouble with doing time was that ever afterwards the time you'd done hung round you like one of those dreadful shirts made of nettles that Teutonic virgins were always running up in Grimm's Fairy Tales and the like: once on, only the kiss of another virgin could remove it. Except the Brothers Grimm had fouled up. Got the facts wrong. Because though he'd kissed quite a few virgins of one sex or another in his time, none of them had removed the indelible stain of his prison record. Which was why, although he was over here on perfectly legit business connected with the big Antiques Fair being held up in San Francisco, he was still kind of leery about calling the fuzz. If the English police decided to pass on his F-11/40, he'd be in irons before he could say 'Habeas corpus'.

But he'd have to call them. He had no choice.

Thank God he wasn't here on his own.

He turned away from the dead girl out there in the mist. *She died young.* Someone had written that about another dead girl. He supposed he ought to cover her face. Find a sheet or something. It seemed wrong to leave her there to stare up at the invisible sky.

'Hey,' he said. This time he did raise his voice.

'Mmm?' The person on the big double bed humped over, dragging the bedclothes out from under the mattress. From where he stood, Barnaby could see a single bare foot, a rhomboid of sanded pine flooring, the rose-budded sheet. Red ones. Red roses for a black lady. The shock of his first sight of her was still there inside his head, beating at his skull, hammering to get out. The pain was so intense that when he first reached the window – three minutes ago? three years? – and seen what was lying out there, he'd thought he would keel over. There was absolutely no way he could handle a Pennyless future. In that first stunned incredulous moment, he'd seen grief, loss, loneliness. He could still feel the panic, knowing that without Penny he couldn't survive. Not whole. Not as he wanted to be.

'Get your ass out here,' he said.

'Why?'

'There's something you better see.'

'I know what I want to see. Why don't you bring it right back in here and show it to me?'

'No.'

Something in his voice reached the girl on the bed. She slid out from under the rose-spotted sheets and came into the long living room.

She was tall.

She was black.

She was beautiful.

She was very much alive.

Penny Wanawake. Her stomach was firm, her breasts elegant. In the weighty light coming through the early-morning windows, her skin gleamed. He never failed to get a thrill out of that long lean body.

'What goes on?' she said. Her mouth smiled.

Barnaby stepped to one side. Penny took in the topaz-tinged mist. The plants, their leaves wet with moisture. The body.

'Jesus Christ,' she said.

'Or something.'

'Is she – uh – is she dead?'

'Yes.'

'You sure?'

'Take another look,' Barnaby said. 'I'm sure.'

Penny stepped closer to the window. She was silent for a moment. Then she said, 'This is unreal. Bizarre.'

'Yeah.'

'Who is she? *Was*.'

'You may find this kind of incredible, but I don't know.'

Penny snicked the catch. She slid open the glass doors and stepped outside. The air was dankly chill, sun-suffused but still opaque. Her bare feet made black footmarks in the mist-drops on the wooden deck. The mist packaged her like a Christmas present, pressing tightly back into the spaces she made as she moved. The cold sea smell of it sidled up her nose. Somewhere far away a fog-horn sounded bereft. At her feet, the dead girl smiled. However many times Penny closed her eyes and opened them again, the body just stayed there. How could a smile stay in place after death? Or was it like a baby's smile, the product of escaping gases?

Don't think like that. About death. Decay. The process of rotting.

Especially not when the person doing the rotting could have been your twin sister. Well, almost. At first glance. A second one reduced the likeness to similarities of bone-structure and skin-colour rather

4

than a fundamental resemblance. Nonetheless, a casual observer would easily mistake one girl for the other.

Mist wraithed the redwood rail around the deck. Penny bent to look closer at the wound. The girl's hair was pearled with tiny drops of water. From the right angle, it looked almost white. She lifted one slim brown arm. It was very cold. When she let go, it fell away from her grasp, flaccid, the meat shrunk away from the skin which covered it. Not recently dead, then.

Without straightening, Penny looked up at Barnaby, standing in the doorway. 'How'd she get here?' she said.

'Pass.'

'She remind you of anyone?'

'Yeah.'

'Me too.' She looked once more at the girl. 'More than remind. If I looked in a mirror, that's almost what I'd see looking back at me. She could just about be my double.'

'All those black girls look the same to me.'

'Like you honkie men do to us sisters.'

Barnaby began to shiver violently although behind the mist there was heat. 'Oh Jesus, Pen. What's going on?'

'Whatever it is, I can tell already I don't like it much.'

He stepped out on to the misty deck. 'Come here.'

Penny went.

He put his arms close around her. So close her lungs were squashed. Didn't matter. She wouldn't have been breathing right anyway. A dead girl. Her own sort of age. Gone. Finished. She thought: *Cover her face; she died young.*

'I thought it was you,' Barnaby whispered into her hair. 'I knew it couldn't be. I knew you were back there in bed. But I still thought it was you.'

'Is it accidental,' Penny said, 'that she looks like me?'

'Seems unlikely.'

'Is that why she's dead?'

Barnaby said nothing.

Penny took in a deep, deep breath. Who'd want her dead? She'd never done anything to hurt anybody, had she? A few bad jokes. A certain amount of indecorousness. But nothing that deserved the death penalty. She thought of the muggers who killed for two quid and an Irish penny. Was there a moral equivalent that might provoke a person into murder?

Barnaby let her go and sat down on the damp cushions of the swinging seat. His face was white, the lack of colour emphasising the freckles which went with his red hair. 'I really thought it was you,' he said. His voice shook. He drank some of his cold coffee and made a face of disgust.

'If someone offed her in mistake for me,' said Penny, 'why was she here in the first place? What did she have in mind to do, before she got killed?'

'Must have come by car.' Barnaby leaned back and squinted round the edge of the house. Close to the cliff, the mist was no more than a thin veil. There was nothing to see up on the hard-top parking near the road. Which was hardly surprising. With the subsidence round there, if you parked too close to the edge, you were liable to find by next morning that your car had floated halfway to Hawaii.

'Natch,' said Penny, 'no other way to get out here.'

'And she couldn't have hitched a ride,' Barnaby said, 'not in that outfit.'

'Somebody better go call the cops.'

'Somebody?'

'You. While I take a look around.' Penny walked towards the corner of the house, where steps led from the deck up to the hard standing.

'You going to look around like that?' Barnaby said.

'What's wrong with me?' She looked back at him over her shoulder.

'Far as I'm concerned, not one damned thing. But anyone driving past is probably not prepared for several feet of black lady standing stark naked in the driveway.'

'Six,' Penny said.

'Six what?'

'Feet.'

'And every one of them on show.'

'OK.' Leaving wet prints behind her, Penny padded back inside the house and across to the bedroom. She came out again, wrestling her way into a jumbo T-shirt. A four-letter word was printed in bold black capitals across the front. As she crossed the deck, she paused to look briefly down again at the face so like her own. She began climbing the steps up to the hard-top. Barnaby watched her for a moment. He went in and dialled the police. Then he followed her.

'Did you get the police?' she asked. Her voice wavered. Her eyes took on a glassy shine. He knew she was holding back shock-tears.

'Yes,' he said. 'They reckoned it'd take them at least half an hour

6

to get here. The highway's blocked solid with traffic heading down the coast.'

'Good.' Penny swallowed.

'What's good about it?'

'Gives us time to poke around. Check things out. See what's what.'

'I've seen all the what I want to see,' said Barnaby.

'You realise what this means?' Penny said.

'Sure I do. A pretty girl's just been knocked off right outside our back door.'

'Is the resemblance to me deliberate? That's what I really need to know. Or is it maybe something to do with my father?' She frowned. Benjamin Wanawake had been staying at the house himself until a couple of days before. They'd been expecting to have some time together with him but he'd been called back to San Francisco before they could join up with him.

'Don't know,' Barnaby said. He put his arm round her shoulders. 'Honey, you're asking the wrong person. Until we find out more, we just don't know the answers.'

'That nail varnish . . .'

'Gumps was having a promotion. She could have bought some too. Probably doesn't mean a thing.'

'Except that she might be from San Francisco.'

'Unless she's visiting. Same as we are.'

'The thing of it is, maybe she was killed because someone thought she *was* me.'

'Why would anyone want to kill you, sweetheart? You can be kinda feisty if you miss out on your three square meals a day but apart from that . . .'

'How did she get here?' Penny said. 'And why doesn't she have any baggage?'

'What I want to know is, what kind of a girl goes calling in half a bikini in the middle of the night?'

'You talking social breeding?' said Penny. 'Or motivation?'

'I mean, not even you would be that dozy.'

'Thanks.'

'Perhaps she was planning one of these life exchanges. A complete takeover from Tampax to tennies.'

'You need the agreement of the other party for one of those.'

'If you're right, if she *was* here for some specific reason to do with you, what would she have done if you hadn't played ball?'

7

They looked at each other. 'What would *you* do?' said Penny.

'I don't know. Would I knock you off?'

'Maybe. Maybe not. She isn't all that like me. Couldn't really pass for genuine Wanawake.'

'Except to someone who didn't know you.'

'Jeez.' Penny brushed her hands together. It hid the fact that they seemed kind of trembly all of a sudden. 'No bags, no ID. But I guess if you were going to assume someone else's identity, you'd want to have as little of your own previous identity hanging round your neck as possible, wouldn't you?'

'Sure. Even so, she must have had some nerve to be travelling in a bikini at midnight,' said Barnaby.

'Half a bikini.'

'Suppose the traffic-cops stopped them.'

'Them?'

'Stands to reason there must have been someone else involved. Someone had to've driven her out here and dropped her off.'

'Unless she hid her car somewhere along the route and walked the rest of the way.'

'Dressed like that?'

'Mmm . . .' Penny tried to imagine it. 'Weird. And even weirder is that once she got here, someone else should have turned up and killed her.'

'Why bother to wait until she was out here?' Barnaby walked across to the edge of the cliff and looked out to where the sea would be if the mist wasn't in the way. Somewhere beyond it, a gull screeched. Others screeched back.

'Either,' said Penny, 'they didn't realise you and I were coming down. Or else . . .'

'Yeah?'

'The killer thought she was me.'

At the cliff-edge, Barnaby turned. 'Tell you what's bothering me,' he said.

'What's that?'

'If you're right, what's he going to do when he finds out he screwed up on the ID?'

'Come after me again, I should think.'

'What do we do when he shows up?'

'We go get him.'

Barnaby kicked at a loose stone. It disappeared into the mist. He hunched his shoulders. 'Would you say I was good at my job?'

'The best.'

8

'OK, so there's some would call it operating on the wrong side of the law . . .'

'A lot more than some.'

'. . . but I only steal from those that can afford it. And the money goes to a good cause.' He didn't bother mentioning the little extra bits and pieces that sometimes disappeared along with the insured diamonds he was so adept at removing from their rightful owners. 'But murder – that's heavy. That's *serious*.'

'Yeah.'

'I don't get any kind of a kick out of dead bodies, you know,' he said.

'Hey,' Penny said softly. 'Hey.'

He turned. She walked towards him. 'Neither do I,' she said. 'But I get a kick out of you.'

Across her breasts shimmied the four big letters. He took his time reading them. L. O. V. E., they said. They moved into each other's arms. Held each other. Tightly.

Inside the house, the telephone began to cry.

2

By the time Penny reached it, it had stopped ringing.

'Perhaps it was the cops,' Barnaby said, 'saying they can't make it after all.' He could feel his insides beginning to clench. He wished he hadn't seen so many movies where someone is thrown into jail and has a hell of a job proving his innocence. Particularly since he couldn't remember when he'd last been innocent.

On the deck, the dead girl still lay sprawled. Penny tried not to look at her. When a person travels all the way from Chelsea to California for a vacation, when a person really needs a break after five arduous months on safari taking photographs for a major exhibition plus setting *up* that exhibition, the very last thing a person wants is a corpse on their hands. Let alone a corpse that is practically their twin. She wished she could figure out why anyone would want to impersonate her, if that, indeed, was what the girl had planned to do. Deep down, round about where her stomach left off being her stomach and became her appendix, she felt a niggle of apprehension. Was this, in fact, nothing to do with her at all? Some kind of vicious reprisal? Had Barnaby Midas, South-African-born antique dealer, art thief and conman, been up to something? He'd been so keen on this trip. Insisted that he had to attend. All the top dealers would be there, he'd said, and there'd be some magnificent jewels coming with the French contingent. He'd even managed to get himself on to one of the organising committees, nearly a year ago. He'd had to fly over on committee business several times since then which gave him plenty of opportunity, if he wanted to set something up.

She loved him. Absolutely. She might not trust him with her jewel case, but she would with her life. And her heart. Yet she was always conscious of the fact that if you were trying to describe his morals, loose was probably as useful a word as you were going to come up with. Not that she minded. Her own were nothing to preach a sermon about. On the other hand, she didn't have a criminal record as well. Barnaby did. He'd told her once that he'd been known as a hard man during his time in Parkhurst. He'd said it was the only way to survive. Suppose some other Parkhurst alumnus was now after him, seeking revenge. On the whole, ex-cons with a grievance tended not to be the types who would listen nicely if you tried to explain that the Lord had definitely cornered the vengeance market. Or had he tried some kind of sucker deal with the antiques he'd brought over from England for the Fair? She'd always thought that where antiques were concerned, he was an honest broker. Maybe he wasn't. Maybe the demand for old-type stuff was so great that he'd been tempted from the narrow path of righteousness. Nobody said it wasn't easy. Or it might be that one of the people he'd robbed in the past had recognised him and had planned to revenge themselves in some deeply subtle way.

Come on, she told herself. Subtle-wise, a dead body was a bit over the top.

While Barnaby showered, she stuck a disc into the CD player. Brahms's Requiem. She waited for the first sonorous chords. Then unstuck it. With the girl out there dead, music, even appropriate music, was out of place. In the kitchen she set water boiling, squeezed oranges via the Juice-O-Matic, popped bread into the toaster. A person had to eat. Especially a six-footer. Thinking about how much eating a six-footer had to do, she put a couple of frozen Danishes into the microwave. No sense going hungry. Wouldn't help the girl out there in the mist.

She leaned against the counter and closed her eyes for a moment. She didn't believe too much in God. Only in Man. On the other hand, just in case there was a Someone up there somewhere, she floated a bit of heartfelt thanks that even though it was apparently meant to be, it wasn't her out there dead. Nor Barnaby. And added a plea that it wouldn't be in the near future, either.

'Never saw her before in my life, man,' Barnaby said. He sat with his legs stretched out in front of him, crossed elegantly at the knee. Penny saw a Mickey Mouse on the ankle of his black silk socks. Where'd he bought those?

'Even though she could be Miss – uh – Wanawake's twin sister?' asked the detective who sat at the table, staring at the two of them. He pronounced Penny's name wrong, even though she'd said it slowly, emphasising all four syllables. He had the blank-eyed look of a man who has trafficked too long with death. Doctors often have it. It signals that the heart no longer cares. Someone ought to tell him that when death becomes commonplace, it's time to shut up shop and go home. This didn't seem the right time.

'Could have been,' said Penny, 'but wasn't. I don't have a sister. And merely because, when you think about it, merely because she looks a bit like me's no reason why I should ever have seen her before.'

'It's just it has to be more than some kind of weird coincidence, doesn't it?' insisted the detective. He'd told them his name was Fredo Santini. He sounded as they were supposed to recognise it. They didn't.

'What does?'

'That there's a stiff right out there on the deck who looks near as dammit like one of the people sitting right here in this room.'

'But not ex*act*ly like.' Penny set her dimples to work. She wasn't too keen on wasting them on turkeys like Santini but she knew Barnaby was getting edgy. Worrying about his darn criminal record. She moved into her British mode. 'I mean, if this young woman was hoping to impersonate me, for some reason that neither Mr Midas nor myself can at present comprehend, she'd have had a hard time. Because quite frankly, she'd never be able to pass. Not now.' Her Majesty could hardly have done it better.

The cop was wearing man-made fibres. Both cut and colour caused Penny's blood to race. 'What're you saying?' he said. 'Not now?'

'Saying it used to be I had braids, too. Just like . . . her.' Beyond the picture window, men were kneeling round the dead girl. One of them had a videotape back-pack. He kept lifting the camera above his head and firing off ten-second bursts. She put a hand on the back of her neck. She lifted the mass of hair which hung there and let it fall again. The change was still recent enough for her to miss the white beads which used to rest against her face. And being able to swing them about when she got mad, make them clash against each other. 'I changed hairstyles a couple of days ago.'

'My wife'd *love* to know the name of your hair-stylist,' simpered Santini, leaning on the sarcastic button. 'Jesus.' He raised exasperated eyes to the ceiling. 'Look, lady. I'm a helluva lot more interested in knowing who that is out there than in swapping beauty hints.' He let his eyes linger on the neck of the white singlet Penny wore tucked into white jeans. It was a real practised linger. It reduced Equal Rights legislation to a mockery. Likewise the 14th Amendment. It made her wonder how he'd treat her if he had her alone in an interrogation room with a length of rubber hose in his hand.

12

'Keep in touch,' she said. 'We are too.'

'Anyway,' he said, 'how do I know you aren't the fake and she's the person you're pretending to be?'

Penny frowned. 'I need to work on that one.'

'You *don't* know,' said Barnaby.

'So what's to stop me hauling you both in on —'

'But there are plenty who do.'

'Name one.' Santini reached for a packet of Marlboros and tapped one out on to the table. Penny'd already asked him not to smoke. She'd explained that one whiff of tobacco and she became a raging animal not responsible for her actions. She opened her mouth to say it again. He saw her. He replaced the cigarette in the packet and the packet in his pocket. He took out a plastic pen.

'The owner of this house, for starters,' Penny said.

'Who's he?'

'His name's Wanawake, like mine,' said Penny. Again she gave all four syllables equal weighting. 'Dr Benjamin. Works at the UN.'

'Isn't that some kind of crap organisation trying for global peace or something?'

'That's one way of putting it.'

'What the hell's the point of world peace when we got war on the streets?' said Santini. 'Only way we'll ever keep the inner-city areas safe for ordinary citizens is when we got four times the cops we got at present.' It was a beef he'd obviously aired many times before. Why was it that wherever you went, the fuzz always saw things through bigot-coloured spectacles? Must be because they saw more of the dark underside of humanity. Walk down too many mean streets and you end up mean yourself.

'I bet you'd bring back disembowelling,' Penny said.

'So would you, lady, you saw some of the animals out there.' He tapped his pen on the table. 'I'll tell you what I think.' He paused. Maybe so they could congratulate him on being able to.

'What do you think?' said Barnaby.

'Fuck world peace. That's my honest-to-God opinion. Fuck it.'

'Good of you to share that thought with us today,' Penny said.

'World fucking peace.' Santini turned to look at the men out on the deck. 'Jeez.' He shook his head.

'My father, luckily, doesn't agree with you.' Penny used her prim voice. The one that went with a wimple and demurely cast-down eyes. She leaned forward and prissily straightened a pile of auction-house catalogues. Wherever he went, Barnaby dropped a trail of them like fancy fewmets.

13

'Your father,' said the cop. 'That's this Benjamin Wanawake, right?'

'Right.'

Santini reached inside his jacket for a flip-up notebook then turned his head towards the bustle centred round the body outside. 'Married man, is he?'

'Very.'

'Happily married?'

'Yes, thank you.'

'So he wouldn't be the kinda guy gets a kick out of something on the side?'

'If you mean a mistress,' Penny said with what she hoped was dignity but felt more like indignation, 'certainly not.'

'You'd know, of course.'

'So would you, you'd met my father.'

'Where would we get in touch with him?'

'At the Sheraton-Regis, in San Francisco.'

'Where they had those jewel robberies a couple days ago?' Santini paused meaningfully in the middle of writing it down. He shrank his eyes to thin lines on either side of his face, as though he thought that if he did it for long enough, someone would break down and confess.

'I do hope you're not implying that my father had something to do with them,' Penny said. From the way she said it, no one would have guessed how her heart had lurched.

'Not yet, I'm not.' The pencil tapped again. 'There's one thing kinda bothers me, though.'

'What's that, officer?'

'How come you didn't hear anything? Either of you?'

'It doesn't make much noise,' said Barnaby. 'Killing someone.'

'She was hit on the head,' said Santini. 'That's noisy.'

'If she wasn't expecting it? If she thought the person who hit her was a friend? Or more. It would only take a couple of thumps to finish her.'

'Even so, there musta bin cars driving about. Maybe a bit of screaming. And the body being dumped on the deck – you ought to've heard something.'

'We only got here late last night,' Penny said.

'So?'

'I'd say she was killed some time before that. Like maybe a couple of days ago.'

'Oh, you would, huh?'

14

'Yeah.' Treat a sarcastic question like it was genuine and it took the heart right out of it.

'And I suppose you know all there is to know about dead broads, huh?'

'Not all. But some. Not just broads, either.'

'How come?'

Because I was the one, cheesebreath, who found Monsignor Capet in the swing at Hurley Court, thought Penny. I was the one who identified Marfa Lund in the LA morgue. I was the one who found handsome Kendal Sartain with the dead goose at his side. I was the one who – the *hell* with it. Each time she met up with it, death looked her in the eye with an ever-colder stare.

She didn't say any of that. She played it cool. Smiled kind of enigmatically. 'Let's just say I've been unlucky,' she said.

It worked. Santini changed the subject. Which was fine. One thing she hated to do was remember those times. And the others. 'So you didn't look outside when you got here?' he said.

'No reason to. It was dark. We were tired. We ate and went to bed, said Barnaby.

'After listening to some music,' Penny said.

'Is that all?'

It wasn't but neither Barnaby or Penny was going to explain. *Carmina Burana.* Music to boff by. They had suited action to sound. As the music had climaxed, so had they. It took the edge off the memory to think that while they were doing so, the girl had been lying out there in her shroud of mist.

The detective stood up. His clothes settled themselves round his body. Free of wrinkles. Free of class, too. Lester Polyester. He walked towards the door and looked out at the activity taking place on the deck.

'So what's your father – this big cheese in the peace game, right? –'

Penny nodded.

'– what's he doing in San Francisco?'

'Various things. Some official, some not. Mainly he's flown in from the East Coast to visit with an old friend of his.'

'Who's the friend?'

'Guy called Pilot Whitman. Owns a couple of restaurants up there. You ought to be able to get hold of my father at the Sheraton-Regis. If not, he'll probably be at Whitman's place in the Napa Valley. I have the numbers somewhere.'

Out on the deck the police surgeon stood up. The two other officers who had hunkered down beside him looked up expectantly.

15

He said something, writing quickly in a notebook. They nodded. One of them got up and disappeared round the side of the house. He came back with a collapsible gurney. They rolled the girl's body on to it.

The mist was receding. Penny could make out the green-blue of the ocean now. Surfers in black wet-suits were standing thigh-high at the water's edge. A whitecap or two sparkled in sunshine she couldn't yet see. What she could see was people. Lots of them. Down on the beach. Staring up at the house. Their bodies had that curious cast compounded of avidity and relief which afflicts even the most compassionate in the face of another's misfortune. Not me, today, thank the Lord. Not me. So much for Barnaby's suggestion that they get away from it all for a couple of days, before the Antique Dealers' shindig got started.

Any man's death diminishes me, Penny thought. How much more so does a woman's? She wondered who the girl out there had been: where she lived, who she'd loved, who had loved her. Was she white hat or black? She'd probably never know.

Unless Santini chose to keep her informed. She watched as he slid open the door to the deck. He stepped out and closed it behind him. He peered back into the room, like a biologist examining an entirely new life-form. Still watching Penny and Barnaby, he spoke to his men.

'Lovable guy, isn't he?' Barnaby said.

'Intensely.' Penny put her hand on his thigh. 'And a long way from dumb.'

'Very.'

'For instance, he knows about that jewel heist at our hotel, although, way I understood it, Security killed it before it even reached ground-floor level.'

'Clever fellow,' said Barnaby. Very non-committal.

'Were you involved?'

'*Moi?*'

'Don't bullshit me, Midas. Yes or no?'

'I'm pleading the 5th Amendment.'

'Yes, then.' She shook her head. 'No wonder you're getting so antsy.'

'What makes you say that?'

'I live with you. Remember?'

'Always.'

'Just as a matter of interest, where's the haul?'

'Just as a matter of interest, I don't know.'

'But you did.'

'Two days ago, as you so astutely guessed, it was in my attaché case. In our hotel room.' Barnaby put a hand into the pocket of his shirt and pulled out a piece of chamois. He unfolded it. Inside was an ornate diamond bracelet. In the centre of it was a brooch-like ornament. He looked at her and grinned. 'Whoever took it the other day must have missed these.'

'How come?'

'Because, anticipating the snatch, I'd kept them about my person.'

'Jesus, Barnaby, what've you got us mixed up with this time? Or who?'

'Don't say you think there's some connection between that . . . girl . . . outside and the theft of my jewels.'

'They are not your jewels.'

'Possession is nine-tenths of the law.'

Penny looked at him. 'It would certainly seem logical to posit a connection,' she said.

'You sound like Mr Spock.'

'Long as I don't look like him.'

'Only round the ears.'

Penny looked down at the chamois. The diamond bracelet glittered. She was a pearl person, herself. Diamonds were too cold and hard for her. 'Are you going to tell me about them?' she said. 'They sound as if they might be kind of special.'

'Believe me, sweetheart, they kind of are.'

Santini came back into the room, sliding between the door and the jamb. A wisp of fog came in with him.

'Neither of you got any idea why someone should be sneaking round looking like you?' he said. His voice was a tad less surly than before.

'None whatsoever, officer,' said Barnaby. His hand closed over the chamois, hiding the gems.

'But I aim to find out,' Penny said.

Santini stroked the underside of his jaw. It was already dark with shadow, although it wasn't yet ten o'clock in the morning. 'Sure,' he said. Real sceptical.

'Because,' said Penny, 'if someone killed the girl thinking she was me, it makes it kind of dangerous to *be* me, wouldn't you say?'

'So all I got to do, right, I got to find out why someone would want to off you. Then I've got the guy offed the kid out there.'

'Right.'

17

He spread his hands. 'It's a cinch.' He shrugged in Italianate style. 'Any theories?'

'Uh-huh,' said Penny. She shook her head.

'By the way.' His eyes, colder than diamonds, moved from face to face as though searching for hidden meanings. 'You were right.'

'What about?'

'Time of death. The doc says the same thing. A couple of days. Minimum.'

'There you go.'

'Are we at liberty to leave now?' Barnaby said. He stood up. 'I have important business appointments up in San Francisco.'

'Long's you keep in touch.'

'So we're not under suspicion?'

'Way I figure,' Santini said, 'if you'd done the killing, you wouldn't have bothered calling us in.'

'Could be a double bluff,' said Penny. He smiled, Meanly. 'But it's not, is it?'

'No,' said Penny. 'It's not.'

3

It was warm in San Francisco. The usual on-shore breeze was off-duty for a while, giving the air a chance to heat up. Along the steep streets of Chinatown, cars were parked with their wheels pigeon-toed into the kerb. Tourists jostled the smartly dressed Orientals who crowded the sidewalks. The cable-cars belled. From the bay came the small of sea water to mingle with the scent of fried duck.

It was several sweaty hours since Penny and Barnaby had finally been allowed to leave the beach house. Every one of them had left its grubby fingerprints. The long lickety-split drive through the hills, the encroaching shopping-malls, the acres of tract houses packed in on either side of the road had been depressing. Somehow, the sheer huge fact of the North American continent never seemed so inescapable as on the Californian freeways. Under that ever-blue sky, Penny's feeling that not for anything could she live permanently out here was always doubly, trebly confirmed. She needed shadowed places, cobwebbed corners, driving rain. She needed England, London, Chelsea. Not shiny newness and everlasting sunshine.

On top of that, they'd been driving an unfamiliar hire-car, since the police wouldn't release her father's BMW until it had been tested. That hadn't helped. Nor had the psychological downer caused by finding a corpse on the doorstep first thing in the morning. In anyone's dictionary, that had to be a good definition of a bad start to a vacation. The drive had included passing three major pile-ups, one involving visible blood. Plus Penny's neck felt like it had come off its hinges from all the twisting round she'd done to see if they were being tailed. As far as she could see, they weren't. That didn't prove a thing. A good tail wouldn't be spottable.

When they arrived at the Sheraton-Regis, Barnaby hurried into the hotel, leaving Penny to park the car in the underground garage. Not her favourite job. In those vast oily acres, you never knew who you were going to meet. Nor, once you'd met them, what they were

19

going to do to you. She cased the place pretty thoroughly before she got out of the car, but all she could see, way down the other end, was a guy leaning against a concrete pillar with a bucket at his feet and a cigarette in his mouth. If he planned on mugging her before she reached the lifts, he'd have to move some.

Upstairs, a lot of people were discussing sixteenth-century *netsuke* and the boom in Continental statuary. Among them was Barnaby. She could see him talking to a small Japanese man in large hornrims. The place was full of priceless heirloom furniture fenced off from the general public by thick crimson braids of rope. It was even fuller of security guards. Most of the antiques were encrusted with ormolu. All the guards were encrusted with guns.

Penny went over to the reception counter. The girl behind the desk had a neat waist, neat buns and minimal boobs. So did the girl changing the menu outside the dining room. And the young student-type guy with the long-handled dustpan sweeping non-existent litter from the mock-marble floor. An hour off the interstate and already she felt as though she was the runner-up in a Mrs Michelin contest. Hadn't they heard of curves round here?

She expected that eventually she'd be able to handle the fact that half of San Francisco looked like a Barbie doll. Right now, she wasn't sure she could handle anything, period. Given a choice between a couple of hours' sleep and all the riches of the world with Robert Redford thrown in for good measure, she'd have dumped Bob and the cash without a second's thought. She asked if Dr Wanawake had left a message for her. He hadn't. She asked if he were in his room. He was.

As she turned away from the desk, Barnaby came over.

'That's Yawasata,' he said.

'What is?'

'That man I was talking to.'

'Ah so.'

'The name doesn't ring any bells?'

'Should it?'

'He's the one who recently shelled out a cool fifty million plus loose change for something pretty to hang on the drawing-room wall.'

'*That* Yawasata.'

'And I've got him all pumped up about Fereghan rugs.'

Penny always enjoyed seeing Barnaby *qua* working man. It fleshed out the lover. Gave substance to the jewel thief. Also added the legitimacy that sometimes she was all too conscious he lacked.

20

He looked at her now with apology behind his freckles. 'So I guess I'm going to be tied up for the next few hours.'

'Keep in touch. I'm real good at undoing knots,' she said.

He laughed. 'How about a date some time?'

'Maybe later. Right now, I aim to have a quick visit with my father, then crash out. I'm bushed.'

Barnaby looked over his shoulder. Yawasata had removed his eyeglasses and was examining the underside of an unattractive piece of Delft tin-glazed maiolica. A big man came out of the ballroom-turned-exhibition hall, calling over his shoulder to someone still inside. His voice made Penny's bones rumble, as though an organ was being played in the basement under her feet. He must have been six foot seven. He needed to be, to support some 250 shiny black pounds of solid meat and muscle. The white linen suit he wore would have to have been personally built for him. The same went for the yellow silk shirt underneath it. He carried a white borsalino with a yellow band round the crown.

'My God,' said Penny. 'Who is *that*?'

'Professor Ralph Nkasa.'

'What is he? President of Pimps International?'

'One of the world's leading authorities on African primitive art, as a matter of fact. You should see him in tribal dress.'

'I'd need to rehearse for that one.'

Nkasa caught sight of Barnaby and Penny. He stopped short for a moment, frowning. Something that could have been fear and something that was definitely surprise showed briefly in his eyes. Then he lifted a palm large enough to pitch a tent on, and waved it from side to side. 'Hey, Midas,' he said. 'How ya doin', man?'

'Just fine,' Barnaby said.

'Found anyone to take those sandstone carvings off your hands?'

'Not yet.'

'Don't forget my offer still stands.'

'That was an offer?' Barnaby said. 'I thought you were telling me what the charge here for coffee is.'

Both men laughed. Neither of them did it with sincerity. Nkasa moved off.

'Where's he from?' said Penny.

'Funnily enough, from Senanga. He knows your father. He just flew in from Harvard.'

'What was he doing there?'

'Giving a couple of celebrity lectures to the Faculty Club.'

'He's famous, is he?'

21

'Really, Penelope. Priding yourself on being apolitical . . .'

'I prefer to call it neutral.'

'. . . is one thing. Not knowing who Nkasa is, is just plumb ignorant.'

'So who is he?'

'The Senangan Minister for the Arts, dumbo. And an aspiring Presidential candidate.'

'The Senangans are holding elections? I thought they just did that.'

'So? That doesn't stop someone aspiring.'

A man in granny glasses and a full head of soft permed curls stepped out of one of the elevators. Even across the lobby, Penny could tell he was older than he looked. Seeing Yawasata, who was bending over a glass-topped display table full of jewelled time-pieces, he set off towards him.

'Oh Christ,' Barnaby said.

'What's up?'

'That's Svante Svinhuvud.'

'You're kidding.'

'He's a dealer from Stockholm and he's about to horn in on my territory.'

'Your Japanese territory.'

'Right.'

Penny patted him on the rump. 'Go on, sweetheart,' she said. 'Beat him out.'

'You'll be OK?'

'Sure.'

Barnaby moved fast towards Yawasata, neatly cutting off the Swede. Smiling, Penny took the elevator to the third floor. She tapped on the door of Room 312. Her father's voice told her to come in. As always, on first seeing him again after an absence, she was struck by the nobility of his features, the benevolence of his expression. As he was Senangaland's Permanent Ambassador to the UN they might have been no more than necessary tools of his trade. In fact, they bespoke a genuine integrity. Penny had once seen him referred to in a newspaper as the Good Man of Senanga. She went all the way on that one.

'Hi,' she said. 'How ya doin'?'

It was the standard Californian greeting. It did not receive the standard Californian reply. Instead, Dr Wanawake's face broke into a smile that did nothing to hide its worried expression. 'It's lovely to see you, darling,' he said heavily. His well-modulated voice gave each syllable its due weight, each letter its sharpest pointing.

Penny could tell he was preoccupied. He'd have said the same thing if an armadillo had just walked in.

'What's up, Doc?' she said.

'Uh – nothing.'

'Cut it out, Pop. I know when something's bothering you and when it's not. Right now something is.'

'Well . . .' He hesitated. 'I had a rather curious telephone call.'

'Hey. I've had some of those,' Penny said. 'What you do is, you blow in their ear with a police-whistle.'

'I don't think that would have been appropriate in this case, Penelope, since the call was from Pilot Whitman,' Dr Wanawake said drily. He often found himself being dry around his daughter.

'The restaurateur?'

'Yes.'

'This guy you flew in from New York to see?'

'Exactly.'

'What was the gist?'

'Sorry?'

'Of the rather curious phone call.'

'Ah yes,' said Dr Wanawake. 'As you know, we were planning to meet here in San Francisco. He now says that he would prefer it if I would travel up to his home in the Napa Valley as soon as I can, since something has come up that prevents him from coming here.'

'Did he say what the something was?'

'He was about to when we were abruptly cut off. When I tried to call him back, there was no answer. I've been trying for the past half hour and he doesn't reply. Nor has he rung me back since. I must admit I am somewhat perturbed.'

'Don't exaggerate.'

'How do you mean?'

'Somewhat perturbed is what you are when the bottoms fall out of international markets. Or war is brewing in Middle Eastern trouble-spots.'

'Naturally I am disturbed at being unable to reach Whitman,' Dr Wanawake said. 'Particularly . . .' He broke off.

'Particularly what?'

'Nothing.' As far as he was able to, he looked embarrassed.

Penny put on her Sexton Blake expression. 'Sounds like the kind of nothing that means loads.' She sat down beside her father and put her arm round his shoulders. 'Come on, Pop. You can tell me. Particularly what?'

Dr Wanawake heaved a sigh. 'Particularly in view of the subject I came out here to discuss with Whitman.'

'Which was?'

'I am not at liberty to tell you.'

Penny raised her eyebrows. 'Oh?'

'No.'

'Is it something political?'

Like a man accepting the fact that the only way he's going to escape from the mad axeman is to jump down a well full of man-eating sharks, Dr Wanawake said: 'Yes.'

'I just saw the Senangan Minister for the Arts down in the lobby.'

'Nkasa?' Dr Wanawake made a face. 'A man I can never quite believe in.'

'Larger than life.'

'That. But also difficult to read. Is he corrupt or isn't he? I don't know. But until I do, he's not someone I'd want in my house.'

'I take it that the political something you want to discuss with Mr Whitman is not Professor Nkasa.'

'Precisely.'

'What is it?'

Resignedly, her father said: 'As you probably know, the President of Senanga is arriving in a couple of days' time to take part in a high-level conference in Boston. I really have to be there too.'

'So what's stopping you? Doesn't take that long to fly back east.'

'Of course. But . . .'

'What exactly's bugging you?'

Her father frowned. 'As you are aware, Penelope, your mother and I knew Whitman years ago when we were all in Senanga. Nkasa too, as it happens, but that's beside the point. It was just after we were married. Your grandfather was still at the Embassy then, and Whitman had been seconded from Whitehall to act as a military adviser to the Senangan cabinet, of which I was a junior member.'

He stopped. 'Yes,' Penny said encouragingly.

'Occasionally there would be trouble. Riots, minor uprisings in the provincial areas, the odd tribal killing. Nothing very major in itself, but calling for a firm hand before it got out of control. When

24

that seemed likely to happen, Pilot would alert us using a — a personal sort of code we had devised. A particular phrase to warn that there was trouble pending.'

'And?'

'That's the only reason I agreed to come out here in the first place. I hadn't seen or heard of him for years. But when he used the very same phrase . . . And then his telephone call being terminated so abruptly this morning . . . It's very worrying.'

There was a silence. Penny said: 'What was the phrase?'

'It really doesn't matter,' said her father uncomfortably.

'Come on, Benj. Don't be shy.'

'It sounds like something out of Bulldog Drummond.'

'I promise not to laugh.'

'Oh, all right,' mumbled Dr Wanawake. 'We used to say that his shoes were too tight.'

'And Whitman said that when he called you in New York?'

'Yes.'

'Couldn't he have been making conversation?'

'He *could*.' But Dr Wanawake clearly didn't believe it.

'You aren't just trying to get out of our dinner engagement tonight, are you?' Penny said.

'Penelope, I assure you that such a thought had not —'

'Just a joke, Pa.'

'A joke?'

'You must have heard of them.' Penny swallowed a sigh. Her father was a stand-up guy. Straightest of straight arrows. No question. Someone she'd back against all comers. But a sense of humour was definitely not part of his personal baggage. As a UN Ambassador, perhaps it wasn't a life-skill he'd felt the need to develop.

'In fact, why don't you go ahead and make reservations somewhere for us?' her father said. 'I'll probably be back from Napa in time to dine with you, if you don't mind eating late.'

'You're going to go on up there?'

'I think so.'

'In spite of the footwear?'

'Yes.'

'Where shall I book us in tonight? One of Whitman's places?'

'Why not.'

'OK, Pop. I'm going to catch up on some sleep while you boogie on up to Napa and —'

'Boogie?'

25

'– drive on up to Napa, like Mr Whitman asked you to. And don't worry about things. What kind of trouble could there be for him to warn you against?'

'That, Penelope, is precisely why I came. For all I know, it could have some bearing on Senangan security. And with the President's visit coming up, I couldn't afford to ignore it.'

'You could have misheard him.'

'Mmm. You're probably right,' Dr Wanawake said nonchalantly. It was the kind of nonchalance a man who'd just slammed his finger in the car door might have used. 'I do wish your mother was here.'

'If the wind gets up, she probably will be.' Lady Helena was somewhere between the west coast of Ireland and the east coast of the North American landmass, taking part in a single-handed transatlantic yacht race. Not exactly incommunicado, but you wouldn't ring her up to discuss the merits of rival washing powders, either.

Penny decided it was probably better if she didn't mention the corpse back at the beach house. For her own sake, as much as her father's. Boy, was she whacked. Besides, the police would catch up with her father soon enough. And if they didn't, she'd bring it up herself at dinner later. Anyway, he sounded like he already had enough problems on his plate. A body in the backyard might push the perturbation counter from a handleable somewhat to a fraught seriously.

'I'm going to catch up on some sleep,' she said. 'I'll talk to you later.' She turned to go.

'Uh – Penelope.'

'Yes?'

'While you're here, there's something I'd like you to do for me.'

'What's that?'

'There's a dealer here with an item I am particularly anxious to acquire. However . . .' The pause was delicate.

Penny understood immediately. Barnaby Midas gave a lot of people pause. Especially people like Benjamin Wanawake, who was deeply fond of the man his daughter shared her house and her heart with, and who therefore kept discreetly silent about his own small but extremely valuable collection of snuffboxes.

'You want me to beat this dealer down for you?' she said.

'The price he's asking *is* somewhat excessive, considering the item's value.'

'But you don't want a certain person involved?'

'Without wishing to give offence, that's more or less what I mean.' The gravity of Dr Wanawake's expression lightened for a heartbeat or two.

'Even though the certain person might have more leverage on the dealer with the snuffbox than you or I?'

'Precisely.'

'Because if that certain person knew you were after that snuffbox, he might start asking himself why you wanted it, and then come rapidly to the conclusion that where there is one snuffbox, there might well be others?'

'Since you put it like that, yes.'

Penny would like to have burst into loud protestations about the impossibility of Barnaby stealing from the father of the woman he loved. They would have rung hollow. She refrained.

'Who's the dealer?' She said.

'A Swede. Called Svinhuvud.'

'I'll do my best.'

'I know you will,' Dr Wanawake said with gratitude. 'You always do.'

Penny gave him a quick hug. 'Don't worry about Mr Whitman. I'll bet he just bought himself a pair of shoes that didn't fit.'

'And wanted me to be the first to know?'

Penny stared. Was that a joke? Nah. Couldn't have been. She went away.

4

Next time she consulted her watch, it was nearly ten p.m.

Whaaat? Last time she'd looked, it had been five. Which meant she'd slept for five hours. Standing under the shower, she wondered what Barnaby was doing. And why her father hadn't called her about dinner. Shimmying into a white silk pant-suit, fastening pearls round her throat, she went on wondering. Perhaps they'd both decided she needed to catch up on her beauty sleep. She examined her face in the bathroom mirror. Nope. Couldn't be that. She didn't look any less beautiful than usual. Nor any more.

She called Benjamin's room. There was no answer. Maybe he was downstairs, having a drink with Barnaby. Maybe he'd given up on their date and decided to eat without her. She took the elevator down to the lobby. A medium-to-serious search of the various bars failed to unearth either of them. She asked at the desk if Dr Wanawake had left a message for her and was told he had not. She thought about it. She walked over to the bank of phone booths. Squashed inside one, she dialled Information. A woman with a voice like Bambi's mother answered. Penny asked for Pilot Whitman's home number and got it back before she'd finished asking. She called the number she'd been given. No one picked up. She asked Bambi's mother for the number of both the Whitman restaurants. Neither had seen him for a while. The guy who answered at the second one said he hardly ever did anyway. He laughed in a Not-that-I-really-care kind of way. He said he guessed Mr Whitman had better things to do these days than bother stopping by to see what a good job they were doing down there for him, though frankly, in view of the economic situation and all, he'd have thought the boss would want to keep a pretty close eye on things. Penny said when she caught up with him, she'd be sure to tell him.

She hung up and went back to the desk.

'Are you sure there's no message for me?' she said. 'Wanawake?'

'I'm sure,' the girl said. 'Your . . . father, is it? . . . went off in quite a hurry.'

'When was that?'

'Some time around four thirty. I remember it because the two of them seemed in an awful rush.'

'Which two?'

The girl shrugged. On her lapel, a rectangle of mauve plastic had the name *Donna* picked out on it in white. 'Your father and the friend that stopped by to pick him up.'

Friend? But Whitman had changed their plans, hadn't he? Specifically asked Benjamin to come up to his place in Napa? 'Which friend was that?' Penny said.

Donna raised her eyebrows and turned down her mouth. 'He didn't say.'

What was going on? None of this made any sense. Even if Pilot had changed his mind yet again and reverted to the original plan to come into San Francisco after all, there was no way Benjamin would've taken off without leaving a message for her. She told herself there was some rational explanation. Then tried to think of one. She failed.

Barnaby appeared. 'How's it going, sugar?' he said. He wasn't really interested in the answer. She could tell by the way he kept his eyes on a leatherette-covered bench where Svante Svinhuvud sat. The Swedish dealer was being charming to an immensely fat lady with mauve hair and a matching chiffon muu-muu. The muu-muu looked kind of tacky. The diamonds she wore on top of it were one hundred per cent. Both she and Svinhuvud held brandy snifters an eighth full of what was probably Armagnac. Triple X, if Svinhuvud's smile was anything to go by. Or was it just the reflection from the diamonds? Behind them stood two gorillas with folded arms.

'Terrible,' Penny said. 'I was just raped in the elevator by a guy wearing a lampshade.'

'That's too bad,' murmured Barnaby.

'But I'm just fine, thanks.'

'Good.'

Penny gave up. 'Who's the ocean-liner in purple?' she said.

This time Barnaby took in what she was saying. 'A rare sight,' he said. 'The Contessa di Sforzini. She lives in Paris, deals mainly in historic jewellery. Seldom seen in public but known wherever two or three gentlemen thieves gather together.'

'What do they say about her when they gather?'

'Mostly how impossible it's so far proven to part the little lady from her wares. She's only here because the Fair Committee agreed to pay for round-the-clock bodyguards.'

29

'She seems to be wearing quite a bit of her stock.'

'She always does,' said Barnaby. His eyes were hungry.

'Was she the victim of the jewel heist the other day?'

'Uh . . . ' He wasn't going to say.

Penny wrenched him round to face her. 'Listen,' she said. 'Have you seen Benjamin?'

'No. Why?'

'He seems to have gone.'

'He's a big boy now.'

'He's also a punctilious one. He'd never leave San Francisco without telling me. Especially when we were going to eat together tonight.'

'You're tried Reception, of course.'

'Of course.'

'So what next?'

'I don't know. It's kind of weird.'

'I'm sure it's nothing at all.'

So was Penny. Almost. 'Listen,' she said. 'Did you eat already?'

'Yeah. Yawasata took me to a Japanese restaurant near Union Square. Tried to butter me up in order to beat me down.'

'Did he succeed?'

'No. But I let him think he did.'

'How about keeping me company while I eat, then?'

'OK. Where?'

'You'll see.'

They walked up the angled streets towards Nob Hill, through the fragrant smells of boiling bean-curd and sweet-and-sour. The street life was wide awake. It could have been high noon rather than closing in on midnight. The tourists were packing the sidewalks, eyeing the trashy shops selling blue-and-white rice-grain porcelain and teapots with cane handles and tasselled lanterns. Small one-room stores overflowed on to the pavement, displaying fruit and vegetables that were only distant cousins of the things on the greengrocery counter in Safeway. Old men in mandarin hats sat beside piles of Chinese-language newspapers trapped inside wire cages. Younger ones in sharp suits lounged in doorways, smoking. Behind them, pictures of oriental girls in exotic undress incited passers-by to lust.

In a quieter side-street, they stopped in front of a restaurant. Orange drapes were drawn across the windows so you couldn't see if anyone was in there or not. Upward-directed lighting from somewhere at windowsill level generated a subdued glow that reminded the would-be diner of camp-fires out under the stars and the crackle of thorns beneath a cooking-pot. A pair of horns carved with skilled primitivity stood on a small plinth between pane and drape.

'Why here?' Barnaby said.

'I've got reservations. Besides, the African Queen is one of Whitman's places.'

'And what are you hoping to find here?'

'Something to eat would do me fine.'

'Anything else?'

Penny looked at him sideways and squeezed his arm. 'Maybe a side order of what Whitman and my father are doing.'

'A house-speciality, I'm sure.'

'Someone might know something,' Penny said. The chances of finding Benjamin and his friend inside, enjoying a dish of groundnut stew together, were small. She was here because some instinct told her to get as close to her primary sources as she could. And for the moment, this was as near as she was going to get.

The foyer of the African Queen was small. With Penny and Barnaby in it at the same time, it seemed overcrowded. Jungle grasses grew in it, set into sand edged with ethnic-type stones. Further inside, rhinoceros-hide shields hung on the walls, along with spears and clubs made of knotted strips of skin. The ceiling was low enough to make Penny careful where she put her head in case she dislodged some of the rush-matting with which it was covered.

'Darn it,' she said, looking round. 'Why didn't I wear my shrunken-head necklace?'

'Whitman must have borrowed the set from *Roots*,' Barnaby said.

'I can't believe my father could once have been friends with a man who'd do this to four inoffensive walls.'

Partitions topped by small balustrades made the room seem more crowded than it was, though very few of the round tables were empty. Most of the faces were white. Nearly all of them were male. More or less. At one end of the room was a low dais with some long drums standing on it next to three-legged stools. Other instruments, stringed and keyed, were close by. No one was playing them.

A guy straight out of *King Solomon's Mines* approached. Tall and stately, he walked with that distinctive Watusic stance which always implies chronic back trouble. He wore flowing tribal robes. A round embroidered cap sat on the back of his head like a muffin.

31

He carried a fly whisk made from the coarser hairs of some animal's body. Why? As far as Penny could see they were in a fly-free zone. Despite the Dark Continental trappings, the language he spoke was pure Californian.

'Hi there, I'm Earl,' he said, his voice soft. It was the same voice Penny had heard earlier on the phone, being querulous. 'Welcome to the African Queen.'

'In person?' Barnaby said.

'We-ell . . . get you,' the guy said archly. 'How about a drink before dinner?'

He showed them to a booth and they ordered dry Martinis.

'If I catch up with my father and his friend and find they're in trouble, I may just rescue Benjamin and not bother with Whitman,' Penny said, when he'd gone. 'Don't you hate waiters who tell you their names?'

'Now, now. Earl was only trying to be friendly.'

'I don't go to a restaurant to buddy-buddy with the help, for heaven's sake. I go to eat. Which I hope I'll be doing fairly soon.'

A slim youth wearing not much more than a loin cloth and an earring brought their drinks and a rough wooden bowl full of misshapen nuts. Barnaby watched him thread between the tables. 'I wonder when *he* gets off work,' he said. He picked up his glass, then turned to look at the rest of the room. 'Well, looky over there. It's Professor Nkasa.'

Penny peered round the side of the partition. The big African was seated at a central table on the very edge of the small space in front of the musicians' dais. He still wore white linen, but he had replaced the yellow silk shirt with a cerise one. His wide-brimmed hat, on the chair beside him, had a rolled band of leopard skin round the crown. Penny would have taken bets the leopard never stepped off the production line.

'Yeah,' she said. The corners of her mouth were turned down.

Barnaby put a hand over hers. 'Don't worry about Benjamin,' he said. 'I'm sure he's OK.'

She tried to smile at him. 'Maybe it's not him I'm worried about,' she said. 'Maybe it's me.'

'Still think someone's after you?'

'Don't you?'

'I might, if I could think of a logical reason why someone should trail that girl down to Big Sur and then murder her. Or why anyone wants to get rid of you.'

Someone brought a menu and Penny ordered without much care.

A woman joined Professor Nkasa, putting her hand briefly on his shoulder and sitting down without speaking. She was black, in a loose robe of scarlet embroidered with borders of black silk. Her hair was tied up in a big handkerchief which glinted when she moved her head. Round her neck was a piece of silverwear, elaborately asymmetrical and studded with semi-precious stones. It was the sort of thing a crusader might have picked out as being a perfect deflector of heathen arrows. Silver earrings to match hung from her ears. She must have weighed close to two hundred pounds but she was tall enough to carry most of it off gracefully. The rest you were glad to forget about: one look from those eyes and you'd be glad to forget anything she didn't want you to remember. Although she sat quite still, her hands beneath her chin as she listened carefully to the professor, there seemed to be a lot of emotion surging around inside her massive body, pressing against breast and thigh and upper arm, eager to emerge and start causing trouble.

'Is that his wife?' Penny said.

'I don't know.'

'On second thoughts, it can't be. How could two people that size possibly make it together?'

'There are special positions for the heavily built,' Barnaby said primly. 'I could demonstrate a few of them when we get back, if you like.'

Penny's order arrived. Some kind of very tough meat wrapped in leaves and sprinkled with chopped nuts and mangoes. She chewed for a while, staring round the room. The meat was either goat or horse, she decided. Or possibly donkey. The taste was better than she had expected.

From the gloomy shadows behind the dais, three men appeared. Two wore white shirts open to the navel under leather jerkins. The third wore an outfit similar to the big woman's. A spattering of handclaps came from the tables as they picked up various of the instruments and began handling them in a way that made it clear they would shortly play them. The woman rose gracefully to her feet. She touched Nkasa on the shoulder again, then surged across the floor and stepped up on to the dais.

The man on the drums began stroking them with broad black fingers. They rattled briefly, then boomed, then whispered. A thin flute-like sound joined in and wavered alongside them. A stringed instrument began to splatter plucked thrums in and out of the rhythmic line. Finally, the woman opened her mouth. The voice

33

that came out was startling. Goosepimpling. The primeval anarchy of it clutched at the roots of Penny's hair.

Earl passed by. Penny beckoned. 'Earl, honey,' she said.

'Yes?'

'Mr Whitman's not here, is he?'

'No.'

'When did you last see him?'

Earl looked tough. Or tried to. 'Who wants to know?' he said.

It was one of those damn stupid lines that came straight out of a Thirties gangster movie. Ordinarily Penny would have pointed out that since she'd asked the question, the chances were that she did. Instead she smiled her special smile. The ass-kissing one. The one that said you could put on your spiked shoes and stomp all over her and she'd still be happy to lick the soles of your feet. Even after you'd just cleaned out a stable. She didn't use it very often so it felt rough round the edges. Earl didn't seem to notice. He looked as if he wouldn't mind an encore. 'I do,' she said. She gave him one.

'And who're you?'

'Let's just say I used to be a friend of his,' she said. 'A close friend, if you know what I mean.'

Earl seemed to. 'But not any more, huh?'

'You know how it is, Earl. I been out of town a while. Thought I'd see what was going down with ol' Pilot – Mr Whitman, that is.'

'He hasn't been around for a while,' Earl said.

'That's too bad.'

'It was Mr Whitman you wanted to see? I mean, if you were thinking of a job waiting tables, or something, guess –'

'Waiting tables? Honey, I don't even wait to be asked.'

'– you should talk to the person who handles that kind of stuff for him.'

'Could you arrange that for us, Earl?' Barnaby said. He moved a little, just to give his shoulders room to breathe inside his shirt. Earl's eyes opened a little.

'Oka-a-ay,' he said. 'I'll pass on the message.'

'Perhaps your naked friend could bring us another bottle of wine, while we wait,' Barnaby said.

'Hunky, isn't he?' said Earl.

'Definitely.'

'You're not bad yourself,' said Earl. He widened his eyes suggestively. Three tables away, someone called petulantly. 'I'll have to go.' Earl moved off, his robes rustling in the tropical darkness.

'Dammit. He was putting the make on you,' said Penny, 'with me sitting right here. What a nerve.'

'The way you were talking, I guess he had you labelled All Rights Reserved.'

Penny drummed her fingers against the table, staring impatiently round the room. 'I don't expect that this guy who handles the waitresses has seen Whitman any more than anyone else has.'

Professor Nkasa, bigger than an avalanche, was standing up. He turned, taking them in. His face grew jolly. He came over to their table, his body almost blocking out the light.

'Hey, Midas,' he said. 'How are ya?' His eyes were on Penny.

'Just fine, Professor,' Barnaby said.

'And who's the young lady?'

'I'm Penny Wanawake,' Penny said. She put out her hand and the big man took it between his own.

'Wanawake.' He nodded, as if he'd thought as much. 'Dr Wanawake's daughter.'

'Yes.'

'I knew your father,' he said.

'Knew?' Penny said, sharp as a mussel-shell.

'Out in Senangaland,' Nkasa said. He spoke the Oxford-accented English of a public schoolboy. He turned round to hoick a chair away from a neighbouring table so that he could sit down at theirs. Close to, Penny could see that his eyes were lighter than they ought to have been. They gave him the look of a being from another planet. 'Before he was appointed Ambassador to the UN.' He laughed. 'A while ago now. It was a great pleasure for me to meet him again in the hotel lobby the other day. I had no idea he would be here at the same time as I was.'

'If you knew my father, you must have known Pilot Whitman,' Penny said.

'Pilot!' he said warmly, his smile a deflector from further questions.

'Some coincidence, huh?' Penny gave him a shot of the dimpled charm. 'Did you know that Whitman lives in Napa Valley? That this was his restaurant?'

Nkasa's eyelids dropped slowly over his eyes like cashpoint-shields. He didn't quite hesitate. But his answer was fractionally delayed, as though he was rapidly trying to calculate what reply to make. Whether affirmative or negative would land him in the deepest trouble. 'Of course,' he said. 'Of course I did.'

'You haven't seen him tonight, have you?'

Nkasa slowly moved his big head from side to side. His alien's eyes stayed in place, staring at Penny. At their depths was a light as hard and brilliant as quartz. 'I'm afraid not. Why? Is something wrong?'

If there was, did she want this guy to know? 'No, nothing,' she said, smiling brilliantly. Little Miss Carefree, enjoying a joke with friends.

'When did you arrive from Senanga?' Barnaby said.

'Some time last week,' said Nkasa. 'I had to spend a couple of days on the East Coast before I flew out here. I'm hoping to pick up some things while I'm here.'

'Things?' Penny said.

He spread his big hands. 'You know.'

'Actually, no.'

'I collect African art. Particularly the early Senangan stuff.'

'I wouldn't have thought you'd find much in California.'

He smiled secretly. 'You'd be surprised.'

'Haven't the Senangans put an embargo on the export of native artefacts?' said Barnaby.

'Indeed they have,' Nkasa said. 'I was chairman of the advisory panel which drew up the regulations on import controls in the first place. There was far too much leaving the country. For years we've been letting irreplaceable items disappear into private collections overseas.'

'Which must increase enormously the value of whatever's already floating around, I guess,' Barnaby said.

'You could say.' Again Nkasa's face creased into a smile of which the main characteristic was crypticity. He laughed a lot as he talked, his big hands sliding through the air, as graceful as the necks of swans. Looking at them in mid-flight, Penny wondered whether they could recently have clubbed a girl to death.

For the first time, she asked herself whether the body had anything to do with her father. Like it or not, it more or less had to. It was his house. His daughter's lookalike. Perhaps she'd been wrong in thinking the death was in some way aimed at herself. Perhaps it had some bearing on what she was trying not to think of as Benjamin's disappearance. Even though, so far, her only ground for even the mildest frisson of surprise was the fact that he had failed to inform her of his movements. No one said he had to. And as Barnaby had reminded her, he was an independent entity. Think rational, she told herself.

36

You could rationalise yourself right off the planet if you tried hard enough. It didn't alter the fact that she felt something was wrong.

'Your own collection in Senanga, for instance, must be worth something now,' Barnaby said.

'Possibly,' said Nkasa. 'Though in my experience, the true collector of art – whatever form it takes – is swayed by aesthetic considerations rather than financial ones and is therefore not interested in values.'

'Is yours a large collection?' asked Penny.

'Small,' said Nkasa. 'Very small. And of course doomed now to remain so, except for the odd pieces I can pick up here and there. Senanga is being particularly careful since they let so much get out before Independence.'

'What about the stuff Mr Whitman has here?' Penny said.

'Stuff?'

Penny waved at the shields and masks which decorated the walls. 'Aren't these valuable artefacts?'

Nkasa made it clear that only breeding kept him from throwing up on the spot. 'Certainly not. Cheap imitations, for the most part. Probably made in Taiwan, for all I know. Nothing more than tourist rubbish. Decoration intended to convey a certain atmosphere for the people who come here to eat.'

Behind them, the singer's sound throbbed beneath the drums, rich as a double-malted fudge sundae. Voice and instruments wove together via disharmony and counterpoint to produce a single scalp-singeing sound. And then suddenly it stopped, dissonance rising into the straw-mat roof, leaving a sense among the listeners of something suspended rather than ended.

The singer stepped down from the dais and walked over to the table where she had been sitting with Nkasa. She picked up her glass and watched him over its edge. Her glance flickered over Penny, rested briefly then dragged away.

Earl approached and spoke briefly to her. She set her glass down and came towards them.

'Hello,' she said in the bright tones they teach at car-salesman school. 'Earl tells me you want to speak to me.'

'Do I?'

'I'm Eve. Pilot Whitman's partner. How can I help?'

One of the drums began to beat softly. The intervals between the beats were irregular. Any minute now, the natives would drag in some guy in a topi and light a bonfire under him.

'I purely don't know where to begin,' Penny said.

'Try,' the woman suggested. She massaged her silver ornaments with a finger as big as a courgette.

'For a start, I've been trying to get hold of Mr Whitman,' Penny said. 'Would you have any idea where he is?'

'He doesn't keep me posted of his movements,' Eve said. She moved one big hip towards Barnaby and he slid to the other end of the banquette. She squeezed in beside him. 'He has a small apartment above the restaurant, of course, for the nights when he stays late here in town. But he did say he was going up to his home in Napa.' Her eyes kept bouncing off Penny, as though she wished to stare but knew it was rude.

'I've tried there, and nobody's home.'

'You're sure he's not upstairs now?' Barnaby said.

Eve played some more with the big earrings which brushed her shoulders. 'Unless he climbed up the outside of the building, I'm sure,' she said. 'He'd have to come through the kitchens to get up there, and the staff would have reported to me or to Earl if he had. They always do.'

'Would he take off without letting you – or someone here – know?' asked Penny.

'He might. He's a free agent. And the managers we've put in at both the restaurants don't need to refer to him – or me – for every decision they take. That's why we appointed them. So there's no reason why he should feel obliged to keep us informed of his whereabouts.'

'As a matter of fact, it's not so much Mr Whitman I want to find, as my father,' Penny said. Did she imagine it, or did both the big bodies tense up at the words?

'Find?' Eve's eyes briefly brushed Nkasa and came back again to Penny. Both of them were hostile. 'Has he gone missing?'

'Probably not. It's just he's with Mr Whitman and I can't raise either of them. Which is why we came here, to see if anyone had any idea where they might be.'

Professor Nkasa opened his mouth but Eve got in first. 'Look, Miss Wanawake, I can assure you Mr Whitman is not lurking about in his apartment upstairs, with or without your father. You'll have to look somewhere else.' She eased herself back on to her feet and stood above them. Her gaze lingered on the green and silver varnish which covered Penny's fingernails. 'But I'm quite sure it's nothing to worry about. He's probably gone off to Lake Tahoe or somewhere for the weekend. He's perfectly entitled, after all. And

38

what would be more natural, when an old friend like Dr
Wanawake comes to town?'

She smiled. She slid out of the booth and walked away from
them. Under the scarlet silk of her robe, the two halves of her
buttocks rode like ships anchored in a swell.

She was right. Of course. The only thing that bugged Penny was
that at no time had she identified herself to Eve as Penny
Wanawake. Nor had she said that her father was an old friend of
Whitman's.

So how had she known?

5

Because of her long nap the evening before, Penny found it impossible to sleep that night. At about 7.30 a.m., Barnaby started stirring, at which point she fell into a log-like slumber. It was the middle of the morning before she was once again in the lobby. Through the open doors into the Exhibition Hall, she could see the Antiques Fair dealers drinking coffee from plastic cups and giving the hard sell to such San Franciscans as paused for breath near their stalls. She saw the Contessa seated behind a glass-sided cabinet, inside which were various pieces of expensive jewellery. On either side of her stood the hired muscle. They looked as if their combined IQ would barely make double figures. Be nice, Penny told herself. They'd hadn't been hired for their brains but for their brawn. There was plenty of that showing beneath and inside their short-sleeved black shirts.

Barnaby was near the door. She waited until there was a temporary lull in front of him. He seemed pleased to see her. 'If there were dreams to sell, what would you buy?' he said.

'My father, right here, standing on my toe,' she said promptly.

'Still bothered about him?'

'Yeah.'

He blew air heavily out of his lungs. 'You're taking off, then?'

She nodded. 'Think I'll head on up to Napa. See if I can locate him.'

'Locate, as in look for?'

Penny shrugged. Acted casual. As in allaying suspicion. 'Just to make sure he's OK.'

'Are you seriously worried?'

'Only slightly,' Penny lied. Sure she was worried. Benjamin was almost boringly predictable. His sudden departure wasn't. But if she told the truth, Barnaby would worry. He wouldn't enjoy the Antiques Fair, which was his main reason for being here. And she would therefore feel guilty. Nothing she hated more than guilt. 'No more than that. Just seems like a good excuse to drive up there. I've never been to the wine area before.'

'I don't think you should go now.'

'Why?'

'Because of the possibility that it was you who was supposed to be dead down there in Big Sur. We don't know who the murderer is. Or where.' He looked out into the lobby. Two gays in tight cream cords were twittering over a Crown Derby tea-service. A party of short-sleeved Hawaiians listened to a courier in a red dress and Reeboks. A frizzy-haired girl with a small child slung across her back stood by the desk. Three lawyer-types swapped papers at a low table. There were no heavies in black suits and shades. No Mata Haris lurking behind potted palms. No potted palms, even.

'Think they could be watching us now?' Penny said.

'Just because nobody's openly glomming us doesn't mean they aren't here somewhere,' said Barnaby.

'Even if they were, I'd still take off.'

Barnaby sighed. 'And I couldn't stop you, could I?'

'That's right.'

'Will you be OK?'

'Sure.'

'And careful?'

'Aren't I always?'

'No.'

'I will be this time.' She pushed a kiss through the air and smiled. 'I'm out of here.'

She went over to Reception. Donna was on duty again. She leaned over a newspaper spread flat on the wooden counter, tumbled blonde hair falling on either side of her face. Penny could see headlines: *Drought Conditions Worsen* and *Presidential Visit – Capital Prepares*. She asked for directions to Napa. Donna blue-pencilled a map of the area for her, marking the route with as much serious attention as if Penny planned to recreate some trail-blazing transcontinental trek. She told Penny she loved her accent. She reminded her three times to drive on the right-hand side of the road. She added that there was a speed restriction in force.

Penny went down to the basement parking area to retrieve her car. A young black guy was about to slap a STOP AID TO THE CONTRAS bumper-sticker on the front.

'Don't even think about it,' she said.

'Aren't you concerned about the situation in Nicaragua?' he said. Most of his face was hidden beneath the brim of a baseball cap of dark blue cotton.

'Desperately,' Penny said, 'but even more do I care about what the rental agency will say if you mark up their car.'

'Pretty car,' said the man.

'Which is just the way I aim to keep it.'

'And you some kinda pretty lady.'

Penny smiled at him. She slid behind the wheel. The *Female Eunuch* crowd would probably have stamped on his instep. Woman as Object. Personally, she rather liked compliments from strangers.

'Goin' north?' he said, leaning intimately against the door.

'Napa,' she said.

'Have a nice day.' He slapped the side of the car and she drove up to street level.

Traffic on the Bay Bridge was light, the weekenders not yet ready to think about starting home. A few wisps of fog floated between the spans. On the other side of the Treasure Island tunnel, the sun was gold in a blue sky edged with yellow haze. Once the density of Marin County started to thin out, shivering pepper trees lined the road, screening shopping centres, gas stations, small developments of just-flung-up-yesterday housing. Hills rose abruptly out of the earth and as abruptly subsided. There were cypresses and palm trees. The air was mild, occasionally fragrant with the cough-medicine smell of a rogue eucalyptus tree shedding long peels of bark. Although the temperature was still low it hinted at future fierceness. The lines of traffic thickened, running together, moving away, their paths parallel, intersecting, joining and unjoining. There had to be a moral there somewhere.

After she'd turned off on to Highway 29, the road that ran straight through the centre of the Valley, Penny checked out the guide which lay open on the passenger seat beside her. Seas of vineyards, it said. Twenty-four thousand acres of them. She was prepared to take the figures on trust. Hip-high leaves spread across the valley floor towards rugged hills footed by tree-covered slopes. The sun shone without falter. There were red-painted barns. Rustic white houses. Signs begging her to stop by and visit wineries, to taste, to picnic, to buy. She kept on going, her thoughts on automatic, enjoying the traffic-free ride north. At some point, a road-sign mentioned Sonoma. It was a place Donna the desk-clerk had told her to be sure to take a side-trip to. Said she could find some real easy drinking wine over there. She'd confessed to being something of a wine-buff herself. Most everyone Penny'd met up here was. Including the twelve-year-old kid who gassed up her car when she got to St Helena. He asked where she was headed. When she told him, he said she didn't want Napa at all but Mendocino.

'If it's Whitman's place you want,' he said. 'Say. I dig the car.'

'So do the car-rental people,' Penny said. 'Mind leaning someplace else?'

'Kinda small outfit he's got up there,' the kid said. He stroked the car's silver flank. 'I'm gonna buy me one of these, one day.'

'It'll cost you.'

'I already got me a lawn-cutting concession,' said the kid. 'Three guys working for me. Yeah. 'Sa real one-horse place, Whitman's. Losing money like crazy, I'll bet. Stands to reason.'

'Does it?'

'Sure. Way he runs it, not enough return on capital. One man op, right?'

'I'm afraid I don't really know —'

'What's he got, fifteen, twenty acres?'

'Uh . . .'

The kid snapped his fingers. 'I got it. Pinot, right?'

'Possibly.' What the hell was Peeno?

'Released for the first time two years ago, right?'

'From what?'

'Huh?' The kid's immature brow wrinkled.

'What was Mr Whitman released from? I didn't know he'd been —'

'Jesus,' said the kid. He'd obviously never run across ignorance on the scale of Penny's. 'Released for sale. You know?'

'Frankly, not really.' Penny found herself on the defensive. 'I understand Mr Whitman makes a terrific wine.'

'Sure,' said the kid. Many an older man would have envied the way he did derisive. 'About enough to, like, cover the bottom of a tasting glass.'

'Listen, kid. He's going for quality, not quantity, OK?'

The hell with him. Not that she knew much about wine – matter of fact she didn't know *squat* about wine – but she knew what she liked. Which was lots of it. A name swung into her head. 'His Zinfandel,' she said. She made an appreciative noise.

'Nah,' said the kid. He shook the end of the gas-hose as though he'd just used it to pee. A few drops joined the oil slicks on the tarmac. 'Zinfandel sucks. Might as well drink grape Kool-Aid. You want a good wine, go for the Cabernets, want my advice.'

Gaahd. Snotty little wiseacre. Penny tried to imagine a kid in

England offering his elders oenological advice. She failed completely.

She followed the route marked out for her. She would have to turn off the main highway and head for a town called Santalina, the nearest kick-off point for Whitman's place. She'd been assured she would only have to ask for Whitman's when she got there and someone would put her on the right road. Driving across the valley floor, she dredged up what she knew of Whitman from her parents' reminiscences.

English. Sandhurst-trained. Sent out to Senangaland as a young military attaché. He'd spent thirty years there. When the country went independent and two centuries of colonial rule were expunged overnight, the white man comprehensively kicked off the land he'd originally annexed from the black one, Whitman had still managed to stay. According to her father, however, he'd seen Independence coming and was able to get some of his accumulated assets out in time. She'd never met him. With a name like that, she imagined him in a faintly nautical cap, his gait rolling as befitted a man who'd spent years at sea, his eyes far-reaching and blue, an albatross somewhere close to hand.

He'd bought some acreage up here in Napa where he produced a small amount of choice wine each year, intended only for friends. He also owned a couple of tony restaurants. She'd already seen the African Queen. The other was the Zebra Stripe, down in the Castro. Both of them specialised in African dishes. In trend-hungry California, both had been overnight sensations. Never mind that the cuisine — leaning heavily on yams, goatmeat and groundnuts — could hardly be said to be typical since large numbers of the continent's inhabitants were starving. In a vague way, San Franciscans felt they were doing their bit for Third World famine by eating there.

Why did she have a feeling that he had once been, or was about to be, or possibly that very minute *was* engaged in some kind of shady dealing? Guns? Drugs? Sex? She couldn't remember what. If, indeed, her father had ever said. He always spoke of Whitman with the kind of exasperation that showed he'd disapproved of him.

Why wasn't he answering his phone? She'd pretended to scoff at the question of Whitman's overtight shoes. But even if his footwear was killing him, would he bother ringing New York after all these years to tell his former friend about it? 'Course not. And as an old soldier, he'd never have used a phrase that had special meaning unless he really was in trouble. Was he warning Benjamin too to

44

look out? If so, what for? And did any of it have anything at all to do with the dead girl at the beach house?

So many questions. So few answers.

She looked at the map. Any minute now, she would have to branch off the main road and take a subsidiary through the hills which continued northwards up the continent, range after range of them, dark green with ridges of sand-coloured rock breaking through the tree-line, growing steadily bluer until they merged with the sky. According to the guide. Down here, every square inch of land that could support a vine did so. The sky itself was huge and utterly blank. A long way up in it, a bird hovered motionless above something. Something dead, probably.

A sign that even Blind Lemon Jefferson couldn't have missed informed her that the minute for branching had arrived. She checked the mirror. Behind her were half a dozen cars. She turned left. Slowed. Checked the mirror again. No one turned off after her. The road behind was empty. So was the road in front. She floored the gas-pedal, enjoying the countryside smell that came in on the rushing wind. Five miles, and she was slowing down at a yellow sign informing her she'd reached the city limits of Santalina. Not that she could have missed them, clinging to one side of the highway as uncompromising as a wasps' nest. Not exactly trail-blazing stuff, she thought, poking the car into a parking slot and leaving it in gear, the way the desk-clerk had reminded her to be sure to do.

And if you were going to blaze a trail, she further thought, getting out and looking about her, Santalina was the sort of place you'd blaze it right on by. Talk about one-horse. Calling it a city was going it some. From where she stood, she could see what seemed to be the entire downtown district. There was a large grassy square, ringed with orange trees. On one side it was bounded by a Walgreens, a discount carpet saleroom and a liquor store specialising in local wines. Opposite was a gentlemen's outfitters and a gift shop called the Laughing Monkey where you could buy wind-chimes, scented candles and anything you could possibly want made out of abalone shell. There was also an eating place made of redwood and glass, called the Oyster Inn, and a bank with a digital clock on the roof which alternately flashed the time and the temperature. A large brick church with an integral parking lot and a white-painted bell-tower containing a bell took up the whole of the other side, apart from a motel built in Spanish Mission style, its walls blindingly white in the sun.

The fourth side was the highway.

The town was very quiet. The only noise came from the occasional car passing on the road, and an angry bird shooting off its mouth in among the oranges. If the citizens of Santalina were making whoopee, they were doing it someplace else. It was very hot.

Two skinny Mexican kids rollerskated the brick paths bisecting the square, fingers clicking, hips moving to the rhythms coming from their Walkmans. Some old men in white cotton caps came out of the drugstore, clutching brown paper bags, and watched the kids, their jowls tremulous. As often before, she tried to decide whether the old really wanted the backwaters of daily life into which society was so keen on shunting them or whether they yearned secretly for excitement, for adventure, for brassy women in suspender belts, for speakeasies with sawdust on the floors and drug deals going down in the padded booths. For love. For fear. For any kind of heartstopping, throat-clutching feeling. All passion spent. But maybe not by choice.

Santalina went on being quiet. All round her, things were growing in profusion that in England grew in pots. Riotous was the word. Penny walked over to the motel. Geraniums tumbled down its wall, also something that she told herself was probably bougainvillaea. Through an arched doorway marked 'Office', she found a coffee-coloured man in a neat striped shirt with short sleeves. He seemed glad to see her.

'Back again,' he said.

'Not me,' said Penny.

'Must like us,' he said. He smiled, showing a silver eyetooth.

'I'm sure I will when I get to know you.'

'Keep on coming back like this and you soon will.'

'When was it I was here before?' Penny said. She wrinkled her forehead like someone trying to remember number thirty-eight of the Thirty-nine Articles.

'A while ago now.' He laughed. 'But I couldn't forget a girl like you.'

'Perhaps that's who was here before,' Penny said. 'A girl like me.'

'Nah,' he said. 'I reckernise you. Even if you do look diff'ent.'

'Different?'

'Your hair. You changed it.'

Penny felt distinctly unthrilled. She frowned to herself. Was he one of those guys who thought all black people looked the same? Being one himself, it seemed unlikely. So who was he mixing her up

46

with? She had a feeling it was a corpse. A platoon of apprehensions goose-stepped slowly down the middle of her spine. How many Penny Wanawake lookalikes could California hold? She thought of the dead girl lying in the mist. Was she the one who'd been up here the time before? And if so, what had she been doing, this close to Whitman's place? This close to where her father ought to be and probably wasn't?

'Tell me,' she said. 'How do I get out to the Whitman place?'

He told her. When he'd finished, he wrinkled his nose. It gave him an expression she recognised. The sort people put on when they want to be asked what's wrong.

'What's wrong?' she asked. Nothing if not obliging.

'Whitman,' he said.

'Yeah.'

'I mean,' he said.

'What, exactly?'

'I told you last time, you looking to buy yourself some wine, you don't want to go to no Whitman.'

'I'm not.'

' 'Sides, Whitman don't do none of the tourist stuff. Tours. Tastings. Stuff like that.'

'Who says I want it?'

'He don't like no visitors up to his place, neither. Says so, right there on his mailbox.'

'Private kind of guy, is he?'

'So private, I guess we don't see him in town much as once a year. So private, he does his grocery shopping in the city, just so's he won't have to say "Hi" to people.' He leaned across the counter, scratching an elbow. 'Say, you're English, right?'

'Right.'

'You ever meet the Queen?' He shifted gum inside his mouth.

'Not exactly.'

'How come?'

'Basically,' said Penny, 'because she runs with a different crowd from me. She doesn't ask me to dinner, and I don't ask her.'

'Okaaay.' He smiled at her. 'Hey, ol' Mr Whitman, he's so darn private, I don't 'spect I'd reckernise him, he came walkin' through that door carryin' a trayful of toads.'

Penny could tell that, given his head, the guy would go on telling her how private Pilot Whitman was until the Late Night Movie came on.

'Guess I'll just have to hope he lets me in,' she said. She eased her

47

feet on the cool tiled floor. Heat always made them swell. He came round the side of the counter and walked her to the door.

'No problem,' he said. He held it open for her, letting heated air into the air-conditioned cool. 'I'd sure let you in, you came knocking at *my* door.'

Penny hoped Pilot would feel the same.

But not as much as she hoped he was still around to feel it.

6

A grey-haired old lady in a Chevrolet was hogging the road which led north from Santalina. The car was so big, she had to look through the steering wheel instead of over it. Every time Penny tried to overtake, the Chevvy swerved right out over the centre line. There was a sticker in the rear window that said I ♥ MEN. At her age, her mind should have been on higher things. It was kind of nice that it wasn't.

Ahead, the outlines of the hills were misty against the sky. The bluffs on either side were heavily wooded with pine and oak. It seemed a long way from the crowded streets of San Francisco. Especially for a sidewalk freak like Penny. The Valley was green and cool-looking. Only by looking up at the sky, metallic with heat, was it possible to see how hot it really was. The wineries were fewer now. Most appeared from the come-on signs to be several miles into the country on either side of the road. The only one she passed that fronted the highway was called Bonami's. She caught a glimpse of a long red-painted wooden barn, a Victorian house covered in wooden trim, some arthritic oak trees with picnic tables underneath.

A couple of miles further on, the Chevvy suddenly turned left across the road into the driveway of a big old house covered in cedar shingles. No hand signals. No indicator. Penny was proud of the way she kept on going without taking time out to have a heart attack. She thought about following the Chevvy and rousting the old lady about road courtesy. Big house meant big money, but that didn't given you the right to be a roadhog. She might have pointed this out, except Nanny Simpson had brought her up to respect her elders. By the time her heart had slowed down, she was at the turn-off which led through the contours to Whitman's place.

The land was wilder here, rounded, rising in dumpling curves, falling away into miniature canyons. Trees hung with trails of Spanish moss lined the road. It followed the twisting course of a narrow stream, crossing and recrossing it by means of small stone

49

bridges. Penny was never fully at ease in the countryside. She always hoped that nobody would ever give her a home where the buffalo roam. Place like this, if a person wanted to run out for a takeaway, she'd better have her jogging shoes handy. It'd be a long haul to the nearest pizza-to-go.

Her big leather duffel lay on the passenger seat. She took a hand off the wheel and hefted it. Because Hasselblads didn't come in a summer-weight version, it felt reassuringly heavy. If there was some kind of a bad scene going down at Whitman's, she'd have something to whip somebody round the ear with. Maybe it was dumb to move in without more protection, but what kind of protection was there? She didn't mess with guns. Not any more. She used to. But not since Zimbabwe. Not since she had spent the longest night of her life, lying beside a dead man. A man she'd killed. It wasn't something she was ever going to forget. Outside her tent the African darkness had been loud with noisy life. Inside, she lay with a gun in her hand and listened for what seemed an eternity to the deep silence the dead give off. He'd held a knife to her throat, his fingers stroking her breast. It had been self-defence, although she had never meant for a minute to kill him. Justifiable homicide. But to die for the sake of an expensive camera and the momentary physical invasion by a stranger's body? She knew that if his two friends came back to finish what he'd begun, she would never be able to fire the gun again. If it was kill or be killed, better to die herself than take another life. She must eventually have fallen asleep because in the morning, the body was gone. She had waded out between the thin reeds into the shimmering water of Lake Kariba and thrown the gun as far as she could. She had never touched one since.

If she wanted protection, she'd have to rely on what she'd learned at her Tai Ch'i classes. Pity she'd just missed eight in a row. She made a war-paint-type face at herself in the car mirror. Oh, hey. Real scary. Might terrify a baby or two. She told herself that the reason she couldn't raise Whitman and her father was probably because there was something wrong with the telephone line. She didn't fool herself. Americans might not be too red hot when it came to choosing Presidents but there was nothing wrong with their phone system. When the line had gone, somebody would tell you. If not Bambi's mother, at least his aunt.

The entrance to Whitman's house was discreet. A small sign carved in oak was set to one side of a track so inconspicuous it could have been a deer trail. A metal mailbox stood on one leg beside it. Both carried a sign saying 'No Visitors'. She followed the track up the slope of the hillside between fields of vines. At the top, trees began again. Big dark ones, which cut out most of the light. An avenue of them led past a small lake where exotic ducks floated. The water had the sheen of satin-finished stainless steel. A flock of gulls had settled together at one end of it. On the other side, backed up against the hill, was a fairytale castle. It was not much bigger than a suburban house, yet contained at least one example of almost every architectural feature known to the RIBA. If Ludwig of Bavaria had been on the look-out for somewhere to be mad in, this would have suited him down to the ground. Turrets and pinnacles and mansard roofs jostled above a stone facade of heavy architraves and mullioned windows criss-crossed with medieval-type bars. It only needed Rapunzel to let down her hair. About five years ago, someone had painted the whole thing flamingo-pink.

Penny slowed to a stop. The house floated in the dark water above a perfect reflection of itself. Instead of being an eyesore, it blended like an overblown rose into the surrounding green. With the engine off, rural sound effects filled the car. Unseen things jerked and clattered in treetops. Others chirped in nearby herbiage. Somewhere close at hand, water was moving slowly, the sound muffled as though running over dead leaves. She could hear sheep whingeing. She parked her car beside some bushes and got out. She thought for a moment then got back in and drove around the bushes so they screened the car from casual observers. It paid to be careful.

Between the castle and the lake was a wide turning area covered in wood chippings. She walked down to the water's edge. The hills were closer here, more crowded. She felt shut in. To the left of the house, dark-green vines spread to the sky. She began to walk along the wood-chip path which led around the lake. Beyond the castle there were other buildings: a big metal vat with a rounded top standing like a cigar case among the trees; two long redwood sheds with corrugated asbestos roofs standing side by side; at right-angles to them, a third, more functional, that could have been a laboratory of some kind.

In front and to one side of the main house stood a small octagonal cottage painted Williamsburg blue, its gingerbread trim picked out in white. She guessed it to be some kind of gazebo or folly. Beyond that, where the land rose, an arched semi-circular opening had been cut into the hillside and a huge redwood doorway hung across it. The cellars, presumably.

A short flight of wide stone steps lay spread before the house. It led into a buttressed porch. The front door looked as though someone had spent several years of his life hammering four-sided metal studs into it. There should have been a drawbridge. Maybe even a portcullis. Someone had left a large flat package leaning against an open seat. A piece of intricate ironmongery hung down to one side. Penny gave it a hopeful tug before she saw the neat electric button on the other side which told her to press. She did.

If she'd been in a Hammer film, this was when a whole lot of things would have started happening. Footsteps would have shuffled on the other side of the door. Bolts would have slowly been pulled. Hinges would have creaked. As she wasn't, what happened was nothing. She waited, turning to look back over the lake. At its edge, the flock of gulls was busy getting outside its afternoon feed, screeching a lot and kicking each other in the beak. The ducks were being better bred, pecking decorously, occasionally diving upside down then righting themselves with a neat flick of water from their feathers.

After a while, Penny stepped back to look up at the facade. The windows were dark, the rooms behind them already starting to fill with the approaching dusk.

'Tell them I came and no one answered. That I kept my word,' she said. If there were phantom listeners inside, let them make what they would of that. She walked slowly down to the water again and followed the wood-chip trail around its edge. She wondered how far the nearest house was. The ducks made low noises of alarm in their throats. The gulls took not a blind bit of notice. Too busy foraging. It was difficult to see exactly what on. Perhaps some vandal had emptied a garbage can into the lake, or a sheep had come down here to die. She walked nearer them. Single gulls rose and fell above the main mass, wings flapping, beaks insolent. Unlovable birds, on the whole. Closer to, she saw that they had settled on to a log that had drifted into the shallows. A log in blue jeans and a T-shirt that said 'San Diego Fun Run'. A log that had — gulp — once been a man.

Shee-it, she thought. Why me? Why, when someone wants to bump someone else off, do they always do it around me? How in the world did she get into these situations? Nobody could possibly say she went out looking for them. There was a dogwood near the water, its leaves flaming with autumn. She dragged off one of its branches then waded into the water, beating at the gulls until the bulk of them had risen into the air to hover sourly above her head. Not wanting to much, she took a close look at what lay floating face down among the reeds. Gulls didn't mess around. Given a corpse, they'd certainly made a meal of it. Whatever uncovered skin there had once been now looked as though it had fallen into a blender. The arms and hands were raw meat. It looked like nothing so much as 150lbs of hamburger stuffed into a couple of moth-eaten pillow-slips. Without actually touching it, rolling down the jeans or up the T, she couldn't tell whether it had been a black man or a white. Matter of fact, at first she couldn't even have said for sure whether it was male or female. Not wanting to, she looked more carefully. OK. Male. Gingerish, therefore Caucasian. Fiftyish. Mouth twisted in disgust, she turned away. One more thing. It hadn't been there for too long. The outline was still recognisably that of a tall, slimmish human being. There was no bloating. The tattered arms lay half-in, half-out of the water, fingers drooping. Cause of death wasn't immediately obvious, though from the angle of the head *vis-à-vis* the body, Penny guessed the neck was broken.

She looked up into the fading sky, remembering the single buzzard floating above the air currents that morning. She did not want to ask herself who this was. Had once been. Not that she'd know the answer, however much she demanded one.

She got back on to dry land. The gulls immediately swooped down again, raucous, insatiable. Above their noise, she heard the sound of a car. It was pulling off the road to take the track leading up here to the castle. To do that, it would have to pass the bushes where her car was half-concealed. If they saw it, they'd stop. Examine it. Wonder who it belonged to. Come looking for her.

Call it instinct. Call it the rule of survival. Like any dimwitted heroine in any Gothic novel you cared to name, she knew instinctively that if they found her, they would almost certainly be mean to her. That whoever was in that car was not good people. That it was time to assume a low profile. She ran fast towards the octagonal cottage. A pillared gingerbread porch spread around five of its eight sides. She eased herself underneath, into the leaf-mould-smelling space between the wooden floor and the earth. Couldn't get a profile much lower than that. Several spiders immediately took up residence on her face. A couple of neurotic beetles ran about in her hair. Bleeeh! She wanted to scream and beat at herself until the intruders scuttled off somewhere else. With heroinic restraint she stayed absolutely still.

From where she lay, she had a clear view of the front of the castle. A Cadillac as long as a railway carriage pulled up. Someone got out from behind the wheel and slammed the door. He looked like the sort of thug the Mafia would have turned down as being bad for their corporate image. He had more hair than the average yak, most of it greasy and hanging off his head, the rest arranged above his upper lip. If he had a forehead, it wasn't worth mentioning. His face seemed recently to have received the attention of an apprentice plastic surgeon.

Penny tried not to groan. No prizes for guessing his job description. Life, like a cheap novel, was full of clichés. And she'd never seen anyone who more clearly came under the heading Hitman. She told herself not to be so prejudgemental. He could have been a visiting flautist. A brain-surgeon on his way to the operating theatre. A wine-lover dropping by for a couple of cases of Zinfandel.

Sure he could.

She elbowed closer to the overhang of the porch-floor. There was a wisteria growing round one of the pillars, its trunk halfway over the opening through which she was peering. On the far side of the car, another man got out from the front passenger seat. He looked up at the sky and stretched, lacing his fingers above his head. The head was black, the hair on it cut close. The rest of him was hidden by the Caddy.

'I guess we'd better get started,' he said. It was a preppy voice, the 'r's reduced to a minimum. East Coast, not West.

'Just a cotton-pickin' minute here,' said the other one. 'What about the auto back there?'

'Which one?'

'Din't you see it?'

'No.'

'Chrissake, man. It's parked right there, in among the shrubbery. Shoon't we check around a little? Someone must've drove up while we was away, could be hanging around someplace. Watching us, maybe.' He shifted his eyes around without moving his head.

Rats, Penny thought. Just showed that lack of brains didn't necessarily go with lack of forehead. Because he was one hundred per cent correct. Someone was watching them — Penelope Wanawake. And wondering what the heck the two of them were up to. Whatever it was, it couldn't be kosher. Stood to reason. If it was, they wouldn't be worrying about checking the place out. Which kind of argued that neither of them was Whitman.

The other guy came round the car and stared out over the lake.

He was black. He sniffed hard a couple of times. 'Jesus. Don't you hate all this open space?' he said.

'Uh-huh,' said the gorilla, still staring round the landscape.

'Well, I do. I get agoraphobic just thinking about it. Plus it sets my sinuses off.'

Penny was on to that one right away. Lightning brain at the ready. The guy was a town-dweller, right? Liked the feel of sidewalks under his shoe-soles. Store windows full of consumer durables. Uncollected garbage. The knowledge that if you got hungry, Col. Sanders and his colleagues were standing by. She could sympathise. She felt the same way.

Something was crawling slowly up the inside of her thigh. It felt like a slug. If there was one thing she absolutely could not *abide*, it was –

'Still think we should beat the bushes a little,' the Mafia reject said.

'You get beating then,' said Preppy. 'I'm allergic to leaves.'

'Cheez,' said his friend. 'You guys really think you're sump'n else, don't you?' He looked out towards the lake where the gulls were a shifting white blur. 'What the fuck those goddamed birds screamin' about?'

'I thought noise was what birds did,' said Preppy. 'What are they? Robins or something?'

'Robins?' said the hitman. '*Robins?* Don't they teach you nuthin', where you come from? Robins, for Chrissakes.'

'Just get on with it, Dezzy, will you,' Preppy said. 'I didn't take the red-eye out here to catch a lesson in ornithology.' He walked towards the door of the house and pulled out some keys. A dark sweater was slung over his shoulders, the arms knotted across a collarless white shirt, open at the neck.

'Seagulls. That's what they are,' Dezzy said. He shook his head. 'Robins. Cheez.' He opened the rear door on his side of the Caddy, started to lean inside then straightened again and spread his arms along the car roof. 'Just don't say I din't tell you when some bozo turns out he's inside waiting on us, that's all.' He bent down again and reached in, dragging at something on the back seat. Something heavy. Something that didn't want to come but had very little choice.

A body.

Dezzy pulled it out feet first. Penny saw expensive loafers, white sport socks, pale pants cut close at the crotch. The torso followed: a snakeskin belt, a white tennis sweater, a 24-carat coffee bean hanging from a gold chain round his neck. A man. When his feet had hit the ground, Dezzy pulled him to a sitting position then hunched down to get a shoulder into his midriff. When he straightened, the body was over his shoulder in a fireman's lift.

'Cheez,' he said. 'Guy weighs a ton. Got the keys?'

'Hold your water, Dezzy. Of course I have the keys.'

'Then opena friggin' door. I don't wanna stand about with this round my neck any longer'n I have to.'

Preppy set a key into the front door. It opened without a single creak. He went in. Dezzy followed. Over his shoulder, the body dangled, loose arms flopping against his back. Whoever it was would be tall when he stood on his own two feet, Penny thought. And burly. Well-nourished to a point that stopped just short of gross. All he was now, however, was out. Not dead, or so Penny reasoned. Nobody would bother lugging a corpse into a house, would they?

A few minutes later, Dezzy returned to the car. He opened the nearside door and ducked down out of sight. With the car hiding him, Penny couldn't see what was happening. She guessed he was repeating the performance. Sure enough, when he straightened, he had another body over his shoulder. A black man, this time. Dressed in a conventional business suit, with white shirt and tie. The tails of the shirt had pulled out of the suit pants and now fell over the man's back. The tie dragged along the wood chippings as Dezzy went back inside the house. It was a silk tie. From an exclusive boutique in Rome. Penny knew because she had bought it last summer as a present for her father. From where she lay, she could just make out the designer's subtle logo, slightly right of centre. Like Benjamin himself. Who at this very minute was being carried unconscious into a storybook castle, slung over the shoulder of some cheapshit gorilla.

What the hell was going on?

The door shut. She reached down and flicked away the creepy-crawly now edging past her panties. Then she scrambled out from under the porch. She didn't bother brushing herself down. The dirt was camouflage. She ran silently across the wood chips and looked in at the window to one side of the front door. It was made of small squares of coloured glass leaded together. Difficult to see out of but fine for peeking in through. Inside was a noble baronial hall, several storeys high. There was a minstrels' gallery but no minstrels. There were various heads attached to the walls. Animals, as far as she could see. Some had horns, some did not. There were escutcheons.

56

Banners. An oriflamme or two, probably. Even a suit of armour. There was also the kind of sofa King Arthur might have lolled about on after a hard day's jousting, if he hadn't been into Sieges Perilous. It was covered in the skin of several African beasts. On it were slumped two middle-aged men. All she could see of one was a deep sun-bed tan and the kind of white hair that looks deliberate rather than natural. Whitman?

No need to ask who the other one was.

He stared at the man who sat on a hard chair, facing them, his legs suave, his slouch nonchalant. Since it was not Dezzy, Penny guessed it must be Preppy. Preppy would be hitting thirty some time in the next couple of years. He had the move-over-Harry-Belafonte lean good looks that film stars are made of. Penny had seen his eyes before, more than once. Mainly on Easter Island statues. Large, that is. Blank. And absolutely stony.

Rage flamed inside her. It pushed its way through her veins to the ends of her body. She'd never seen her father vulnerable before. She didn't want to see it now. However much you were intellectually aware of parental fallibility, you still didn't need it thrust at you. And fallible was what Benjamin looked right now. No longer the veteran of a score of indignant walk-outs, the indefatigable fighter for further Grants-in-Aid. There was a greyish tinge to his skin. When he closed his eyes, his eyelids shone plum-coloured in the light from a cresset or something on the walls. His hands lay helpless beside him, one curled upwards as though hoping for alms. She wanted to burst in through the door, beat the shit out of Dezzy and Preppy, knock their teeth down their throats. She restrained herself. Partly because there were two of them and only one of her. Partly because Preppy had a gun on his hip. And, seen in the full light, he looked as though he knew how to use it. Looked as if he'd already used it, more than once.

What did he and his sidekick want with their prisoners? Should she hang around and see? Or should she get back to the car and go find some cops somewhere? Staying suited her better. Someone had abducted Benjamin and she wanted to abduct him back. On the other hand, unless one or other of the abductors succumbed to a sudden fatal disease, there were always going to be two of them and one of her.

As she watched, her father opened his mouth and said something. She couldn't hear what. From where she was standing, it looked like a plea for understanding, for tolerance, for compromise in the face of the great difficulties facing them which, if they pulled

57

together, they could overcome but which, if they presented a disunited front, would inevitably swamp them, sink them, bring them down. It was a rhetoric he'd employed many times before the UN General Assembly, with favourable results. Preppy didn't seem to go much on rhetoric. A couple of times while Benjamin spoke, Preppy said something brief that was clearly a plea for silence. When Benjamin ignored it, he finally got up from his chair and went over to him. He waved his gun around. He pushed it against Dr Wanawake's forehead and flexed his trigger-finger. Dr Wanawake stopped talking. He looked greyly up at Preppy. Preppy returned to his seat.

Penny didn't like it much. As a matter of fact, she didn't like it one single bit. She'd have gone in there and sorted Preppy out at the drop of a hat, no question. But she didn't. It wasn't so much that she was frightened. More the thought that if Preppy mowed her down, then there would be no one at all left to help her father and Whitman. She wished she knew where Mafia Man had got to. Since the Cadillac was still out front, he must be somewhere about the place. But doing what? Oiling the thumbscrews? Repointing the Iron Maiden?

Better to go. And fast. She hurried across the wood chippings towards her car. The keys had buried themselves at the bottom of her bag. She fished for them. As she found them, something hit her very hard on the head. She heard the descending swish. Felt a split second of diamonding hurt inside her skull. Felt her ears sing. Then dropped forward painfully into darkness.

7

'Catch a falling star and put it in your pocket,' someone sang. The song came either from a far-off planet or from right inside her head. 'Catch a falling star' . . . but she had a star already, a bright star, in her silver car, in the pocket of her sweater, a falling star to warm her hands by, warm her body by, and if she didn't get her sweater soon, catch the falling star, warm herself, it was going to be too late, she'd cease upon the midnight clear, the midnight star, 'cos star quality gets you to the top, to the very top of the water in which you're lying, crying, dying, born under a wandering star, and likely to die there, too, unless star quality gets you to the . . .

Penny surfaced. Water. Cold water. And stars. Above her, the night sky was full of them. There seemed more than usual. Night has a thousand eyes. She moved her head from side to side and at least half the bright points of light moved too, swinging slowly across the navy blueness the way a boat does in a deep swell. And with much the same effect on the stomach. Disregarding the pain in her head, Penny turned it sideways and neatly decanted the vomit that burst from her throat into the freezing water in which she was lying.

Gaahd. How disgusting could a person *be*? The answer to that was, pretty damn disgusting. Especially when a person seemed to have lost control of a person's stomach and the sky was zooming about, full of unfocused movement that reminded a person far too forcibly of the lowest moment a person's life had so far reached, i.e. crewing for a person's mother in the Fastnet Race, up to the neck in freezing water and being seasick every five seconds into a bucket. Just like now. With one small difference. There wasn't a bucket.

Only the dark waters of the little lake in front of Pilot Whitman's sugar-candy castle. Only the tiniest whisper of sound as the cold water moved among the sedges and night creatures rustled. Only the feel of ooze beneath her as she lay a yard from the shore, her elbows touching bottom, something sharp nudging one knee.

Gagging, she got to her feet. Moved away from where she'd been.

Rinsed out her hair. Moved further away and thought about washing out her mouth. She also thought about dysentery bugs, cholera germs, bird shit. No thanks. Her mouth could wait. At least she hadn't been pecked to pieces by man-eating sea gulls. She strained her eyes into the blackness and saw darker darkness lying further round the lake. The dead man.

She bit hard on her lower lip to stop the terrified shivers ringing round her like hula hoops. Who was he? Who'd killed him? And why? One thing was obvious: it couldn't be either Preppy or Dezzy. Even if Preppy wasn't too clear on the difference between gulls and robins, he'd have known what the birds were cheering about.

She wondered what time it was and who the *fuck* had slugged her, and then dragged her down here and thrown her in? She tried to remember who said he'd called the New World into existence to redress the balance of the Old. Her brain refused to mesh. Something you had to say for the Old World: this kind of thing didn't happen in it. At least, it never had to her.

Frankly, if this was God's own country, God could stick it in Her ear.

She must have been out for a while. The hills all around were solid and dark against the remains of a sunset-pink sky. Long shadows chilled the water and folded up against the front of the house, leaving only the rooftops still golden. What ought she to do? Start all over again was probably best. Peek in the window, check Benjamin was still OK. Find her car. Go like a bat out of hell to wherever the nearest phone/cop/Jack Daniels – in that order – was. How, in all this rural blackness, was she supposed to know where that might be? Even supposing her car was still parked where she'd left it and was still running. She started up the bank towards the house. One of her shoes had gone. She took off the other one. Shit. They were white suede, a favourite pair. As for her skirt, it would only be fit for polishing brass after this. Under her bare feet, the wood chippings were warm with residual heat.

More questions buzzed. Why had someone bothered to knock her out? Was the blow Wanawake-specific? Or was it simply aimed at eliminating whoever it was that had been snooping, regardless of race, creed or colour? Had the knocker-out intended to murder her by throwing her into the water?

She shuddered. Not just with cold. Her hair hung behind her and dripped on to her back like a hank of seaweed. It was all too easy to imagine her own neck skewed away from her backbone, like the body by the lake's. She decided the tap on the head couldn't have been aimed at her just because she was Penny. After all, no one knew she was heading this way. Except, of course, for the clerk at the motel in Santalina. And the wise-ass kid at the filling station.

And Barnaby.

Once again she wondered about his past. Was it catching up with his present? Why had he seemed so unfazed about the theft of the jewels he'd stolen? Could this whole thing be something to do with him, her father an innocent pawn in a high-rolling game of catch-thief?

She turned and looked into the darkness. The lake was a broad smear of silver against the increasing darkness. She could make out the solid shape of the octagonal house, its wooden decorations gleaming dully. Trees were black against the darkening sky. Otherwise, she could see almost nothing. She listened. Could hear nothing, either. Nothing out of the ordinary. She moved silently towards the house. Still wet, the inner sides of her thighs chafed together as she listened for footfalls, a sudden breath, movement.

She looked in again at the hall. A light had been left on beside the big sofa. Carefully she turned the handle of the door and pushed it open a little way. She listened for voices. There were none. Not a sound. She pushed the door open further and slipped into the hall, still listening. But there was no point. You can tell when a place is emptied of humanity. The air is stiller. She walked towards the back of the hall, where, beneath the minstrels' gallery, three doors gave on to the rest of the house. One opened into a study-type room. The next, into a dining room, where a long table of calamander gleamed like tyre tracks in wet sand beneath three portraits of austere ladies with contemptuous mouths.

The third led to the kitchen. Hi-tech. State-of-the-art decor. White tiles. Utilitarian cooking implements hanging from a central steel frame. A custom-built butcher's block. There was a bulletin board on the wall beside the icebox. Wine labels. A by-the-week diary. A faded photograph of two kids, girl and boy, grinning. The girl had a gap where her two front teeth were missing. Notices of concerts, art exhibitions, wine tastings. An invitation to a private viewing from something called the Fontaine Gallery in Berkeley, with the words *Do try to come – Josh* scrawled across it. A sheet torn from a memo pad, bordered with stylised harebells. *Ketchup*, it said, *instant coffee Salt.*

The room smelled of Africa. Spices, rotting fruit, vegetables with pungent leaves. Close her eyes and she could be back there, in the middle of the noise, the brightness, the dust, the despair . . .

61

The rest of the house was large and luxurious. Carpets curled over the ankle. Bathrooms were plentiful. Furnishings approached sumptuosity. Art with a capital 'A' hung from many of the walls, mainly in the form of drawings. They were all modern, all Western. Of Whitman's years in Africa there was no other sign at all. Cautiously, as she searched the place, Penny sniffed. The smell she instinctively dreaded was the thick metallic scent of blood. It wasn't there. Not in the bathrooms, bedrooms, closets, utility rooms. Nothing. By the time she had finished, she realised just how long she had been holding her breath. She fetched up in the study again. It was small, windowless, lined with books. A lot of them were the outsize kind that mean books on art. Looking more closely, at the titles, Penny saw that Whitman seemed to have a fairly comprehensive library of African art. Including several volumes by Ralph P. Nkasa.

There was no point staying any longer. What she needed to know now was where they'd taken Whitman and her father. She walked back into the kitchen. Was there anything useful on the bulletin board? Difficult to be sure. In the end, she unpinned the invitation to the private view and put it in her bag. She went outside, pulling the door to but not shutting it. A person never knew when a person might want to come back again.

Amazingly, the car was where she'd parked it. The keys were in place. She swung into the driver's seat and turned on the ignition. Reversing in a splatter of wood chips, she took off down the drive. She felt ill, drunk, exhilarated. Adrenalin sang like champagne through her veins. She was going to do something, anything, everything.

She was also going to heave again. Luckily she had time to pull up by the side of the road. Gaahd. One thing being sapped made you realise was the improbability of the Tough Guy school of literature, where the hero comes to five seconds after being slammed unconscious by a beating that would have felled an elephant. Especially as he usually goes on not only to eliminate the opposition with a series of lethal upper cuts but also to screw the heroine three times in half an hour with the stamina and skill of Casanova, create some gourmet sauce for the steaks he's found time to stick under the grill and deliver a dialectic of stunning morality while laying the table for two. No guy's that tough. Nor was she. Realisation of how untough she was, how very much she hated being hit on the head, made her nauseous again. Once more she threw up.

When she'd finished, she felt better. She decided the best thing she could do was to stay on this road and make for the nearest house. Although lights glinted here and there in the darkness on either side, she had no way of knowing the best route towards them. And they might turn out to be just street lamps. If the worst came to the worst, there was Bonami's only a few miles away. She looked at her watch. Six fifty. Maybe she should just head straight for the winery. There might still be someone there.

Ten minutes later, she passed a house. Behind a beech hedge which fronted the road, she could see that the windows on the ground floor were all lit up. A light over the front door was on, illuminating the black cedar shingles which covered the house. She'd forgotten the old lady in the Chevvy. Maybe this was a chance to teach her a thing or two about hand signals.

She pulled off the road and into the driveway, which ran on round the back of the house. A yellow compact with a black convertible roof sat on the gravel in front. The gravel hadn't been raked in weeks. It had a lumpy look and weeds were pushing through. The Chevvy wasn't on view.

The house was fronted by a broad porch with a swing seat suspended from the ceiling above. She ran up the wooden steps and across the boarded floor to bang on the door. The door panels were of Tiffany glass. Swirls of reds and blues and yellows. Art Nouveau. She'd dated a French-Canadian guy once at Stanford called Zeke Nouveau. He kept saying that Art was no relation. The joke soon wore thin.

Footsteps sounded in the hall. A woman opened the door a crack. The old lady? Seen from the front, she was slim and sixtyish. Not really old so much as not young. No wonder she still loved men. Men probably still loved her. Who wouldn't? Her hair was silver-grey and smoothly coiffed over the beautiful bones of her face. Behind her, was a square panelled hallway, furnished with Shaker spareness: one wooden chest, one wooden rocker, one wooden blanket-box. Preparations for Christmas were already evident in a bowlful of shiny silver balls with a bayberry candle planted in the middle of them and an arrangement of gilded pine cones. Warm. Comforting. Especially when you'd just got out of a lake.

'Hi,' Penny said. Her head ached like crazy. For two pins she'd have fallen forward on to the rag rugs which were spread over the polished planking of the hall and gone to sleep. 'I wonder if you could help me.'

The woman showed little emotion. None at all, really. That was

63

because she was already busy looking shell-shocked. As if Nemesis had recently tapped her on the shoulder and said, 'OK, lady. You're next.'

She stared at Penny without moving. She was a perfect size 8. 'What exactly to you want?' she said. There was a ghost of long-ago Britishness about her vowels.

'I wondered if I could use your phone,' said Penny. 'I need to call the police.'

'I'm sorry but I haven't got round to having it connected yet,' said the woman. 'I've only just moved in.' She started closing the door.

Penny didn't blame her. She might have done the same, if some black chick she never saw before showed up on her porch after dark, trying to be social. She stuck her foot out.

Somewhere upstairs a door opened. For a moment it leaked the sound of hollow television voices which spoke direly of the current financial crisis. Then the noise was cut off as the door closed again. Someone was upstairs, listening to the conversation. Doing nothing.

'Listen,' Penny said. 'I have a —'

'Would you mind moving your foot,' the woman said. It didn't seem to faze her that the foot in question was bare. That a person'd have to be pretty desperate to use a shoeless foot as a door-wedge. Maybe there was a lot of that sort of thing up here in northern California. 'Otherwise I shall have to call my – my friend down.'

Penny noted the lack of the word husband. The friend might be fine-boned and wimpish, easily manipulable. On the other hand, he could be big and a bully. Either way, he was almost certainly thirty years younger. She didn't waste time checking him out.

'Why don't you do that?' she said. 'Maybe he can help me.'

'What exactly do you want?' the woman asked. Simon Legree couldn't have been cooler.

'Just want to croon a verse or two of "Swannee Ribber", miz,' Penny said. 'Needed someone to join in on the chorus and hoped you and your – uh – *friend* might oblige.'

The woman's face twisted. She looked like the last time she'd obliged was when the man who usually turned on the current for the electric chair was held up in traffic. Resolute as Cerberus, she held the door against Penny's instep. She said: 'I have guard dogs on the premises which I am perfectly prepared to let loose if you don't leave at once.'

'Which way to the ice-floes?'

'I shall call my friend,' threatened the woman again.

'Please,' said Penny. 'Call him. Maybe he'd be more helpful.' She leaned suddenly on the door. It opened. The woman jumped back as though expecting Penny to club her to death. Penny was past clubbing anything. She stepped just over the threshold and stood on the mat. It said *Welcome to our Home* in green bristles set into red ones. They tickled the soles of her bare feet. 'Do you mind if I just wait here until he comes down?'

'Yes,' the woman said. 'I do.' She glanced up at the unseen listener then back at Penny. She might have been going to faint. 'And you're dripping all over my floor which I've just had professionally stripped.'

'Gee,' said Penny. 'I've always wanted to meet a professional stripper. You must give me his name.' She was beginning to feel like Toulouse-Lautrec. As though there wasn't a lot between knee and ankle. 'I've just driven here from Pilot Whitman's place. I believe he and my father have been abducted against their will. Also, there is a dead man in the lake.'

'Your father?' the woman said. She cleared her throat. Twice.

'Yes. Dr Benjamin Wanawake. Won't mean anything to you but he's with the UN.'

'Benjamin Wanawake,' said the woman. She frowned as though trying to remember where she'd heard the name before. Somewhere under the ice, something stirred briefly.

'Do you know him?' Penny said.

'I've heard of him,' said the woman. Defrosting began. Behind her a long-case clock which showed the phases of the moon suddenly tinkled a couple of times. 7.15. 'Look. I can't help you. But there's a winery just down the road. Try them. They'll be on the phone. I'm sorry.'

Penny shrugged. 'So am I.' She moved backwards out of the door. She walked down the steps of the porch and stepped sideways to avoid the yellow compact. As she passed she put a hand on the hood. It was still warm. From the doorway, the woman watched her, as though worried she might leave marks on the finish.

She got back into the sopping seat of her hire-car and swung out of the drive. There'd been a phone in there. She'd seen it through the crack in the door. So why would the woman claim that she wasn't yet connected? She shrugged. There was no law said you had to let soaked strangers across your threshold. Just because the Good Book said 'Knock and it shall be opened unto you' didn't mean they had to let you in.

It was another ten minutes before she could see in the distance a string of coloured bulbs. Closer to, she saw that they bounded the edge of Bonami's Winery. They swayed back and forth on unseen cables, each with its own nimbus of fuzzy light. The big barn appeared deserted but brightness spilled from the Victorian-style wooden house behind it, painted peachy brown with trim in a darker shade.

Penny rattled the knocker. After a while, a woman opened the door. Her hair was done in a sculpted Californian tangle. In this light it was hard to tell whether the blonde streaks were sun or Clairol. Whichever, Penny was prepared to bet her father's collection of snuffboxes that no one had thrown up near it in the last twenty-four hours.

Penny smiled at her. 'Hi,' she said. 'I'm Penny Wanawake.'

The woman seemed confused. 'Oh. It's you again.'

'I'm sorry to trouble you,' said Penny. 'I urgently need to use the phone.'

A man with a face inclined to geniality appeared behind the woman. Late fifties, paunchy, plentiful hair of the wild kind. He wore a pair of shorts that were a bad mistake, and a white knitted shirt which featured crossed tennis racquets at nipple level. 'I thought you were going to come back,' he said severely.

'When was I?'

'Whenever it was. Months ago. You said you were. I waited over an hour in my office for you.' He looked at her more closely. 'That *is* what we arranged, isn't it?'

'Not me,' Penny said. 'Honest.' Her teeth began to shake against each other.

'Not you?' the woman said sharply. 'Don't be ridiculous.'

'You're mistaking me for someone else,' Penny said. This had to be the dead girl cropping up again. Her double. Doppelgängers can be bad for your health. Your mental health. They can start you wondering about the nature of reality. Whether the who you think you are is really an illusion. Whether it is the other who that is the real one and you, the image.

'If we're mistaking you for someone else, you must have a twin sister,' said the man. His tone was heavily sardonic, as though he knew she was lying but couldn't prove it either way.

'I know the person you mean,' Penny said. 'I'm not her. Far's I know. She's dead.'

The man's genial face paled. It was obvious that until now, he'd lived a life entirely free of black girls who got themselves killed. It was also obvious that the life he'd lived until now was the sort he preferred.

The woman put a hand to her mouth. 'Dead?' she said squeakily. Her eyes bulged like a toad's.

' 'Fraid so.'

Her husband swallowed lumpily. His face had all the glow and vigour of a tapioca pudding. 'Sure,' he managed. 'And I keep my second head in a hatbox in the closet.'

'It's true. I saw her. Someone had beaten her brains out and then left her on the deck of my father's beach house.'

He looked like he'd just heard Ronald Reagan had been elected to a third term in office. 'What?' he said.

'Listen,' Penny said. 'Could you call the police? There's been some trouble up at the Whitman place.'

'What kind of trouble?' If there was trouble, the woman wanted to make it clear she thought Penny was at the bottom of it. 'You look as if someone just fished you out of a lake.' She made it sound like a synonym for slurry pit.

'It was a do-it-yourself job,' said Penny.

'Really?'

'Someone dumped me in Mr Whitman's lake.' It had to be Dezzy, didn't it? Creeping up behind her in the dark, sound hidden by the wood chips.

They looked at each other.

'He's been kidnapped, see. And my father along with him. I saw the guys who took them.'

The wife squawked for a second or two. Then she turned and went away.

'Kidnapped?' the man said.

'Yeah. Some bozos brought the two of them to Whitman's place in a Caddy and then drove them away again.'

'Why would anyone do that?'

'I guess because they found me snooping around,' said Penny. 'They had to take them someplace else after that.'

'What for?' He'd obviously had more than enough excitement that evening.

'Ah,' said Penny. 'There you have me. I think someone's going to use one or other of them – or maybe even both – for some pretty intensive bargaining. And it's no use asking me what they're going to want in exchange, because I haven't worked it out.' As yet, there seemed to be no direct connection between the dead bimbo in Big Sur and the kidnapping of a diplomat plus the friend he hadn't seen

67

for years. There might not even be one. Yet all roads seemed to lead to one or other.

The wife came back. 'Ed Lutz is on his way,' she informed them both. For Penny's exclusive use, she added: 'He's the local sheriff. And a very good friend of ours.' Just in case Penny decided to try apple-polishing her way out of trouble.

The husband seemed suddenly to decide that Penny was on the level. 'Look, honey,' he said to the wife. 'Why don't you ring Ed back, tell him to meet us at the motel in Santalina?'

'What for?' the wife said. 'Where are you going?'

'I'm going to drive this young lady back there, book her in for the night. She looks all worn out and she's soaking wet, too. Before we go, you could give her a towel so she can dry off.'

The woman shrugged and started up the stairs without speaking. The lines of something cutting into her body at waist and buttock were clearly visible under her pink pants. She came back with a green-striped towel and pushed it at Penny. Ask and it shall be given unto you.

'OK,' the man said. 'Let's go.'

'No,' said the wife. She clasped her hands together. 'Honey, you don't know what you're getting mixed up in. Dead bodies. Abductions. It's like something off *Cagney and Lacey*. Don't get involved.'

'What?' the man said.

'That's just what they told each other while Kitty Genovese died,' said Penny. ' "Don't get involved." Well, I am involved, so I'd better get back, see what I can do to help my father and his friend.' She flashed a look at the man. 'And please don't bother asking me to drop by again, because the answer's always going to be no.' She marched across the porch and down the steps.

The man came after her. 'Just a minute here,' he said. 'I'm not my wife's keeper. And no more is she mine. You see what I'm saying?'

'That your wife sucks?'

'You probably do too, sometimes. Everybody does.'

'Right.'

'What I'm saying is, I'm on your side, lady.'

Penny decided to be forgiving. It was supposed to be divine, wasn't it? 'OK,' she said. 'Your car or mine?'

'Mine,' he said. 'Your driver-seat is all wet. For another, I don't think you could drive straight. That's a hell of a lump on your head.'

From the porch, the woman wailed: 'Hon-eeeeh.'

'A real Pass-by-on-the-other-sider,' said Penny.

'She's not so bad,' the man said. 'Sounds it sometimes, but she's OK. I guess she's just kind of soured, living the public life we have here, always on show here for the customers, front woman, like that. It's not her scene.'

'What is? Selling package holidays in Siberia?'

He frowned. 'That's my wife you're talking about.'

Penny like loyalty. Even if misplaced. 'Sorry,' she said. 'It's just it's been quite a night.'

'As it happens,' the man said stiffly, 'my wife did a course in oenology at Davis after we got married. She makes most of our wines. She's won all sorts of diplomas.'

'Any of them for congeniality?'

'She's OK,' he said again. 'You know how to handle her.'

'You're Carlo Bonami, right?'

'Right,' he said briefly. He drove competently fast. In front of them the road stretched black and empty. A highway to nowhere.

They were in sight of the lights of Santalina when he suddenly stamped on the brake. The car slewed into the side of the road. He grabbed her wrist and squeezed so it hurt. 'OK,' he said. 'Confession time.'

'I'm not Catholic.'

'Cut the crap,' he said. The genial face was no longer genial. The wild hair menaced like the Gorgon's. 'What kind of game are you playing?'

'Not,' Penny said, trying to wrest away from him, 'a contact sport.' His grip was disconcertingly strong.

'What are you really after?' he said.

'I really told you. My father.'

'I heard what you said. That doesn't mean I believe it.'

'Why not?'

'Because although it took me a while to be certain, I know you're not the girl who came here before. Even though you look pretty much like her. You're taller. And you have that British accent.'

'You've got it all wrong,' said Penny. '*She* looks just like *me*.'

'I want to know why you're going round pretending to be someone else.'

'She was the one faking it, for chrissake. If anyone was.'

'Prove it.'

'How? What would you accept as proof? My passport? I could have stolen it from her. Same with any ID I offered.' She turned in her seat to face him. 'Tell me, did you and this girl talk much?'

'No.'

'Did she say what she was doing up here?'

'She asked about Pilot Whitman. Just like you have.'

'Did she say why?'

'She said he was an old friend of her father's.' His hold on her wrist had relaxed. She wrenched her arm away, edging over towards the car door.

'That's right,' she said, 'he is. At least, no, he's not. Not of *her* father's. Or I suppose he could be, but I don't know about that. I do know he's an old friend of *my* father's. At least . . .' Penny had to think about it. '. . . he's definitely an old friend of Benjamin's.'

'Who's Benjamin?'

'My father. At least, I think he is. He certainly used to be.'

'This whole set-up's getting kinda confusing.'

'I'm a little confused here myself,' Penny said. 'Why did you make an appointment to see her, for instance?'

'Like I said, she wanted to know about Pilot. We're good buddies, Pilot and me. At least, we used to be.'

'Aren't you any more?'

'I guess. But he's been keeping pretty much to himself lately. I know how it can be. Money troubles. Makes you want to keep away from those who haven't got them. I've been there myself, believe me.'

'Why didn't you tell this girl to talk directly with Mr Whitman? Why have her come to your office?'

He seemed uncomfortable. His hand played with the steering. He pushed in the cigarette lighter and waited until it popped out before replying.

'If you really want to know, this girl strung us a line about her parents being in the catering business in Boston. Wanted to talk about us supplying them direct. Discount for bulk buying, that sort of thing.'

Penny didn't say anything. Mainly because she could think of nothing to say. Had the girl been lying? Was Carlo?

He went on: 'Nobody's so big that they can afford to turn down a possible business deal. In times of recession, it's the mid-market luxury businesses that go to the wall. Wineries. Restaurants. Jewellers. It's not the rich rich who suffer when the economy's bad but the poor rich.' He shrugged. 'You go where you think the business is. It wasn't a lot of my time, and talking to the girl could have led to something.'

Once again he pushed in the lighter. Penny guessed that Carlo

70

Bonami was embarrassed by the fact that he'd fallen for what might have been a scam of some kind. What she couldn't even begin to guess was what the girl had really been after.

'It's not going to lead to anything now,' she said. 'Not now she's dead.'

She heard him swallow. 'It's really true?

'I'm afraid so. And before you start wondering, I didn't kill her.'

'Dead,' he said. 'Jesus.' He put one hand on his mouth for a moment. 'God. That's terrible.'

'Matter of fact, I was the one called in the cops. If you don't believe me, call Detective Fredo Santini of the Monterey Police Department.'

'What exactly happened?'

Penny filled him in. When she'd finished, he said, 'If it's murder, Ed Lutz isn't the guy to handle it. He's got the intellectual impact of an oyster.'

'I always thought oysters were pretty smart. Look how hard it is to break one open.'

'Break old Ed open, and you'll find solid cement.'

'This whole thing is getting dangerous,' Penny said. 'Whoever it was dunked me in that lake was hoping I'd die. Or that I was already dead. Whoever it was may already have killed two other people.'

'But this is terri —'

'And may be the same person who's holding my father and Mr Whitman.'

They arrived at Santalina. Carlo nosed the car into one of the slots in front of the motel and got out. He came round and opened the door for Penny. 'Will you be OK?' he said.

'I guess.' Penny tried to smile above engulfing weariness. It probably had a lot to do with the crack on her head. 'I'll have a shower, get the gunge off my hair.'

'I'll hang around, wait for Sheriff Lutz. You might feel better talking to him if I'm there.'

'Sounds good to me,' she said. She showed him her dimples. He deserved it.

Back in her room, she showered. Something was niggling her. Some detail that didn't quite fit. When her hair started to squeak, she stepped out of the tub and swilled it clean. Then she filled it up and lay submerged. She was still niggled, irritated as though by a mosquito bite. The more she scratched, the more it itched.

Wound up in a bathsheet, she sat down on the edge of the bed

71

and dialled the hotel in San Francisco. She asked for Barnaby's room. She let it ring fifty times before she put down the receiver. Wherever he was, it wasn't here beside her, putting his arms round him, comforting just by his presence. She despised herself for the emotional dependence. She told herself that we are all ultimately alone.

Some time later, after talking to the sheriff, she picked up the phone and dialled Whitman's house. For a while she listened to the telephone bleeping itself hoarse in an empty room. She called Whitman's restaurants. The Forlorn Hope ploy. The first said they hadn't seen him. The second said he hadn't either. He said so in a pouty voice, adding that Mr. Whitman didn't seem to realise you got a lot more out of people if you gave them a bit of encouragement and that just because —

'Belt up, Earl,' Penny said. She put down the receiver.

She took in the four bare walls. Climbed into the fresh-laundered bed. Lay down on her side. When you thought about it, ultimate aloneness was a bit of a bore, frankly.

8

The invitation to a private view of works by local craftsman Joshua Peters, Worker in Precious Metals, was for a couple of weeks back. That didn't faze Penny. She'd tell them she had no sense of time. It had a good creative ring to it.

She left the car in a supermarket parking lot and walked back up Telegraph Avenue towards the Berkeley campus. The sidewalks were crowded with people chatting to each other or themselves or, in one case, a tree. Stalls were selling all manner of luxury goods, from costume jewellery made out of tortured forks to sexually precocious eggcups.

It was like moving into a *Star Trek* episode. A warp where time had stood still and only the humans got older. The street-people were out in force today, clustered round the entrance to the head-shop, squatting down with their backs against the walls, rolling joints. Hippies mostly who came here back in the Sixties when it was cool to be hip, when love and freedom sounded as if they might acquire some global credibility. Trouble with freedom is, it's too close to aimless. And these middle-aged guys in their jeans and earth shoes, long grey hair pulled back in an elastic band, middle-aged paunches hiding behind black Bob-Dylan waistcoats, *were* aimless, their eyes vacant, their faces florid from the years of trying to fill the emptiness with the drink and the drugs. Reeds who'd bent before a non-existent storm and never quite straightened up again.

They milled around, along with the faculty wives and the dead-beats, while the scholastic young moved purposefully past the instant photo places and the drugstores and the book shops and the nail boutiques, wearing shorts and running shoes and deep-down all-over tans. Penny watched them for a while, marvelling at that heightened sense of future hope which hangs like incense round places of higher education.

She made her way through Sather Gate into Sproule Plaza. Here it was, the home of found causes – or had been, back in the Sixties, during the great wrenching away from the Victorian umbilical.

Before Robert Kennedy died. And Martin Luther King. When there still seemed some hope for the world if only people believed enough. Now there were no riots, no tear gas. Just a man holding a foam-rubber microphone and miming a Beatles standard to a tinny cassette player. She checked the big tourist map which stood to one side and found where she was headed. The Fontaine Gallery turned out to be on the second floor of a green-painted stucco building between a video shop and a mini-market. Underneath it was a bookstore. Lightly varnished open-tread stairs led to a glass door acid-etched with a stylised fountain spraying equal amounts of water to right and left. In front of the door sat a guard dressed in the uniform of some security firm. He was eating French fries from a polystyrene box.

The gallery was small, only two rooms. Both contained plenty of light and air and quite a lot of unframed canvases painted in the kind of colours that leaped off the wall and jabbed at the viewer with the insistence of a sparring partner. Coir matting covered the floors. All the woodwork had been stained black, including the five sharpened pencils which stood in a pot on the table by the door. Large hand-hewn vases containing dried wheat-heads and pampas grass stood here and there. The place smelled as though it had recently been sprayed with roach repellant. Penny wrinkled her nose to stop a sneeze forming.

She was still wrinkling it when a woman appeared from behind a giant artefact of rude pottery. She wore a peasant blouse beneath a black velvet bolero heavily encrusted with rotting gold embroidery, teamed with snow-washed jeans and spike-heeled boots of scarlet leather. She looked like a Hungarian gipsy who'd decided to try her hand at street-walking. Hand probably wasn't the right word.

She sat down at a slab of black wood resting on some artful tree stumps and laid a copy of *People* magazine she'd been reading flat on its face. A slim-line version of Liz Taylor radiated from the cover.

She looked up at Penny with the puckered features of a wild rodent. 'Hi,' she said.

'Mrs Fontaine?' said Penny.

The woman tittered. 'Are you kidding? I know life's been a bitch so far, but I'd hate to think people could mix the two of us up. I mean, she's geriatric. Still got her looks, but definitely over the hill.' She grimaced, using a lot of lipsticked mouth on it. 'Mind you, the way my ex-husband used to behave, the jerk, it wouldn't surprise me if I looked like Miz Fontaine's grandmother, sometimes.'

'Uh —' Penny said.

'No. I'm Lisa Druckner,' said the woman. 'General dogsbody, I guess you'd have to call me. Though there sure isn't a lot to do here since nobody much comes around. I guess Miz Fontaine writes it off as a tax loss or something. It's not exactly the Museum of Modern Art, is it?'

She seemed to expect an answer. 'No,' Penny said. It wasn't.

'Still, it keeps me off the streets,' said Lisa.

'Right.'

'Especially while Miz Fontaine's so busy right now, getting herself organised. Personally, most of the stuff she goes in for has me coming off the wall.' She eyed her surroundings critically. 'Right off the wall. I suppose it's from living abroad all those years. But then so did my ex. Drive me nuts, I mean. Him and his women. Jeez. Go-go dancers, and all. Man of his age. Ridiculous, really, but —'

'I've come about Joshua Peters,' Penny said firmly. If she didn't get a word in edgewise, she might never speak again.

'Oh, sure.' Ms Druckner fumbled about in the top drawer of the table and handed Penny a catalogue. 'That'll be a dollar fifty,' she said.

'I'm quite happy to buy a catalogue, but I'm actually more interested in Mr Peters than in his work.'

'Ri-i-ight,' said Lisa. She dragged the word out like bubble gum. She winked. 'I know what you mean. Quite a hunk, isn't he? I like 'em big myself, but he's enough to make you take out property-damage insurance.'

'Is he?'

'I thought you knew him.' Ms Druckner drew back as though afraid of contamination. Her tight little features grew wary.

'Not yet,' Penny said. 'But I'm hoping you'll help me put that right.'

'How?'

Penny held out the invitation card. 'See, he sent me this down in La Jolla, but I couldn't make the opening. And, stupid as it sounds, I can't find his number and they told me on 411 that the darn thing's unlisted. So if you'd just give me his address, I could contact him direct.'

Out on the street, a car alarm sounded, pushing regular whoops of noise into the room.

'Oh no. I'm sorry.' Ms Druckner might have the frail look of a framework tailor's dummy but underneath she was pure steel. 'We

75

can't give out the private addresses of exhibitors. I'm sure you can appreciate our reasoning.'

'Not really.'

'Why, how do I know you're who you say you are?'

'I haven't actually said yet.'

'I give you his address, you could just drive on up there and start bothering him some way. I mean, maybe you sell insurance or something. Or you're some looney-toon like that girl in *Play Misty For Me* want to go on up there and give him some hassle.' She looked at Penny, waiting for her to crumple into sudden violent rage like Jessica Walter.

'Do I look like a screwball?'

'No,' the woman said.

She could've sounded more certain. 'Well, then,' Penny said.

'But that could just be part of your mad cunning.'

'I'm as sane as anyone else.'

Ms Druckner laughed, open-mouthed. Her teeth were un-American. 'Round here, that's a pretty meaningless statement.'

'OK,' Penny said. 'If you won't give me Mr Peters's address, how about his phone number? Like I said, it's unlisted.'

The woman nodded. 'That's right.'

'Any particular reason for that?'

'What do I know? I just sit here, sell catalogues, write a few letters when Miz Fontaine gets her ass moving, which isn't real often. Living abroad, guess she musta lost the ol' American hustle.' She put her head on the side, stretching her mouth into a suggestive grin. 'Maybe Mr Peters gets a lot of obscene phone calls, heavy breathers, like that. Man with his looks, it's not surprising. Makes me breathe kind of heavy myself, you want the truth.'

'So will you give me the number?'

Lisa shook her head.

'But I need to get in touch with him urgently.'

'I just couldn't take the responsibility.'

'OK,' Penny said. 'Here's what you do. You call him for me. Tell him someone wants to speak to him and would he authorise you giving out his address.'

Lisa looked suspicious. Her eyes narrowed. Wrinkles corrugated the skin round them.

'I'll turn my back,' Penny said. 'So I can't possibly see which numbers you punch.'

'Who should I say wants to know?'

'Say I'm a good friend of Pilot Whitman's.' Too late, she realised

76

that she'd slipped up. If Josh Peters was supposed to have sent her the invitation, he'd know her, wouldn't he? She gambled on the fact that like every other artist she'd ever known, he simply sent out invites for the private view to everyone he could think of. Plus their third cousin. Also, that Lisa Druckner was a no-brain.

'Whitman?'

'Yeah. Say I couldn't make the show, but Pilot told me to get in touch next time I was up here.' Penny tightened up her posture. Thought money. Thought cheekbones. 'I have my own gallery, see, down in La Jolla. I'm always looking for new talent. Pilot thought Mr Peters and I could maybe get together, do a deal.'

'Is that right?' Lisa said.

No. As a matter of fact it was a complete lie. One of these days, her tongue was going to cleave to the roof of her mouth, the lies she told. Still, she figured if a person had a talent, she shouldn't let it go to waste. And she was a real talented liar.

'Uh-huh,' Penny said. Wasn't a yes, wasn't a no. Just a sop to her grossly underactive conscience.

'You go look at the stuff on show,' Lisa said. 'I'll call him up.'

Penny walked away as she hunched over the phone. The pictures were undoubtedly impressive. Joshua Peters was a forceful painter of the naive school. And an obsessive one, covering the same themes again and again. Against the rough-cast white walls, his work glowed like Ali Baba's treasure, logging the ease with which a whole civilisation had been chimney-swept into dust. Parrot greens. Hibiscus reds. Egg-yolk yellows. A sequence, women with bright spotted bandanas round their heads, big-eyed black babies, men standing proud and tall beneath a hurricane of wild-game, lions, zebras, elephant and rhino hurtling through a sky as blue as jay-feathers. Everyone was smiling, including the animals. Then the white man came. He was there many times over in the next pictures. Bearded, armed to the teeth, killing. The animals still rushed across the sky, but fewer now, and sadder. In the last picture, the green had given way to grey. The woman wept, the points of their bandanas drooping over children whose bellies were big now with starvation. The animals lay torn and bleeding on the ground. Where there had been trees, chimneys bloomed. Where there had been water, television-screens lay like pools in the grey dust.

You didn't need a catalogue to know the title. *The Rape of Africa. Let My People Go.* Something like that. A simple message. A simplistic one, even. And ultimately dishonest. Because the whites could be blamed for exploitation, for greed, for the imposition of an alien culture and the desire for the goods it spawned, but not for the lack of rain. Not for the way the desert shifted southwards every year. Not for everything.

Penny walked into the second of the two rooms. It was smaller than the first and held less. A trio of landscapes, the same scene taken at different times of the year. Several marine views, painted with a lack of conviction that suggested the artist had not yet found his sea legs. A few portraits.

Admiring them was a large white suit of linen containing Professor Nkasa. When she came into the room, he turned.

'Ah,' he said. 'Miss Wanawake.' He came towards her, stretching out a hand.

Penny was reluctant to take it. Who knew where it had been? Suppose one of the places was round the dead girl's neck. Or smashing in her skull. 'Good morning, Professor,' she said. Breeding always tells.

'I've not come across this man's work before,' Nkasa said. 'Have you?'

'No.'

'Then let us enjoy it together.'

Just what she'd always wanted. Penny bent with him over a glass-sided viewing case which stretched down the middle of the room. It was lined with black cotton velvet arranged into nooks and crannies in which nestled pieces of silver and various bits of jewellery. Most of it was modern, using precious metals and semi-precious stones to create fluidly organic shapes which reminded Penny of Rorschach tests. At one end of the case, however, lay several pieces that were more traditional in design, the kind of thing painters of Elizabeth I used to delineate with such exactitude. There were several necklaces with matching drop earrings, some brooches, a couple of tiaras. Although Penny never wore anything but pearls, one particular bracelet of square-cut amethysts set in gold made her draw in a covetous breath. Had all the pieces been worked by the same hands, she wondered? The modern ones were distinctive enough to be immediately recognisable. Eve, the singer from the African Queen, had been wearing work by the same craftsman. The others could have come from the nineteenth-century jewellery collections of any major museum. Were they deliberate copies, or merely homages to the craftsmen of an earlier time? Whichever, they were very beautiful.

Nkasa murmured appreciatively as they studied the exhibits. 'I imagine that working in precious metals is his first medium,' he said. 'This is a genuinely original and exciting use of materials. The artist has a great future ahead of him.'

'You don't like the paintings?'

'Not all of them. Some of the flower-studies. Some of the portraits. This one may interest you.' He moved Penny towards one. It showed a naked girl. She was stretched out on a divan which had been covered in a shawl of fringed white silk. Behind her a bank of birds-of-paradise loomed. She lay with her eyes closed. One hand was behind her head. Despite the relaxed pose, the artist made it clear that the girl was tense and troubled. The eyes were shut not in sleep but to block out a world with which she could not cope. Looking at that face, Penny felt a frisson of something indistinguishable from fear crackle down the ends of her hair. The painted girl was unquestionably the same as the one she'd last seen dead, wreathed in sea-mist. She lay in the same pose, one hand splayed across her breast, the other alongside her body, emphasising its sleek lines.

Why had Nkasa chosen this one to show her? Was he warning her? Or was she stretching coincidence too far? It was a classic nude pose, after all. And wasn't it a little unlikely that in searching for her father, she'd stepped right back into the middle of the murder she'd left behind at Big Sur?

Of course it was.

'I was struck at once by the model's likeness to you,' Nkasa said. He gave her a smile that she tried very hard not to see as wolfish.

'It was the plants that attracted me,' he said. 'Such brilliant colours, are they not? Your father seems to do particularly well with them, doesn't he?' He stepped back. 'So exotic, so flamboyant. Frightening, almost. Don't you agree?' The silk shirt he wore today was peacock blue. The base of his throat shone. His grip on her arm was too tight.

'No,' she said, 'plants don't scare me.'

'What does, Miss Wanawake?'

'Wild animals, perhaps. Indifference. Fanatics.'

'Ah yes. Fanaticism. Religious, political – it is always the fanatics who cause trouble, in any society. Rushing in without fear of the consequences.' As they moved on, he looked down at her: 'In a small country like my own, fighting for its individual voice on the world stage, fanatics are particularly dangerous.'

'What's the solution, Professor?'

He shrugged. 'Elimination?' He let go of her to examine another picture.

'I gotta go now,' Penny said. 'It's been great seeing you.'

She went quickly back to the first room. At the desk, Lisa murmured into the phone. 'Sure, Josh . . . Gallery in La Jolla . . . Mr Whitman . . . looks loaded . . . yeah . . . yeah.'

Penny turned back to the canvases on the walls. Carlo Bonami had been right about Ed Lutz. He hadn't cut much mustard. Not as an investigator. To imply that his head was solid concrete was to give the building trade a bad name. He'd listened to Penny's account of the evening before with his mouth slightly open, his eyes fixed unwaveringly on the movement of her chest underneath her white singlet. Maybe the guy was investigating whether she wore a bra or not. Even to a small-town cop, it should have been obvious.

Finally he'd stood up and said that Mr Whitman was a private kind of guy, but he'd try to catch up with him, see what was going down. He pulled a stick of gum from his shirt pocket and tore it in half, popping one half back, the other half in his mouth. He had to concentrate to get it right. At the door, he turned, Colombo-style, and said: 'Oh yeah. Something else's bothering me. This other guy, with Mr Whitman: you sure it was your pa?'

Spilling out her troubles to Ed hadn't solved a thing. A jell-head like that wouldn't know what to do with a trouble if it jumped right down his throat. Nor did he seem to have the faintest intention of looking for either of the two men.

What she had to hope now was that Joshua Peters was going to come across with his address. Probably he didn't have the faintest idea where Pilot Whitman was. Hell, he might not even know *who* Pilot Whitman was. Just because he'd sent him an invitation to a private view didn't mean beans. But at this stage in the game, anything went. And there had to be a link between him and the girl, just as there had to be one between the girl and Whitman. Her visit to Napa had just about proved that. All she had to do now was find it.

Suppose she couldn't? Better not think that way. Better not think of her father as she had seen him last night. Grey, reduced, as deprived of potency as a new novel on the Remaindered table. Nor could she bear to think of him being hurt. She was putting all her money on the notion that wherever they'd been taken, Benjamin and Whitman were still together. Not that she had anything substantial to back the feeling up. It was just that Preppy hadn't looked like he was into heavy sweating. And shifting bodies around could generate a lot of perspiration. Could even do some underarm damage to that Armani sweater he was wearing. Which meant he'd probably stick with Dezzy, if only so the goon could handle the heavy work.

Lisa put down the phone. 'OK,' she said. 'Here's the thing. Mr Peters says you can have his address.' She handed Penny a piece of paper. 'Give him a big kiss from me, won't you?' She winked.

9

Joshua Peters. It was a substantial sort of name. And his house, when she'd steered the car there through the Berkeley hills back of the UC campus, was a substantial sort of house. So were its neighbours: luxury-class homes, heavily planted, widely spaced, built to last out of high-quality materials.

Peters's house was set back from the road. The front was dominated by a large tree set into a raised bed and planted with ivy which crawled all over the lower half of the trunk. Orangey ice-plants covered large tracts of the rest of the yard.

Penny rang at the door. It was made of thick varnished wood, with a spy hole set at eye-height. She grinned into it. One thing she really hated was being looked at without being able to look back. After a while, the door opened.

She'd read in the catalogue that after a deprived childhood in a Chicago slum, Peters had been apprenticed to a silversmith. He'd spent a year in Paris, working at Cartier's, and another in Copenhagen with Georg Jensen. Examples of his work could be found in museums and private collections all over the world. Ditto his paintings. There was a black-and-white reproduction of a silver water jug with a lapiz-inlaid lid that had won first prize in some Scandinavian competition.

What the catalogue hadn't said was that he was black. A compact man in white bib overalls who laughed a lot. He was doing that now.

'Hi, Soos,' he said, turning away as he opened the door. It was something you only did to a familiar visitor.

'Hi,' Penny said. She stepped inside the house.

'Got to move,' said Peters. 'Some dame from a gallery in La Jolla's on her way to talk deals. I'm in the middle of picking up in the studio.' He walked away down the dark passage towards the rear of the house, throwing words back at her. 'You changed your hair again. I'd hardly got used to the last lot,' he said over his shoulder.

'Mmmm,' Penny said, giving nothing away. At the end of the passage, green and light showed.

She followed him into a designer kitchen. The fittings were of some kind of dark wood. There seemed to be a lot of small balustrades attached to the shelves. On some of the shelves there were pieces of lustred glass. On others, crude bits of rock lacking beauty. The counter tops were made of black slate.

Large sliding doors of glass led on to a patio so crowded with green plants that it could have doubled as a Tarzan movie set. A redwood picnic table with attached benches stood beneath a cottonwood. Across a patch of tough grass sticking out of soil that was mostly sand, a hot tub lounged beside a single-storey building that seemed to be part-garage, part-workshop. Both the up-and-over doors were up and over. On one side she could see the back end of a pick-up with the flap hanging down. The other showed artistic paraphernalia. Easels. Old coffee-cans full of brushes. A big steel workbench. The top was littered with a variety of implements. She could see welding equipment, a rack of hammers ranging in size from small to lethal, long trails of electric flex attached to objects whose function she couldn't even begin to guess at.

In the middle of the kitchen was a table covered with a Liberty-print PVC cloth. Lady Helena had the exact same cloth back home. Penny felt a homesick pang. Lying about on it, she noted, was a *House and Garden*, an out-of-date catalogue from Sotheby's, several issues of a foodie magazine. Underneath the table stood a cardboard box containing several bottles of Bonami's 1981 Cabernet.

'I'm taking a coffee break,' Peters said. 'Want some?'

Penny nearly said she didn't drink coffee. But that might have made him turn round and look at her more closely. And once he'd done that, she'd be in trouble. Whoever he mistook her for – and it wouldn't require a First in Guesswork to realise it must be the girl she now knew was dead – obviously drank coffee. Indeed, from the way he was already rattling a mug from a kitchen cupboard, had done so with him many times before. Oh shit. And she'd have to end up telling him the bad news. Which would probably mean he'd kick her ass out of there before she'd got any information from him about Whitman.

Under the crossed straps of his overalls the muscles in his back moved. Light shifted on skin the colour of Navy rum. Long thighs. Small buns. Show me a man with a small behind and I'll show you a skilful lover, Penny thought. He looked like he'd go 170 power-packed lbs. Plus another five if you counted in his teeth. They were big teeth. White. Firmly settled. Teeth to dazzle with. When he turned round and smiled at her, she blinked. So did he.

'Susannah?' he said. He peered at her like a tortoise. He felt in the bib pocket for a pair of rimless eyeglasses. He put them on. 'Who the fuck are you?' he said.

'Hi,' said Penny. 'I'm Penny Wanawake.'

'Great,' he said. 'Am I supposed to react in some way?' The manner in which he said it was as near disdainful as made no odds. There were only two conclusions to be drawn. Either he'd never heard the name Wanawake, or he was a world-class actor.

'Not yet.'

He removed the glasses and folded them up again. 'What are you doing in my house?'

'Wanted to know what exactly a deprived childhood was,' Penny said.

'Come on, lady,' he said. His face was full of what she recognised instantly as irritation fringed with anger. 'You've heard of them. Rats as big as water melons. Garbage in the hallways. Daddies raping their little girls. Shit like that. Anything else you want to know before I throw you out?'

'You did invite me in,' she said.

He leaned against the counter. Behind him, coffee whirlpooled inside a glass percolator. 'You look pretty bright,' he said. 'You must have figured out I mistook you for someone else, obviously. I don't make a habit of asking total strangers into my house.'

'Who's Susannah?'

'A . . . friend.'

'A special friend?'

'Sometimes.' He frowned. 'You look a helluva lot like her.'

'Is that right?' Penny said. So the girl's name was Susannah. So how come she was lying in a morgue miles down the coast?

'Would you mind telling me just what you want?' Joshua held up his hand, the palm pale, batiked with darker lines. 'Wait. Don't tell me. You're the chick that ol' Lisa from Fontaine's just called me about.'

'Right.'

'Why didn't you say so?'

'Before we go any further, Mr Peters, perhaps I should say that I don't own a gallery in La Jolla. Or anywhere else, tell the truth.'

'Before we go any further, why'n't I just show you the front door?'

'Because I –' Penny never did have much of a talent for breaking bad news '– I wanted to talk to you about your friend Susannah.' She was ad-libbing here, seeing her investigation taking another sideways leap towards the dead girl who'd impersonated her, rather than a forward one in the direction of her father's whereabouts.

'Why?'

'Because, Mr Peters, she's been trespassing on my space. People are mixing the two of us up. I want to know what's going on.'

He looked her over, the big dark eyes rolling up and down her body with the impersonal gaze of a mortician. 'Wouldn't be difficult to mistake you,' he said. 'I mean, she's got a head start on anyone else'd want to try the same thing. You looking so like her and all.'

'Way I see it, she looks like *me*,' Penny said.

'Whatever.'

'But she doesn't resemble me so much that we could be twins. I mean, if she was planning to impersonate me, it could only have been in front of people who didn't know me that well. Or who'd never seen me in the flesh.'

'True,' he said.

'Is she an artist too?'

Joshua shook his head. 'Uh-huh. Actress. Leastways, that's what she really does.'

'Have I heard of her?'

'Not yet. But you will. She's going to be something, that girl.' She already is, Penny thought. Dead. 'Right now, she's with some hole-in-the-wall company here. The Jumpin' Beans, some shit like that. All garbage cans and masks. It makes me mad, wasting her time like that when she could be really something, if she wanted. If she'd drop all the experimental crap, the street theatre.' He shrugged. 'Going round the neighbourhoods in a potato sack, hassling people till they react – what's it prove? I don't see all this stuff about bringing theatre to the people. If the people wanted theatre, they'd ask for it.'

The coffee blopped and burped. At the same time the kettle began the run-up to a high-pitched scream. 'Still. I do my bit for Art. Buy tickets. Take my friends to see her.' He laughed. 'Sometimes that takes guts, believe me, the stuff they put on.'

'Where is – uh – Susannah now?' Penny said, although she already knew the answer.

'Said she was going down the coast.'

'Where?'

He shrugged. 'She didn't exactly say.' He waved a hand at the side window where the Bay Area spread out below them towards San Francisco, sharp outlines of roofs and buildings easing beyond Berkeley and Oakland into a blue-edged fog. 'Just down the coast. She *said*.'

'You sound like you didn't believe her.'

'In the time I've known Susannah Alphonse, I've learned not to,' Joshua said abruptly. 'The hard way.' He fetched out cups, cream, a cookie jar. There were chocolate chips inside. Homemade. Penny didn't even try to resist. Watching her, Joshua said, 'Jesus. You're awful like her. It's creepy.'

'Same hair and everything?'

'She's been wearing it braided up, the past six months or so. Before that, she kind of held it back with, like, red combs. Or sometimes she wore it in one of those tails, stick out the side of your head like some kind of fountain.'

'How long've you known her?'

'Met her almost as soon as she arrived out here.'

'How long ago was that?'

'A couple of years, maybe.'

'Does she live with you?'

He hesitated. 'Some of the time.'

'What about the rest of it?'

He squashed his mouth together. 'Depends on who she was going with. Guess you'd have to say I'm the one she always comes back to.' He looked like the role had hurt him.

'Do you love her?'

'Man, I love the whole goddamned human race. Long as it leaves me alone to get on with my work. Way I see it, I'm an artist, not some friggin' Messiah sent to save the world. Susannah couldn't see it, could never see I'm an artist first and a black man second. That the best thing I can do for "Mah People" ' – he made the capitals ironic – 'is to be a person. And believe me, the crap that lady hands out, being just a person ain't easy.'

'Hey, Mr Peters, where's your sense of cultural bias?'

He settled the small buns against the edge of the counter. He bent his head to the coffee in his mug. 'I never did see where blacks getting together was black consciousness, while you honkies stickin' together was racism,' he said. 'Me, I don't give a shit what colour a man is, long's he don't hassle me. But say that to Soos and she just about came unglued.'

'Joshua,' Penny said. She sipped at the tea he'd made her. It tasted tenuous. Lapsang, probably. Nice, if your taste buds were attuned. 'Did anything happen to her recently?'

'Happen?' Startled, he stared at her. She could see him wade backwards, remembering. And being made uneasy by it. 'Like what?'

'Some kind of change in her. Like she – uh – joined the Girl Scouts. Came into money. Got religion. Anything.'

'Susannah don't need no religion, man. She already got politics. Says she's gonna be the first black woman President and really show them how. "Babe," I go, "they's already half a dozen black mommas waiting in the wings. Where you think you gonna springboard up the front of the line?" Know what she says?'

'No.'

'She's like: "But *Josh*-yew-ah, none of them sisters is hungry enough." ' He spoke in a falsetto, laughing again. ' "Not like me, *Josh*-yew-ah. Man, I am *stahvin*." ' He waved his fingers about. 'That's what she does, talks with her hands. Always tell her, only way to keep her quiet's to cut them off at the wrist.' For a moment he was still, his cup trembling infinitesimally against its saucer. Then he said softly, 'She in some kinda trouble?'

Not any more. Just a corpse now, skin greyed, eyes dulled, busy fingers quiet. All trouble over. All ambition stilled. And he was beginning to suspect. He stared at Penny. Visibly, he tensed. Muscles bunched along his arms, around his jaw, in his chest. The laughter began to seep out of his body, which gathered into itself under the white overalls, waiting for shock.

'What are you? Cops?' he said.

'No.'

'Why you asking all these questions?'

She told him. Hating it. It wasn't much fun watching the way the blood seemed to recede behind the black skin. Nor how the light dimmed in the eyes. The hands were certainly big enough to have killed Susannah, but Penny could have sworn the man himself was incapable of such an act of violence. He stood in front of her, unmoving, hurting. The only time his stillness broke was when tears came into his eyes.

'How do I know this isn't some kind of a gag?' he asked finally.

'Come up with a real good reason why I'd kid about something like that,' Penny said. 'Besides, you act like you know I'm right. Like you'd been expecting danger to catch up with her sooner or later.'

He dropped his head. His hands curled into fists. He slammed them both down on the slate counters, once, twice, making noises of grief in his throat. He pressed the back of one hand against his nose, pushing back the rest of his pain for later, after Penny'd gone. The big shoulders heaved a couple of times. He said, 'I don't know what she was into, but it was something real heavy. A couple of times, she said things, gave me the impression she'd rather be some-place else.'

'What sort of things?'

'Like, she didn't like being hassled. Like, she was way over her head in something and it looked kind of dirty.'

'This was all in the last few weeks or so?'

'Yeah.' He looked at her. The rims of his eyes were wet, the lashes heavy with tears. 'Why you keep on about it?'

'Because you said she changed her hairstyle about recently. It's not a lot to go on, I know. But until a couple of days ago, I had my hair in braids. I'm wondering whether she might have been wanting to –' it seemed fantastic now, saying this to Susannah's lover – 'impersonate me.'

'Are you kidding? Why'd she want to do that?'

'If I knew that . . .'

'She was in Europe this summer,' Joshua said.

'Was she?' Did it have any relevance? Penny didn't know.

'You asked if there'd been any change in her recently. I guess the trip to Europe was a change.'

'Did she go alone?'

'I don't think so.' He put his hand up again. 'But I don't know who she was with. See, we had this kind of open relationship, Soos and me. Didn't trample too hard on each other's toes, you know what I mean.'

'When did you last go to Europe?'

'This summer, matter of fact. Spent a couple months at the Cité Universitaire.'

'Doing what?'

'Looking around. Visiting the museums, art galleries, like that. Man, I *love* Paris. Thing about California, they've got a terrific climate but you have to go an awful long way to find anything man-made that's more than five minutes old.'

'Were you with Susannah?'

'Some of the time.'

'She tell you what she was doing?'

'Just hanging. Stooging round the place. I know she went over to England a couple of times, see some old family friends, see some theatre. Why you asking?'

'Because like I said, whatever she was doing, it may have involved her taking over my space for a while. Permanently or not, I don't know.'

'Why'd anyone want to do that?'

'My guess is, it has something to do with my father.'

'What is he, some kind of pol? With Susannah that's . . .' he paused, then said delicately, 'that was the real core thing. Politics.'

'He's a diplomat,' Penny said. 'I'm not sure how much diplomacy has to do with politics.'

'How'd you get on to me?'

'Because I saw the invitation to your private view at Pilot Whitman's place.'

Josh jumped. 'Whitman? You thinking he's got something to do with Susannah?' he said. He pushed his glasses back on to his nose. Through them, his eyes were distinctly unfriendly.

'It looks like there's some connection. Did she know him?'

'If she did, it never came up.'

'The way it looks right now,' Penny said, 'someone seems to have kidnapped Whitman, along with my father, and I'm fresh out of leads. Thought I'd try you, see what you knew. Especially after seeing that portrait you did of – of Susannah.'

'I don't know your father,' Peters said. 'Know Whitman, of course. I've been out to his house a bit. Eaten at the restaurants a time or two.'

'Is he married?'

'Used to be. There's a wife somewheres, he told me once. He's been kinda busy this past year or so. I hardly seem to see him these days.'

'Is he political?'

'Not as far as I know. Not like Susannah. But we didn't talk politics, we talked art, and food and Africa, and wine.'

'Sure.'

'Big things. Little things. Life. You know?'

'Yeah.'

'He's bought some of my work. I can tell you I was real flattered he should want to add my paintings to his collection.'

'Which collection is that?'

He looked at her sharply then quickly away. 'Collection's probably overdoing it. He's something of a patron round here, among the up and comers. Fact, they say Whitman buys you, you good as up and come.'

'Mr Peters,' Penny said. 'Someone's pinched him and my father. I want them back again. Before it's too late.'

'This likely to be the same guys who knocked off . . .' Peters cleared his throat. Tears moved into his eyes again. One broke free and trailed sadly down his cheek. '. . . who killed Susannah?'

'I wish I knew,' Penny said softly.

He looked away. With one finger he smoothed the surface of the PVC tablecloth.

Penny walked nearer. She touched the tear-trail on his face. There was some kind of hiatus to do with Susannah and Pilot Whitman. Whatever it was, Peters didn't seem to know about it. Nor could she see that it might be relevant to finding her father. She let it go. 'Listen,' she said. 'I'm sorry about your friend. About Susannah.' Some impulse of sympathy made her add: 'If it is her.'

'We both know it is,' Joshua said. 'You can't have that many doubles.'

'There's a Detective Santini you could contact.' Penny tore a sheet off a memo pad standing under the wall-phone. Each sheet had a happy yellow face in the left-hand corner. She wanted to turn the smiling mouth downward. She wrote down the contact number Santini had given her.

Joshua hunched over the piece of paper. 'I don't want it to be her,' he said. He sounded like a kid.

Penny didn't speak. The dead leave such spaces, she thought. Open wounds. Cancerous lesions that won't heal however many nostrums you try. Time is the only cure. And even then the recovery can never be complete.

'Tell you who might be able to tell you some more about her,' Joshua said suddenly. 'That's the folks at the theatre, the Jumpin' Bean crowd. Might know more about the kind of political shit Susannah'd got herself tied up with recently. Tell the truth, she stopped telling me about the stuff she was into these days. She knew it got me all riled up. Man, I *hate* intolerance. Whichever angle it's coming at me from. Black. White. They's all the same. All into hating other folks. Maybe they'll know down there.'

'I'll drop by,' Penny said.

'You could drop by here again, too,' Joshua said. He looked over her head at the wind-chimes which hung from the redwood frame over the patio. 'If you wanted. If you find anything out. If you want some help.' He looked away from her, his need obvious.

'I'll do that,' Penny said. 'Hey. Is that your studio?'

'Yeah. Come back, and I'll show you round.'

'Is that a promise?'
'Sure is. If you promise to come.'
'Don't worry.'
They smiled at each other. She went.

10

Penny would have been just as happy with a takeaway hamburger. But there were times when you had to settle for more. Besides, Pancho Villa's Mexican restaurant was right across the road from the Jumpin' Bean Theater Company. She went in and ordered a Dos Equis from the kid on the counter. Behind him was a lousy mural of Acapulco Bay.

There were tables in the window. She sat down at one, feeling weary. Boy, did she need a beer. Or even two. Pancho Villa's had raves from the local news-sheets stuck up in the window. That was usually a good enough reason to find somewhere else to eat. Penny stayed because of the location. Over the way, there were lights on in the Jumpin' Bean Theater Company. The premises were kind of two-bit, no more than a narrow converted shop-front, squeezed in between a discount shoe-store and a place selling oriental artefacts. The artefacts were nearly all made of cloisonné.

The Jumpin' Beans had covered the windows of the former shop with black paint so no one could see what was going on inside. Handbills advertising forthcoming local attractions were displayed on the door. You could tell this was a university town by the quality of event they were pitching for. Poetry readings. Displays of Indian Crafts and contemporary Chinese painting. A feminist Evening of Consciousness Lowering with a group called the Untamed Shrews. Sitar recitals. There was a flyer for the Joshua Peters exhibition at the Fontaine Gallery with a fuzzy black-and-white repro of the nude that Penny now knew was called Susannah Alphonse.

She was working her way through her second beer and some tacos, when a woman appeared across the road. Without hesitation, Penny fingered her as a jumping bean. Partly because she came out of the Jumpin' Bean place. Mostly because she was dressed in layers, all of them ethnic, several of them involving two or more types of fabric plentifully strewn with small flower motifs. Penny sighed. People were so predictable. It was a safe bet that at least three out of those associated with a group called the Jumpin' Bean

Theater Company would dress like a cross between a llama and a nosegay. And why did they always wear earth shoes?

She guessed the woman was headed towards Pancho Villa's. Sure enough, she pushed in through the door. A few moments later she appeared with a plateful of refried beans and some enchiladas and took a seat at the next table to Penny's. No coincidence about that. It was the only one vacant.

Penny leaned across. 'Hi,' she said. 'I'm Penny Wanawake.'

'Is that right?' The woman was in her late twenties. She gave a smile that went weary at the corners. Penny could see her thinking that right now, another Berkeley kook trying to be friendly was just a little more than she could handle.

'I wanted to talk to you about Susannah Alphonse.'

'Oh?' Her eyes widened. They widened even more as she took a closer look at Penny and caught the likeness.

'May I join you?'

The woman took a forkful of refrieds. She closed her eyes for a second, savouring the flavour, then nodded, her cheeks bulging. 'Go ahead,' she said indistinctly.

Penny pulled out a bentwood chair with a seat just too small to accommodate the average butt. She sat down.

'I'm Gilly Andersen,' the other woman said. She waved a hand at the theatre over the way. 'ASM and shit-taker for the Beans. What do you want to know about Susannah?'

'First off, I'd better explain something.'

'Explain what?'

That she was dead, was what. Explaining involved a certain amount of emotional expenditure. By the time she'd finished, Penny was close to bankruptcy. There was sweat in her armpits and across her forehead. It was the third time she'd told this particular story. She was beginning to feel like some Old Testament prophet. Or maybe an Ancient Mariner. Prophesying doom wasn't a career you'd want to take up unless you had a true vocation. Plus a glittering eye. Quite apart from anything else, there was the way people looked at you afterwards. As if it was all your fault. As if you could have prevented it if you'd wanted to.

Gilly Andersen was no exception. 'Dead?' she said suspiciously. 'Why?'

'That's what I'm trying to find out. At least. What I'm really trying to find out is what's happened to my father. It seems to be linked in some way with what's happened to Susannah.'

'But she told me she was driving down the coast,' objected Gilly.

'Going to talk to that man who carries all those different bottled waters or something.'

Penny didn't say that murder doesn't take account of people's schedules. Nor that it only takes seconds to smash someone's head in. Whether in LA or San Francisco, or a South African detention cell.

'I know she was involved in all sorts of projects outside the theatre,' she said. 'Do you know anything about her most current one?'

Gilly Andersen shook her head. 'I just can't believe it — Susannah, dead,' she said. 'I mean she was always so alive, so sort of *there*, if you know what I mean. Always into something. Always out front, going for it.'

'What was she going for, last time you saw her?'

'I don't know exactly. Hey. You really do look a lot like her, you know?'

'Yeah.'

'It's amazing, as a matter of fact. The likeness.' She chewed on enchiladas silently for a moment, hoicking in a smidgen of sauce that had lodged at the edge of her mouth. Then she said, 'Shit. We were halfway through blocking out the moves for *Waiting for Godot*.' It always threw Penny, the way Americans put the accent on the final syllable.

So did the monstrous egoism of theatre people. Everything from maelstrom to murder was subsumed in the credo that the play's the thing that counts.

'Did she seem different over the last few months?' she said. 'Was she involved in something new?'

'Only thing I can think of,' Gilly said, 'she fell in love.'

'Who with?'

'Some local guy. He caught her in whatever it was we were doing back in — September, was it? That would have been, yeah, *Hello, OT!*'

'Oh God.'

'It's a radical feminist rewrite of —'

'Don't tell me,' said Penny. 'I can guess.'

'Soos played Mona, of course. A captain at West Point. Lee was OT, the son of her Commanding Officer. We got some rave write-ups in —'

The rumbling sound Penny could hear was probably Shakespeare having forty fits in his grave. 'What about this new man of hers?'

'We never met him,' Gilly said. Her firm white teeth closed

94

around a chunk of enchilada. One thing about the USA: no dentist need ever worry whether he'd make a living.

'Was he white?'

'I don't know. But I can't imagine Susannah making it with a honkie. Not the way she talked. I said to her once I didn't see how she could bear to spend time with us,' she jerked her chin at the shop-front across the road, 'but she said there was no colour-bar in acting.'

'Oh, sure there isn't.'

'All I knew, this guy must've had bucks. He took Soos to Europe in the summer. All over. Paris, Venice, Stratford-upon-Avon. The works.'

'Did she say anything else about him? Apart from the fact that he was loaded?'

Gilly wrinkled her forehead. 'Something, a short while back. What was it? Knowing Soos, it was almost bound to be political in some way. Black/white political. What did she tell me once? They'd really sit up and take notice this time? That's right. A lot of guff about white imperialism and cultural theft. I usually turn off about then, when she starts in on the anti-honkie slogans. Talk about fanatics – Soos really went over the top sometimes. But I do remember that: they'd really sit up and take notice . . .'

Penny felt suddenly cold. She remembered Nkasa's almost casual words. Had someone eliminated Susannah because of her radical ideas? Had *Nkasa*?

'No idea who "they" might have been?' she said.

'Just the usual faceless oppressor that people like Susannah are always fighting in some form or other,' Gilly said. She forked in some more beans. 'Bunch of paranoids.'

'If somebody didn't fight,' Penny said, 'some of us'd still be riding around on segregated buses. Denied voting rights. Toting barges.'

'You think you aren't?' The sound Gilly made was nasal and derisive. 'Not you, maybe. But people like you. Go visit some of the inner-city ghettoes. Take a trip to Oakland. Or East LA. See how free they are down there.'

'I have,' Penny said. Freedom was never so relative as in the ghetto. She remembered the little kids, eleven or twelve, in their high leather boots and mini-skirts, one foot up against the wall behind them as they chewed gum and waited for the customers. She'd seen the dead-eyed boys selling crack on the corners, the armed teenagers, the women with so little to hope for that they didn't even worry about it any more. Better to get on with the chore of living, to accept the money from their children without asking how they got it, to wipe up the blood when yet another kid bought it from a bullet fired by a killer still in the single-figure age group, to close down the eyes at the pimps and the guns and the drugs that had become the only means of survival.

'Then you know it's not radical action that changes things,' Gilly said earnestly. 'It's time. Lots of it. Long slow social revolution.'

'It's easy to talk like that when you're white.'

'Soos could never see that. She wanted everything now.'

Penny didn't want to argue radical politics with Gilly. Or with anyone else, to tell the truth. 'How far was she prepared to go to get it?' she asked.

'Pretty far.'

'As far as stuff like explosives?'

'Well . . .'

'Or murder?'

'Murder? Don't be ridiculous.' Nervously, Gilly stuffed the last of her enchilada into her mouth, at the same time jerking up her chin and smiling, as though to indicate that she knew Penny was only joking. When she had chewed and swallowed it, she said, 'Of course, Susannah was always talking big.'

'What about?'

'Oh, you know. Like, what she was going to do, how she was going to have the world by the balls one of these days. First President of her country, that kind of guff.' Kindly, Gilly added, 'She wasn't an American citizen. Very proud of that, was our Soos.'

'What was she?'

'Don't ask me. All those little African countries sound the same to me.' Gilly swallowed. 'But as far as this new guy was concerned, she never actually *said* anything. Not that there was any need. We could tell, just by looking, that she thought she'd found Mr Right.'

Mr Right. Jeez. Start out thinking you'd found him, and you were buying yourself a cartload of trouble. There were no Mr Rights, baby. Just a bunch of Mr Might-Works.

'I'd guess,' Gilly said, 'that he was political because, over the time she's been with the company, I got to know her quite well, the way she thought about things. I know she was real excited by his ideas, as well as his body.'

Did those ideas include kidnapping? Was that why Susannah now lay dead in a southern California morgue, waiting for formal identification? Almost certainly by a reluctant Joshua Peters? The problem was, Penny couldn't think who'd be likely to sit up and take notice at the disappearance of a black diplomat called Benjamin Wanawake. If, indeed, Susannah was, or had been, involved in his disappearance in the first place.

'Is there anyone else around I could talk to?' Penny said. 'Someone she might have introduced this man to? Or talked about things with?'

'Everyone's away,' Gilly said. 'We usually take a two-week break now, before we start in on the Christmas rush. Besides, she wasn't real tight with anyone in the company. She had this friend, Josh Something —'

'Peters?'

'Yeah. The possessive one. She saw a lot of him. Other than that . . .' She shrugged.

'I already talked to him,' Penny said. 'He didn't know squat.'

'Susannah's trouble was,' said Gilly, 'she was too intense. Obsessive. After a while you start to realise you got better things to do than listen to all that shit about Whitey and his sins. Specially if you happen to be white yourself.' Carefully she wiped the fingers of both hands on a paper napkin. 'Don't get me wrong. She was a nice gal. But she could be a real yawn sometimes. Couldn't seem to realise that she wasn't unique.'

'We're all unique.'

'Of course. But we're also limited. There are only a certain number of ways anyone can be unique. And Soos didn't have the monopoly.' Gilly looked at the watch on her wrist. It featured Mickey Mouse pointing one white-gloved hand at seven, the other at eleven. 'My Lord. Look at the time. And I've only got – what, about eight days left to find a replacement for Susannah. Why the hell'd this have to happen now?'

'That's show biz,' Penny said.

Irony's supposed to be hard to detect. Gilly didn't have any trouble. She flushed. 'Look. Sorry if I sound like a pissant. But it's not going to help any if all the Beans are put out of work because one person quit.'

'However involuntary the quitting,' said Penny. 'I agree with you. Très sad for Susannah, but the show must go on.'

'Why don't you come over to the theatre and look around?' Gilly said. She got to her feet. 'There just might be something over there that could help. Though I can't imagine what it might be.'

Nor could Penny. She walked across the road behind Gilly's broad hips. A tall black guy in a city suit rollerskated past them and down the hill towards Shattuck. He had a small pink and blue back-pack slung over one shoulder and academic eyeglasses. Probably taught philosophy or something. A couple of Japanese ladies in pant-suits came out of the oriental shop, carrying shopping bags. Towards the Bay, the sky was beginning to tinge with pink and gold around a sun like a fireball.

Gilly unlocked the door of the theatre. 'We have to be real careful,' she said. 'We went away one weekend and when we came back, there were about twenty deadbeats dossed down in here like it was some kind of flophouse or something. They'd even pulled down the stage drapes to wrap up in. Gee, that was a scene. Like all these unshaven hoboes sitting up in the middle of a sea of red velvet, staring at us like gophers in the desert. Plus a stench you wouldn't believe.'

The door opened into a narrow hallway. It too was painted black. Crude glass-fronted frames held big black-and-white glossies of the present complement of Jumpin' Beans. A backlit Susannah, hair unbraided and held away from her face in a becoming black cloud, gazed off to the right. She had a professional facial structure. Also, she was prettier than Penny could ever hope to be. Or want. Beauty created its own kind of problems. Most of which were called men. To the right of her, a brawny hunk with a James Dean haircut leaned sideways, eyes fixed on some invisible grail. Above them both was another guy, somewhat older, thin of face, gazing straight at the camera.

'Who's that?' Penny said. Her stomach had dropped.

'Lee,' said Gilly. 'That's Courtney Collins. Real talented. Real dedicated.'

'To what?'

'Courtney Collins, mostly.' Colour rose faintly in Gilly's face. She was the sort of woman who tried to see the best in people.

'And where's he, at the moment?'

'There's an ex-wife and a couple of kids, I think,' Gilly said. 'Living in Thousand Oaks or some place like that. He went down to visit with them.'

'When?'

'A couple of days ago.'

'Was he close to Susannah? Share the same philosophy?'

'Courtney?' The idea seemed to be funny. 'Only philosophy he has is the one that says the world owes him a break. Soos doesn't like him any better than the rest of us. But he's good. That's the only reason we put up with him, sometimes. One of these days he'll make the big time, I'm convinced of that.'

Penny wasn't. Penny was convinced that someone had put their hands round Courtney Collins's neck and squeezed until he could no longer draw breath enough into his windpipe to keep his lungs supplied. Because, despite the hamburger make-up, she recognised him. For his last and positively final appearance, he'd been playing a body at the edge of Pilot Whitman's lake.

She looked again at the guy's picture. Whatever kind of a break the world owed him, he was never going to pick up on it now. She ducked out of telling Gilly Andersen that he too was dead. The news might cause a nervous breakdown. Or hysterics. Penny had never been too good on slapping peoples' faces. Besides, once Josh Peters had identified Susannah, the police would be on to Gilly and the Jumpin' Beans soon enough.

'Hey, I just remembered,' Gilly said, looking off into the distance. 'I said Courtney and Susannah weren't exactly tight. But last time they were here, Susannah was trying to bum a ride off him. Her car was in for repairs so she'd needed transport.'

'To see a man about some Perrier, right?'

Gilly smiled briefly. 'Something like that. Plus a couple of others she was going to take in while she was down there.'

'Take in?'

'You know. Like, interview.'

'What for?'

'Her job.' Penny waited. 'Didn't you know she was a freelancer? Did pieces for various outlets? Magazines, freesheets, underground radicals, the local papers, like that?'

'No.' Why hadn't Josh told her? She should have picked up on it when he said acting was what she really did.

'Well, the Jumpin' Beans is a cooperative, of course. We all share the profits – when there are any. But writing for the papers is how Susannah earned a living. She was always getting these brilliant ideas that were going to win her the Pulitzer. That's why she just had to get down the coast, why she'd go with Courtney, if there was no one else. I wouldn't say she was obsessive, but once she'd got a scent of something, she followed it to the bitter end.'

And ends didn't come much more bitter than violent death. Penny walked on. A journalist, huh? It explained why she was down in Big Sur, but not much else. Further down the passage were photographs of previous productions. Some were recognisable standards – Ibsen, Shakespeare, O'Casey. Others leaned strongly towards backlit plastic sacks and trestle tables. In one, Susannah sat in high-necked grey lace on a throne-like chair, her white-powdered hair piled up on top of her head and crowned with a diamond-encrusted tiara. Strings and chains and brooches adorned her Edwardian frontage. At her feet grovelled a crouched figure in a monkish robe.

Penny stopped. 'What's that? It looks like something to do with the Russian Revolution.'

'It was. One of those Anastasia-type plays. You know?'

Penny had heard of White Russians. But Black ones? 'How long ago was that?'

'About eight months.'

'Looks good.'

'Oh, it was. Very innovative.'

'I can imagine,' Penny said. She peered closer. 'The jewellery looks really authentic.'

'It was. All those pieces are genuine copies . . . well, you know what I mean. She has a friend who lent them to her.'

Penny could feel her own frontage vibrating. There was a brooch pinned to Susannah's grand-ducal dress that was a dead ringer for the one Barnaby had shown her down at the beach house. 'Would that have been the same friend who took her to Europe?' she said carefully.

'I couldn't tell you. But that was one of her best roles. She was really —' Gilly stopped. 'Oh shit. Someone's going to have to tell her mother about . . . you know.'

'I'll do it, if you tell me where I can find her,' offered Penny.

The ASM cum shit-taker looked doubtful. 'Maybe we better leave it to the police. They must be used to handling this sort of thing.'

'It's no trouble. And mightn't it be better coming from me than some cop with other things on his mind?'

'Yeah, I guess,' Gilly said slowly.

Before she could get round to wondering why a total stranger like Penny should be a good bet as a breaker of tragic news, Penny said quickly: 'Besides, I understood the mother lives in San Francisco. I'm going back there tonight anyway. I'm staying downtown.'

'She's never home until late,' Gilly said.

'Oh?' Penny willed her eyebrows not to shoot up her forehead. What did the mother do, for Pete's sake?

'She sings some evenings,' said Gilly. 'In a restaurant.'

'Which one?' asked Penny. The way things were linking together, she had a feeling she already knew.

The feeling was right.

'A place called the African Queen,' said Gilly.

11

The road up Russian Hill pleated the steep terrain like a fan laid sideways. Up here above the city, the roofs of the houses in one street sat level with the foundations of those in the one above. The streets were connected to each other by flights of steps buried in leaves. The Berkeley hills on the other side of the Bay were clear in the golden glow of a setting sun.

Stone steps led up the side of Eve Alphonse's house to the front door. Tubs of flowering plants ornamented one side of them. More waited at the top. Looking at them, Penny frowned. She pressed the bell and heard it ring inside. While she waited, she asked herself how Nkasa could have known that Benjamin was a dab hand at pot-plants, that he grew birds-of-paradise the way other men grew beards? Hadn't her father specifically said that he'd as soon socialise with a rattlesnake?

Behind her, the door opened. Eve stood there, dressed in a robe of navy-blue cotton littered with white leaves. A bandana of the same material was wound round her head, dragging the hair back to reveal the bold planes of her face. Silver earrings the size of manhole covers hung to her shoulders.

'Yes?' she said. She sure didn't sound very friendly. The professional swagger she'd assumed in the role of Whitman's partner yesterday was dissipated. Today, the big body was slacker, the shoulders slumped.

'I'd like to talk to you, Miz Alphonse.'

'What about?'

'Things.'

'Why should I talk to you?'

'Maybe you shouldn't,' Penny said. Down in the street a car door slammed and the sound of an engine roared off between the houses. Somewhere behind a fence of wooden panels a dog whined.

Eve Alphonse thought about it. Her skin was dingy, as though it had been wiped over with a dirty cloth. What she thought must have been positive because she eventually stood aside. 'You'd better come in,' she said.

She showed Penny into a long low room full of mirrors. Three of the walls were painted dark blue. The effect was womb-like and enclosed. The eye was directed as though down a kaleidoscope towards the fourth wall, a single large window which gazed out over San Francisco towards Oakland and Berkeley. An ever-changing pattern of light and sea and sky. A womb with a view.

'Wow,' said Penny. 'Who needs television?'

'I don't,' Eve said.

'Expensive if someone lobbed a brick through it.'

'The glass is reinforced for that reason. Even a bullet would only shatter it.'

As always when she encountered it, Penny double-took at the implicit acceptance that this was a country where all men not only had the right to bear arms, but insisted on it. Under the veneer of high-gloss civilisation there still lurked the primitive instinct of the hunter. The bloodthirsting desire to kill before you could be killed.

She turned away from the window. Candleholders stood on every surface, sometimes singly, sometimes in groups. All the candles they held were alight. The flames sat squatly in their separate pools of melted wax. Some of them must have been scented. There was a smell of warm tallow and country gardens. Lavender, bergamot, oleander, raspberry. And above them, some-thing heavier Penny couldn't identify. Lengths of dark woven material had been flung over most of the furniture like shrouds. A grey cloud of smoke hung just below the navy-blue ceiling.

Eve Alphonse stopped in the middle of the floor and faced Penny. She stood three clear inches above Penny's six foot.

'I had a bad feeling about you from the first minute I saw you,' she said.

As an opening gambit, it was a winner. Penny didn't waste time feeling unloved. Nor in trying to come up with a riposte. 'Is that right?' she said. Adequate, if not witty.

Eve smiled. A broad smile that showed a lot of her teeth. Somehow it slipped right past her eyes without touching them and lost itself somewhere in her hairline. 'Of course, it was a long time ago now,' she said.

'It only seems like yesterday,' Penny said.

'I don't recall the occasion.'

'You wouldn't have done. You were too busy hollering.'

'Where exactly was this?'

'At your christening.'

'Ah,' said Penny. 'I always wondered why my parents got so antsy whenever I picked up a spindle.'

Eve kept on smiling.

The weight of what she had come to say squatted doughily at the back of Penny's brain. 'If last time we met I was in the cradle, how come you know who I am now?' she said. Hope deferred maketh the heart sick. So does the passing on of bad news deferred.

'Let's just say I recognised you.'

'Let's just ask how you could. I've changed a bit since my diaper days.' In the convex surfaces of Eve's earrings she saw her reflection, miniaturised, Rembrandt-shadowed in the dark room.

'I knew your parents, back in Senangaland,' Eve said. Once again she smiled that dead smile. 'Especially your father.'

Penny was suddenly afraid that some kind of truth she did not want to hear was about to be revealed. Bizarre images of Benjamin locked in embrace with this mammoth lady came into her mind. Alongside them lay those of dead Susannah, her sister under the skin. Above it too? Was it possible? Surely Benjamin couldn't once have been Eve's lover. She was aware of the average person's reluctance to think of a parent as a sexual being but even with that removed, it had to be impossible. Didn't it? She could think of no reason why not.

'But me,' she said. 'When you saw me the other night, how did you know it was me?' Once again she was overwhelmed by the difficulty of perfectly grasping the difference between illusion and reality, between what one believes oneself to be and what others believe one is. Which truth is real, which false? 'Who told you? Susannah?'

'Susannah.' Eve sighed the name, shaking her head slowly. 'My daughter.'

'Was she going to pretend to be me?' demanded Penny. 'Or didn't you know about that?'

'Maybe. Maybe not. Maybe I don't remember.' In the time they had been talking, Eve hadn't blinked. Now her heavy lids drooped. She seemed to be on the verge of sleep.

'Maybe you do, Miz Alphonse.' Penny wondered if the smoke round her head was from some hallucinogenic drug. The earrings swayed nearer and back again, and as they did so, the bright reflection of herself swung too. She wanted to reach out and shake the woman's arm, pinch her awake. 'What was Susannah up to? What was she trying to do?'

'She didn't talk to me any more,' Eve said. 'She said she couldn't trust me.'

'Where does my father come into all this?'

'Benjamin Wanawake.' The deep voice intoned the name like a bell. 'The Good Man of Senanga.' A chuckle happened in her throat. 'The only one, I sometimes think.'

'Someone's kidnapped him, Miz Alphonse. Did Susannah have anything to do with that?'

'I doubt it.'

'Who, then?'

'How do I know that?'

'You know something about all this,' Penny said. She knew she'd eventually have to tell Eve about her daughter's death. First, though, she had to extract whatever information the woman might possess about Susannah's involvement. If any. 'Please. My father – I must find him.'

'I can't help you, child,' Eve said.

At the corner of her eye, Penny sensed rather than saw a movement. It came from outside the window, too fast for definition. The jerk of a limb, maybe, or the quiet flash of metal or glass. At the same time, over by the view, the telephone rang. It must have been an illusion that the lines of candle smoke bent momentarily, disturbed by the sound.

Keeping her eyes on Penny, Eve walked across the thick navy-blue rugs towards it. She picked up the receiver. She listened for a while. 'I know,' she said. Carefully she replaced the instrument and came back to where she had been standing.

'That was the police,' she said, 'telling me that my daughter is dead.' The tiny Penny images trembled in the earrings on either side of her face.

'I'm sorry,' Penny said. 'That's what I came here to tell you.'

'I guessed that was why.'

'You knew already?'

'I was – informed yesterday.'

'I see.' Was that before or after Josh Peters had identified the body? 'I'm really sorry.' Penny stepped forward to put a hand on the big woman's arm. Savagely, Eve jerked it away.

Penny's brain flickered like a computer, calculating the odds of getting safely away if this woman suddenly let loose the rage which surged and sloshed inside her like an underground sea. Although it was not directed against her, it wouldn't take much to change that. 'I should have told you straight away,' she said. 'It happened at my father's beach house.'

'In Monterey?'

'Yes.' How did Eve know that? 'I saw her.' Penny didn't know what else to say, whether to mention the gold ring on the girl's finger, or the nail varnish, the attempts to accentuate the likeness to Penny herself. 'It's not easy to break such awful news to someone.' She thought of Josh Peters, heedlessly banging his artist's hands again and again on the tiled counter of his kitchen.

'Georgie,' Eve said harshly. She crossed her hands on her bosom, pressing her fingers against the chest bone until it cracked.

'What?'

'Georgie Lambton killed Susannah.'

'Who's Georgie Lambton?' The tension factor had suddenly risen. It was as though the air was being sucked from the room and replaced with eruptive force. Penny pushed the questions carefully out of her mouth like so many bombs timed to explode on impact.

'Before being kicked out, Georgie swore to get even with us all, however long it took.'

'Out of what?'

'Senanga.'

'Another one?' They were beginning to pile up. Benjamin himself. Pilot Whitman. Professor Nkasa. Eve Alphonse. And now this guy. Georgie. All of which was making her father's disappearance look political rather than personal. Darn it.

Eve Alphonse began to tremble. The high points of her knotted bandana shook. 'Did it have to be this way?' she said. 'Did it have to be this way?' She jammed a fist against her mouth.

'Get even,' Penny said. 'For what?'

Eve wasn't listening. 'I knew Georgie was here somewhere,' she said into the smoke which hung like fog against the dark walls and above the floating candles. 'I felt it.' She stared into Penny's eyes without seeing her. Her own were full of grief. 'I just never thought it would be my daughter who would be harmed. I should have done. Georgie would know that the worst thing anyone could do to me would be to harm Susannah.'

Slowly she raised both hands and held them to her head. She uttered five or six sharp sounds of pain, rocking back and forth on her heels.

Possibilities ricocheted like bullets against the inside of Penny's skull. What kind of man was this Lambton that he could beat a girl's brains out in cold blood? And what was his motivation? If indeed it was in reprisal against some action of the mother's, how long had it taken such bitter vengeance to bear fruit? She opened her mouth to ask.

As she did so, something smacked against the window. Immediately, as though the movement were long rehearsed, Eve dropped to the floor.

'Get down,' she said, hard and fast as thrown stones, her lethargy gone.

Penny did so.

'Over there.' Eve pointed to the couch which jutted out from the wall halfway up the room. The two of them crawled over the long-haired rug towards the safety behind it. Penny was aware as she crawled that whoever was outside could see her entire.

Another sharp crack. The window held. Beyond it, the city shone and sparkled under the last of the sun, and further off still, the white campanile on the UC campus at Berkeley gleamed like a candle among the hills. Penny dragged herself into the shelter of the corner between sofa-back and wall. Beside her, Eve crouched with her head against the shroud-like fabric, her eyes shut. Her dark body trembled continuously. Although the lashes were wet, no tears emerged.

'Is there another phone?' Penny said. She looked behind her at the rest of the house where there might be bedrooms. She wondered why she was whispering. 'I'm going to call the police.'

Eve grabbed her. The pupils of her eyes were dilated. 'No,' she said fiercely.

'Don't be ridiculous. Someone's trying to kill you.'

'Or you.'

'Me? *Me*?' Jesus. How often did bulletproof glass get to stand up and prove itself?

'You. Benjamin's daughter,' said Eve. Her eyes drooped again. The earrings swayed as she nodded her head slowly up and down.

'Then I'm definitely calling the cops.'

'No,' Eve said again, sighingly.

'Why not?'

'It's my quarrel, child. It's for me to end it.' The words came out slowly, as though each one had to be signed for before it could be uttered.

'Not if it's me they're after.'

'It wouldn't be the first time, would it?'

'How do you know?'

106

'One hears things,' Eve said. Her voice was suddenly remote.

'Who from?'

'Here and there.' As though grief were a fast-acting sleeping-pill, Eve's head hung down. The eyelids lingered over the big blank eyes. There was another sharp crack against the glass. This time it shattered, jagged lines spreading slowly out from the point of impact with a noise like ice-cubes dropped into gin. Penny raised her head cautiously and watched the view crackle-glaze in front of her.

'Miz Alphonse,' she said. She clutched Eve's arm and jerked it hard. Extraordinary. Once again the woman looked like she was going to pass out any moment. Penny felt as though she might too. The heavy scent from the candles drifted towards them like a grey fog. In the gloom behind the couch, it seemed as thick as the mist which had wrapped itself round Susannah when she died.

'Yes?'

'Why would someone want to kill me?'

'You're Benjamin Wanawake's only child. But don't worry. It's me they want.'

'Miz Alphonse,' Penny said loudly.

'Mmm?'

'What did you do?'

'When?'

'Back there in Senanga? What got this Georgie Lambton so fired up?'

The big black woman drew in a breath big enough to launch a ship. She nodded a couple of times. 'I helped to kill someone.'

There it was again. Death. Huge and unpredictable. Still the most unforgivable, the most arrogant of crimes. The one for which there was no atonement. 'When?' Penny said. Later, she would wonder why she had not asked who.

There was no answer.

'When?' Penny said again. 'And what does it have to do with anything?' She felt the woman slipping away from her.

A blue flash sent urgent reflections bouncing among the mirrors on the walls. A siren wailed its way up the hill. One of the neighbours must have phoned for the cops. Whoever had been out there, watching them, keeping them within his sights from the flat roof of the house below, would be long gone by the time they got here.

'Do you know why my father's been kidnapped?' demanded Penny. 'Or where he is?'

'Ask Georgie,' mumbled Eve. She keeled over to one side, her mouth slightly open. Penny could smell something sickly on her breath. She guessed it was barbiturates, an overdose, the lethal kind.

'Where can I get hold of him?' she asked urgently.

Something like a smile glossed Eve's inert face. The resemblance to her daughter was suddenly strong. She lolled sideways, her body slack and heavy. Penny shook her hard. There was no response. She pinched the thick flesh of Eve's arm, using her nails. Nothing.

In the street below, there was a screech of brakes. Feet stamped rapidly up the outside steps. Voices uttered short cries of command. The doorbell rang violently and Penny stood up, leaving Eve sprawled at her feet. Down and out. But still strongly breathing. A snort snuffled past her lips and, in unconsciousness, she screwed her face up into a frown. Had she tried to kill herself because of Susannah's death? She opened the door to let in the cops. Several of them streamed past her into the room. For the moment Penny hung on to the only fact she had. Georgie Lambton. If Eve Alphonse was right, and he was at the bottom of all this, then he must be close by. Right on the spot, in fact.

All she had to do now was find him.

12

It was close to nine o'clock in the evening by the time Penny came out of the BART station at Union Street. The sun had long ago slipped into the Bay. Now the high-rises glittered above the velvety blue-black of downtown San Francisco like Christmas decorations.

When she reached the hotel, she walked over to the elevator bank. She pressed all the buttons she could see and watched as the indicator lights reluctantly began to move downwards. Two stopped on the second floor. Another bogged down on the first. When it finally reached ground level, it contained the Contessa swathed in layers of lupin chiffon. Diamonds hung plentifully among them. On either side stood her two bodyguards, massive as gateposts. Neither seemed worried that the guns they carried were plainly visible to the naked eye. The Contessa slid a glance as rough as a vegetable brush over Penny. The help did the same. You'd have more fun in a horsehair shirt than in a confined space with those two.

'Good evening,' Penny said. She tried not to squint in the blaze from the jewellery. The woman was Van Cleef & Arpels on legs.

The Contessa pressed a few of her chins more closely to her chest. Penny took it as some form of greeting. Suddenly the Contessa spoke.

'Hold it, boys,' she said.

The boys did.

'Have I seen you before somewhere, honey?' the Contessa said.

'I don't know,' said Penny. 'Have you?' She was surprised by the woman's accent. Somehow, she'd expected spaghetti-house Italian. What she got was Scarlett O'Hara. Without the looks.

'You sure remind me of someone.'

'If you remember, let me know,' said Penny.

'I'll do that, honey.'

One jewel in particular among the crowd on her massive bosom caught Penny's eye. Before she could do more than register it, the Contessa had moved on. Just a minute there, lady. Penny turned

109

round. One of the bodyguards was looking back over his shoulder at her. Even the shades didn't hide the fact that the synonyms for stony were on double overtime with this guy. She decided she'd let it ride for the present.

Up in their room, she found Barnaby in his shirtsleeves, studying a small notebook. His braces featured stripes of an Etonian kind. A bottle of champagne sat in a silver bucket on the table beside him. He took one look at her face and silently poured her a glass.

She sat down beside him. 'Nice,' she said.

'The champagne?'

'That too. But I meant the glass.'

'Lovely, aren't they? They're Venetian. Seventeenth-century. I bought them from Svinhuvud this morning.'

'The Swede, right?'

'Right.'

'Bet they cost an arm and a leg.'

'Several arms and legs, to be exact. As a matter of fact, a sum roughly equivalent to the annual prosthetics budget for the whole of Scandinavia.'

'They're beautiful.'

Both of them were silent for a moment. The wine shimmered in Penny's gullet, each sparkling bubble a reminder that she was still alive.

'Aren't you going to ask me if I'm OK?' she said after a while.

'Are you OK?'

'No.'

'What happened?'

'I've just been in a shooting match with a total stranger.'

'I bet you showed him who was the fastest draw in the West.'

'I might have done. Except he was using some kind of rifle, and I was fresh out of guns.' Her voice quivered.

Barnaby straightened up. 'What? You're being serious?'

'For once.'

'Who was it?'

'If I knew that . . .' She gave a gasping laugh. 'I don't think I was his primary target. On the other hand . . . yesterday, someone tried to drown me.' At the memory, she began to shake. Dicing with death was not her favourite game. Especially when he kept throwing sixes.

Barnaby knelt and put his arms round her. He murmured soothing words while she shuddered, telling him about everything. When the shuddering subsided, he said: 'That's it. No more. Until the professionals have found your father, you stay right out of things.'

'The professionals don't seem to think he's lost. In spite of eye-witness testimony from me.'

'That's ridiculous.'

'You'd think so. But it turns out Pilot Whitman called into the African Queen this morning to say that he and an old friend from New York were going to drive up to Yosemite.'

'Called in? What does that mean?'

'Telephoned.'

'So they didn't actually see him?'

'No.'

'So it could have been someone imitating Pilot's voice?'

'Could have been. Except apparently Earl swore on his fly whisk it was Pilot himself.'

'Anybody check whether he had a gun to his head when he was doing the swearing?'

'Earl didn't mention it.'

'What about those two guys you saw out at Whitman's place?'

'They think I'm misremembering. They think the conk on the head has given me hallucinations and amnesia and generally turned me into some kind of unthinking vegetable incapable of telling chalk from cheese.' Penny sounded bitter. Mainly because she was. As anyone would be if Ed Lutz, speaking as if he were reading from an autocue, had handed them the same bunch of baloney. 'Even when I called him back and told him about Susannah Alphonse, he kept right on breathing through his mouth.'

'Did he have any theory as to where the lump on your head came from in the first place?' Gently Barnaby's fingers found and soothed the hurting place on the back of her skull.

'Thinks maybe I slipped and knocked myself out on the car door. So when I ask him how come I ended up in the lake, two hundred yards or so from the car, he just shrugs and talks about concussion.'

'What about the body in the lake?'

'Courtney Collins?' Penny swallowed more champagne before she spoke. 'You're not going to believe this.'

'Try me.'

'It's like one of those chiller movies where they're trying to convince the heroine that she's going nuts.'

'Courtney'd gone, huh?'

'How'd you know that?'

'I've seen a lot of movies.'

'Yeah,' Penny said. 'He'd gone. Naturally Ed Lutz didn't believe a word I said after that.'

'Did you tell him about this marksman you been tangling with?'

'Not yet.'

'Hadn't we better?'

'I'd rather tell Santini. He seemed on the ball.'

'I'll do that in a minute. Have some more champagne.'

She did. She picked up his notebook and held it loosely. 'What're you doing?' she said.

'Working out the balance sheet so far.'

'Is it in the black?'

'Very much so.' Barnaby smiled slightly. He took it away from her and refilled their glasses.

'Those jewels you stole in Paris,' Penny said.

'Yes?'

'Where are they?'

'I told you. I don't know.'

'You don't seem too upset about losing them.'

'I'm not.'

'Why?'

'Without the brooch and bracelet I showed you, the whole set's worth about a quarter what it might fetch if it was complete. So eventually I'll get them back. Someone will strike a deal. Having gone to the trouble of stealing them, the person who took them isn't going to drop three-quarters of the value simply because he's missing a couple of pieces.'

'Or she.'

He gave her a glance that was mostly shrewd. 'Right. In the end, it wouldn't have been worth his – or her – while.'

'If the set was complete, what would it be?'

'Fabergé. A parure of white diamonds, designed as a wedding present from the Russian Imperial Family to some minor bit of European royalty. For complicated reasons, the gift was never sent and stayed in the vaults until 1918. It had various owners and was last heard of in Paris, sold to a Mr Lambton.'

Georgie? Penny said nothing.

'At which point, or shortly after which point, it went missing. It only recently resurfaced, back in Paris.' Barnaby sipped thoughtfully at his champagne.

'How recently?'

'A few months. In the summer, to be less than exact.'

'I suppose it's pointless to ask how you got hold of them.'

'Absolutely.'

'I don't remember reading anything about a jewel heist in the past six months. Not one involving historic gems like these seem to be.'

'That's because the person from whom I – uh – acquired them had gotten hold of them in ways that were probably best concealed from the cops.'

'What're they worth?'

'A lot. When complete.'

'Do you have any idea who stole them from you?'

Barnaby frowned. 'I thought I did. But I may have been wrong.'

'Tell me who.'

'The name doesn't really matter.'

'But you're not sure?'

'Not yet.' Barnaby's tone was colder than the Arctic winter.

Penny hoped she wasn't around when he got the answer. Make no mistake: she was one hundred per cent committed to the guy. Had been since the first time they met, when Barnaby was turning over her *apartement* in Paris, hoping to find her jewel case. Yet she was always conscious of what she called his Baked Alaska syndrome. Stick him in a hot oven and he'd heat up, all right. Start to broil. But fundamentally he'd stay the same. The meringue around his heart might brown and bubble but the ice at the centre would never melt. Something she'd learned to live with.

'Show me that brooch again,' she said.

Getting up from the bed, Barnaby walked over to the closet. He put his hand into the breast-pocket of his dinner jacket and came back.

'Here,' he said.

Penny stared down at the complicated flower-arrangement of diamonds and pearls. 'It isn't real, is it?' she said.

Barnaby quickly closed his hand over the brooch. 'Why do you say that?'

'It's a fake,' Penny said.

'How do you know?'

'I don't. I'm guessing.'

'You're doing more than that.' His brown eyes had lost their usual warmth. 'Who've you been talking to?'

She wasn't going to say that there couldn't be two genuine sets of the Fabergé jewels. Therefore one had to be phoney. And of the two, she'd go for the one Barnaby had. The Contessa didn't look like the kind of lady'd be taken in.

'Susannah Alphonse acted with a local drama group called the Jumpin' Beans,' she said. 'A few months ago she played in a local production of *Anastasia* – the Grand Duchess role. She wore the twin of that brooch. I saw the photograph.'

'So?'

'So someone copied the originals.' And I know who, she thought. Joshua Peters. Local craftsman. But what it had to do with the price of tea in China, or of kidnapped diplomats in Napa, she didn't know. Under her hair her head was beginning to ache, streaks of pain centring from the point of impact where someone – Dezzy? It more or less had to be, didn't it? – had slugged her. 'Barnaby. Are you holding out on me in some way?'

'*Moi?*'

'It's just it could be that these diamonds might be the reason that girl was killed. *Stolen* diamonds. Which happened to resurface in Paris a few months ago, just about the time she went to Europe. Does it occur to you that this whole scam, if that's what it is, could be something to do with you? That it's because of *you* that Benjamin is languishing wherever it is they've got him?'

'No.'

'It should. You're known to be connected with me, and through me, to Benjamin.'

'Bullshit.'

'Why is it?'

'Jewel thieves aren't murderers. To them it's just another profession. Same with people who collect them, or deal in them.'

'Don't kid yourself, Midas. It's an *obs*ession. And obsessive people can kill.'

Barnaby shook his head. 'From what you've said, it sounds much more like politics,' he said. 'Black ones.'

Penny was afraid of that. Deep down, she agreed with him. 'Rats,' she said. 'I hate them. Especially pressure-group politics. The thing that really bugs me most about minority groups is that they tend to end up messy.'

'Like people getting killed.'

'Trouble is, I can't think of any other reason why someone would kidnap my father.'

'He's rich.'

'But not that rich.'

'He's powerful.'

'Only to a limited degree. By himself, he can't achieve much. Most he could do is exert a little pressure, no more than that. And the one thing everyone knows about him is, if anyone tries to force him, it's a guarantee that he won't do what they want.'

'Like father, like daughter.'

'He's not due to give any kind of major speech at the UN. There aren't any big resolutions coming up. Far as I know, he's not giving a seminar or anything out here.'

'Didn't he say he'd come out to discuss something with Whitman?'

'Yes. He wouldn't say what. But it has to be tied up in some way with Susannah Alphonse.'

'Why does it?'

'If she was up in Napa, asking questions about Whitman just a couple of days before she was killed on the back porch of the person Whitman lured out here with some kind of a creaky old coded message, I'd say she was connected. And she seems to have been heavily into radical politics.'

'Suppose,' Barnaby said slowly, 'you're right about the diamonds. Would that mean your father was connected with them too?'

'I can't see how.'

'Say he was,' Barnaby said slowly. 'Then this whole kidnap thing might have been set up to get at me.'

'You?' *I knew it*, Penny thought. 'Why?'

'For instance, someone might think that if I was forced to listen to your father's screams while they tore his toenails off, I might agree to let someone have something at a bargain price.'

'Seems like an elaborate way to get a snip. Unless we're not talking Fereghan rugs here.'

'I don't think we can be.'

'More like a missing brooch and bracelet that would complete the set someone stole from you after you'd stolen it from someone else.'

'Much more like.'

'None of which alters the fact that Susannah Alphonse and Courtney Collins are dead. And Benjamin's been snatched.'

A pause. Barnaby sipped champagne thoughtfully. Penny did the same. Anything not to have to think about her father in the care of that cold-eyed young man from back East.

Barnaby shared what remained in the bottle between the two of them. He gave Penny the larger half. 'Unless it's something to do with Whitman,' he said. 'Perhaps the Burgerchef chain is trying to buy out his restaurant and figures a spot of toenail-pulling might induce Whitman to part with the place.'

'In that case, Benjamin's toenails aren't any better for the job than anyone else's.'

'Nor any worse.'

'That is so far-fetched it's out of sight.'

'Can you think of anything better?'

'No.'

The telephone began a discreet buzzing from a low table near the window. Barnaby lifted the receiver. He listened for a while then thanked the voice on the other end. 'By the way,' he said. 'I've got something for you, too.' He described Penny's experiences. He listened some more. 'Do that,' he said. He replaced the set.

'That was Detective Santini,' he said.

'Saying what?'

'That the dead girl's now been officially identified as Susannah Alphonse.'

'Which doesn't do anything but confirm what I already guessed.'

'I didn't tell him that.'

'Thoughtful.'

'He also said a body's been found hidden in the Bonami vineyard, just of the road.'

'What kind of body?'

'Wet. Chewed up.'

'Courtney.'

'I guess.'

'Did he say anything about finding how Susannah got to the beach house?'

'He said they hadn't. Not yet. Also that he'll have to fly up here to talk to us again.'

'Fine. He may look like a one-man crusade against natural fibres, but he's on the ball. Which is more than you can say about Sheriff Lutz.' As Penny spoke, the niggle she'd felt in Santalina returned. Trebled. Tentative as a schoolboy outside the headmaster's door, it knocked politely at the edge of her brain. Then it waited. She knew it wasn't going to go away. 'Barnaby,' she said.

'Yeah?'

'Suppose you built yourself a study, would you design it without windows?'

'No. Only way I ever get my correspondence done is staring out at what's going on outside.'

'Can you imagine anyone would?'

'No.'

'I can.'

'Tell me.'

'If the study wasn't really that at all, but the front for something else.'

Barnaby sat up and produced an elaborate expression of resignation. 'Something which I feel certain I'm going to be checking out pretty soon,' he said.

'Right.' Penny gave him her up-in-the-morning smile. He loved it. 'But before you start checking that, I think you ought to check this first.' She stood up. She slipped off her white T-shirt dress. Apart from panties it was the only thing she was wearing.

Barnaby snuggled her into his lap as she began unbuttoning his shirt. 'Are you trying to disarm me with sex?' he said.

'Yes.'

He held his hand beneath one of her breasts and bent his head. 'I'm very glad you brought this to my attention,' he murmured, his mouth soft against her skin.

They turned off the road up between the moonlit vines to Whitman's castle. Barnaby pulled to a halt outside the archaic front door. He killed the headlights and switched off the engine. A silver stripe of moonlight lay across the pewter-grey surface of the lake.

'I hope this wasn't a wasted drive,' he said. 'I'd do just about anything for you . . .'

'I know that, sweet pea.'

'. . . but perhaps I should state here and now that driving all the way up here at dead of night has stretched my goodwill to its very outer limits.'

'Kiss, kiss.' Penny scrunched her mouth up at him. He smiled.

'If only I didn't find you totally irresistible,' he said.

'Ditto.'

He stared at her. 'We'd better get on with it, then.'

'Right.'

In the dark, some bird squawked softly. Another answered. Apart from that, the silence was absolute. Even the crickets seemed to be taking a huge collective breath. Penny held hers too. She pushed at the door of the castle. It was still open, as she'd left it. Just as well. It wouldn't have been an easy house to break into. Nor would a key have been left with the neighbours. No neighbours. Which meant nobody for the police to ask if they'd seen anything suspicious. In any case, what *was* suspicious? A car stopping by to see Whitman. A car driving off again. Who'd notice? Who'd see

117

anything out of the ordinary in that? Always supposing there was someone to see something in the first place.

She led the way to the study. 'Look,' she said.

'I don't need an invitation,' said Barnaby.

'The bookshelves, dummy.'

Barnaby looked. 'So?' he said, straightening up.

'Do you come to any conclusion?'

'Only that Whitman must have a vision problem if he has to read books that size.'

'Barnaby.'

'Also,' said Barnaby quickly, 'that he seems fairly keen on African art. And the work of Professor Ralph Nkasa.'

'Precisely. And do you see anything that could remotely be described as African art?'

'Apart from you, no.'

'Yet the man seems to be obsessed with it. Wouldn't you think he'd keep some lying about his home?'

'It's probably somewhere else,' said Barnaby.

'Where?' demanded Penny. 'Certainly not in his restaurants. You heard what Nkasa said. It's all junk, that stuff. Besides, nobody in their right mind would keep valuable works of art in a restaurant.'

'Some might argue that, properly protected, it's as good as place as any other. Especially if it's insured.'

'Nuts. Anyway, that isn't the point,' Penny said.

'What is?'

'African nationalism means a lot more than black faces round the conference tables. It means that the African nations have at last learned to be proud of their heritages, and are hanging on to them. If Whitman did put together a collection of African artefacts during his time in Senanga, by now they'd almost certainly be irreplaceable. So where *does* he keep it?'

'Stop me if I'm wrong, but this sounds like the place where the Girl Sleuth reveals all.'

'Stop. It's where the Girl Sleuth asks you to start tapping the woodwork.'

'I'm an antique expert, not a woodpecker.'

'It stands to reason,' said Penny. 'Look at this place. No windows, so it's probably built into the rock. But why? Suppose it's really a guardroom. Then you wouldn't need a view, would you?'

'Um . . .'

'And Whitman obviously kept his collection secret. No one that we've talked to so far has even mentioned it.'

'Could that be because there isn't one?'

'No,' said Penny firmly. 'But it could be because he doesn't want anyone to know about it. Or, if they do know, where it is. Like you and the stuff you keep under your shop.' She was referring to the steel-lined vault beneath Barnaby's Mayfair antique shop. It was full of small but extremely valuable objects acquired in the course of various breakings and enterings.

'There are sound economic reasons for keeping that secret,' Barnaby said.

'The same reasons as Whitman's. Because it's dishonestly come by. Wasn't it Cicero who said that all collectors are crooks?'

'Sink me, ma'am, but you have the advantage of me.'

'Eton's supposed to give you a thorough grounding in the classics.' Penny looked round her. 'Darn it, I know I'm right,' she said. 'And Nkasa knows about it, too. Did you catch the way he said none of *this* stuff is worth beans, as though there was other stuff that was?'

'Not really.'

'I did. So start tapping, Woody.'

Barnaby did so. Penny did too. After a while, he said, 'What exactly are you hoping for?'

'Basically, that a panel of books will slowly swing outwards on creaking hinges,' Penny said, 'revealing a passageway which exudes a whiff of the charnel-house.'

'Cobwebs?'

'Definitely cobwebs. Masses of them, with any luck, veiling the entrance to a hidden chamber crammed with illicit art treasures.'

'And Vincent Price flitting about in a cloak?'

'I'd settle for Joan Crawford.'

'Penelope, may I make a suggestion?'

'Please.'

'Since this is the 1980s, isn't it more likely that − supposing you're right about these art treasures − rather than relying on such Gothic contrivances, Whitman gains access to them by pressing a switch?'

'Keep talking.'

'At his desk, for instance.' Barnaby sat down at it. It was broad, covered with some material that resembled leather to the last imperfection without fooling anyone for even half a second that it actually was. He moved his fingertips over the surface and the drawers. Nothing happened. He stretched his long legs and began to press his feet heavily down on the carpet beneath the desk. 'If I wanted to be able to open my own personal Sesame, I'd use the under-the-rug method,' he said. 'It seems so much —'

A tall portion of the bookcases suddenly moved. No creaking hinges. No charnel-house smell. Sufficiently dramatic for all that.

'Aw-*riiight*,' said Penny. She stepped into the opening left by the bookcase. Beyond it was a room, large, airy, whitewashed, lit by units set flush with the ceiling. A thermostat on the wall maintained a cool dry atmostphere.

Primitive African art was everywhere. Sculptures. Masks. Basketwork. Pottery whose elegance of line and shape brought a lump to the throat. Carvings of horned men and moon-bellied women. Some of it Penny recognised through motif and style as being indigenous to Senanga. She guessed that the rest was too.

'Wow,' said Barnaby. 'MOMA, eat your heart out.' He touched with covetous fingers a pot which stood spotlighted on a plinth of polished grey wood.

'Looks like he's got most of the artistic achievement of Senangaland in here,' Penny said.

'How'd he ever manage to get it all out?'

'Smuggled it. Must have.'

'Must also have had help, wouldn't you say?'

'Quite a lot of that.'

They walked through an arch into another room. Here there were woven tapestries and wall-hangings, and several paintings. The middle of the room was given over to jewellery: exquisitely primitive necklaces and bracelets and rings, body ornaments and earrings, all made of beaten silver or gold. The pictures were mainly examples of naive folk art in various media. Some were in a style Penny knew belonged to Joshua Peters. They treated of the same themes as she had seen at the Fontaine Gallery. There were also some portraits. One of Ralph Nkasa. One of Eve Alphonse. She almost heard the links strengthen in the chain which led from Susannah Alphonse through to Whitman via Eve and her father. She asked Barnaby why Whitman would hang a picture of his partner on his wall. Barnaby didn't know.

There didn't seem to be much more they could do. They swung the bookcase back into position and left.

'I've got a theory,' Penny said. She stared through the windscreen at the darkness. She felt excited, as though it might at last be coming together. The roads were nearly empty at this time of night. A couple of trucks passed, hauling fruit from Mexico and San Diego. A salesman with a rota to complete crowded them, overtook and roared away from them towards the city. They were alone in the darkness.

'A theory?' Barnaby groaned.

'Want to hear it?'

'No.'

'Here's how it goes.' They were passing the black-shingled house. Tonight, there were no lights to be seen, no cars out front. 'Ralph Nkasa wants to be President, OK?'

'OK.'

'He knows about Whitman's collection. Mainly because he was the one who helped to get it out of the country, yonks ago. Now he wants to get it back in. Return it to its ancestral home. Should be worth a few votes in the Cabinet, buy him some popularity. To make assurance doubly sure, he organises the kidnap of Benjamin Wanawake, who he knows won't endorse him. Along, of course, with the owner of the said collection. With them both out of circulation, nobody'll be able to denounce him until it's too late.'

'Sounds like Lycra,' said Barnaby. 'Hides unsightly facts. Stretches to fit all known figures. How does Susannah come into it?'

'Give me a moment to work on that one.'

'You think Nkasa's responsible?'

'This is just a theory, man. I haven't gotten round to the fine-tuning yet.'

'Where does your other theory, the one about the stolen diamonds, fit into all this?'

'Look, I'm big enough to admit that I don't always get things right first time round.'

'Tell me when you do. I'm fascinated.'

13

Early morning. A fine blue sky stretched thinly over the city. Roofs glittered with the damp of early dawn. Penny looked at her watch and reached for the telephone. It beat her how Sherlock ever got a thing done without it. She punched out a Washington number and listened to a dozen rings before she got a reaction.

'Yuh?' a voice finally mumbled.

Some reaction. 'Kimbell,' she said. 'It's me.'

'I can hear it's you,' said Kimbell. 'Question I'm asking is, is this me?'

'Sounds awful like it.'

'This early in the morning, I wasn't sure.'

'You got several hours' start on us California folk. Should be out earning a living.'

'Earning? My brain's still in a glass by the bed.' Kimbell yawned a couple of times. 'It's good to hear from you, babe. You leave that red-headed South African yet?'

'I told you already, sugar. You'd be the first to know.'

'Hoping's the only thing keeps me going. So what can I do for you?'

'You still in the PI game?'

'Unless they drummed me out of the Gumshoe Club while I was in the sack, I am.'

'So you still got the embassy contacts?'

'Got no money and no woman, but I still got the Embassy contacts.' He yawned again. 'Which embassy?'

'The Senangan.'

'Yeah. I know a chick works in Records.'

'So you can find me out some things?'

'What things?'

'First off, anything you can find on some guy called Georgie Lambton. Spent time out there about twenty-five years ago.'

'Why do you want to know?'

122

'He's probably got squat to do with anything, Kimbell. But I'm grabbing at straws.'

'Any special reason you're interested in this particular straw?'

'Because someone's accused him of murdering her daughter. And the daughter looks a helluva lot like me.'

'And you're thinking maybe ol' Georgie thought she *was* you?'

'Gee, Kimbell, you're sharp.'

' 'S how I got where I am today, sugar. So what do you want me to look for on this guy?'

'Everything. From where he is now to what toothpaste he buys.'

'Duck soup,' said Kimbell. 'One of the first things they ask these days, any government form, is what brand of dentifrice people use. Listen, babe. I really miss working with you.'

'Kimbell, honey. You know I feel the same. But we got to keep this professional, we're gonna get anything done.'

'Sure, sure. Anything else?'

'Any dope flying round about Professor Ralph Nkasa.'

'He was just in the papers here.' Kimbell coughed horribly and thumped his chest. ''Scuse me, babe. My lungs don't switch on till noon.'

'In the papers, you say. Doing what?'

'Mr Up-and-Coming, is Ralph Nkasa. Tipped as Senangaland's new President.'

'What happened to the old one?'

'Nothing. Yet.'

'You think it might?'

'Way I read things, he'd have a hard time buying life insurance.'

'He flies in tomorrow for this conference.'

'Right. And the *Washington Post* just did one of their Third-World-in-Political-Crisis numbers on Senangaland, which is how your friend Nkasa got into the act.'

Penny thought about it. 'Did the name of Benjamin Wanawake come up at all while you were reading between the lines of this *Post* article?'

'No,' Kimbell said slowly. 'Not then.'

'When, then?' said Penny, her voice suddenly sharp.

'Guy like me, suave, sophisticated, invited everywhere . . .'

'Yeah, yeah.'

'. . . hears things.'

'What kind of things?'

'Leaks. Rumours. For instance, heard this entirely unsubstantiated don't-quote-me whisper yesterday that somebody would be real

123

delighted to have your daddy out of circulation. Also that somebody from this side had already flown out to your side to see about it.'

Should she tell Kimbell about Benjamin? Misgivings tiptoed about at the base of her spine. Yet she didn't feel that her father could be in any danger for the moment. Stood to reason. Otherwise he would already be dead. In which case there'd – gulp – be a body. What she had to find out was the real purpose behind his abduction. She cleared her throat. 'Permanently out?' she said.

'They weren't saying.'

'Any whispers about the somebody?'

'It's not hard to guess. The buzz round town is, you want to be the big Camembert in Senanga and a guy like Wanawake comes out against you, you can forget it. So who'd be interested in putting him away, at least temporarily, just until things settle down?'

'How's about an ambitious Minister for the Arts who's unlikely to be endorsed by a well-thought-of UN Ambassador like my father?'

'Thought you didn't do politics.'

'I don't usually. Are we talking coups here?'

'Don't know what you're talking, hon. I'm talking strictly off the record. But what Nkasa needs is something that'll boost his popularity back home.'

'Like what?'

'Could be anything, from rescuing the President's kittycat from a tree to improving the annual trade figures. Gotta catch the popular imagination, create a public image if you want to get in there, do something for your country.'

'How about if this ambitious Minister was instrumental in bringing back to Senanga a whole heap of stolen art works?'

'I like the way you think, babe. Matter of fact, I like the way you do just about everything.'

'Gonna pretend I didn't hear that, Kimbell. Could that do it's what I want to know.'

'Why not, sugar? The possibilities are endless.'

'Shit,' Penny said. 'I knew this would turn out to be political. And all I know is, I know nothing about politics.'

'You and me both. 'Cept I do know the President is considered one of your regular guys, while nobody rates Nkasa much. But one thing's for sure. If he and the guys behind him can't get him in legitimately, they'll do it the other way.'

'What guys?'

'The *eminences grises* behind Nkasa.'

'*Grises?*'

'*Noires*, then. Whatever colour, they're the ones pushing and shoving to get Nkasa to the the top.'

'So they can take up position behind the throne? Have first shot at the building options, the communications concessions, like that?'

'So the Senanga-watchers say. The idea being that once Nkasa's in place, they can take over.'

'Kimbell, you're a mine of information,' she said.

'Couldn't I just be a yours, period?'

'You already are, lover.'

Kimbell sighed. 'Anything else you want me to check for you?'

'Yeah. Pilot Whitman. Former military adviser to the Senangans. Also his wife, or ex-wife. Also,' she paused, thinking it over, 'also someone called the Contessa di Sforzini.'

'Where does she fit into the picture?'

'If I knew, I wouldn't be asking.'

'She something to do with Senanga?'

'No. Far as I know, she's nothing more than an innocent bystander. Paris-based. A dealer in antique jewellery.'

'Anything else? A personal message from God, maybe?'

'I ever tell you you're the greatest thing since heated rollers?'

'Thanks.'

'How long'll you need for this?'

'A week, minimum.'

'How about until this evening?'

'Can't be done. You got to be subtle. Got to do the shakin' and shimmyin'. Got to buy the drinks and the cab-rides. Fact, a week's probably not long enough.'

'I'll call back at dinnertime.'

'Yours or mine?'

'Yours.'

'I'll see what I can get for you. I can tell you right now it won't be much.'

'If you find anything – *any*thing, hear? – call me back. Say it's urgent. Make them find me, if I'm in the hotel. If not, I'll leave a message. And I'll keep trying you.'

'I'd like that, dollface.'

Penny laughed. 'Go for it, Kimbell.'

She put down the phone. Looked at Barnaby. Touched him here and there. Especially there. He drew in a deep breath.

Without opening his eyes, he said, 'I hoped you were going to do that.'

She snuggled down beside him. 'Hope you're going to that, too.'

The freeway traffic was moving fast today. Out in the Bay something large and warlike ploughed slowly towards dock in Oakland harbour. The sky was dense with the fog which crept determinedly across the water.

It wasn't much later that she was parking outside Josh Peters's house. Up here in Berkeley it was sunnier, though the fog gnawed at the ground rising from the Bay and obscured the view of San Francisco across the water.

Pulling in to the kerb, she looked up and down the street. It was deserted. A couple of leaves drifted slowly through the sunshine to the pale road. She listened. Nothing but the sound of distant traffic, muffled by houses.

She walked to Peters's front door and rang the bell. No one came. She rang again. After a bit, she went around to the side of the house. There was a gate in the fence that separated front from back. A rolled-up newspaper lay where the paperboy had flung it from the road. She picked it up and pushed open the gate into the backyard.

It all looked just as it had before. Which was misleading. It never could be.

Penny went in. 'You can't put your hand in the same river twice,' she said. She spoke to Josh, who sat sprawled in the hot tub. Chunks of uninspired stone stood here and there round the edge. Steam gathered gently around his waist. He wore headphones and was staring intently at a small bug which strolled across the redwood surround carrying a crumb of Crackerbarrel cheese.

'What?' he said. He took the headphones off, releasing a tiny crackle and thump of house music.

'How're you goin', Josh?'

'OK, I guess.' He looked up at her with red-rimmed hopeless eyes. He was sweating.

'Your paper.' Penny put it down, avoiding the bug.

'Thanks.' Listless, he began unrolling it, his hands stark against the newsprint.

Penny sat down on the edge. 'Did Susannah ever talk to you about her mother?'

'Not really. I believe she worked in some nightclub or something, down in San Francisco. I think she came from one of those small

African republics originally. Matter of fact, I think Soos was born out there. Samangaland, some name like that. But I don't know for sure. Soos kept her lives pretty compartmentalised.'

'What about her father?'

'I guess he must have opted out way back when Susannah was still a little kid. She didn't ever mention him.'

'And she came from Boston?'

'After journalism school.' Josh filled his hands with water and dashed it against his face. 'God,' he said, his mouth strained, his loss clear in his expression. 'I can't believe I'm never going to see her again.'

'You said acting was what she really did. Did she do anything else?'

Peters looked at her strangely. 'Of course. She had to bring in the bread, like the rest of us. Wasn't too much of that round the Jumpin' Beans.'

'So,' Penny said patiently, 'what did she do for bread?'

'She was with one of those foodie magazines they're always bringing out. Where to buy the best lychees in town. The only shop that still stocks dried rat-tails for flavouring that extra-special dinner-party casserole. Stuff like that.'

'Anything else?'

'Some freelance work, I guess.'

'Do you have any connections with Senangaland yourself?'

'Is that the place where Susannah and her momma were from?' He shook his head, water splaying. 'None at all.'

'Why would Whitman hang your paintings in his private museum, as though they were authentic?'

' 'Cos they *are* authentic, lady. Authentic Peters.'

'You ever visit Senanga?'

'Hey, what is this? You trying to catch me out, keep asking the same questions? I already told you, I've never been further east than Europe,' said Josh.

'Travel's supposed to broaden the mind.'

'Guess my mind's already pretty broad. I got everything I need right here inside my head.'

'Do you have any idea how Susannah was going to get down to Monterey?'

'She said she was hitching a ride with a friend. Her own car was at the garage.' He put out a hand and caressed one of the hunks of stone. 'Palaeolithic,' he said.

'What is?'

127 —

'This rock. I picked it up in Scotland last summer.' He smiled distractedly. 'Geology's one of my hobbies. Interests.'

'Whatever,' Penny said. 'Did Susannah say which friend she was driving down with?'

He shook his head. 'No.'

Penny looked across the yard at the garage-cum-workshop. Today the double doors were closed. 'You trained as a silversmith, didn't you?'

'That's right.'

'Which embraces the jeweller's art, does it not?'

He grinned. 'Yes, ma'am.'

'Guess that comes out pretty expensive.'

'Sure does. But there's a lot of money about, whatever they're saying about recession.'

'Who do you sell to?'

'All sorts of people. For instance, I just got an order in from a big insurance company. Wants a whole set of table silver for its head office, from the salts and peppers right through to the wine coasters. Last week some guy wanted me to copy a Victorian silver teapot for his mother 'cos hers was stolen.' He moved his shoulders about shruggingly. 'And people are always wanting wedding presents.'

'What about the jewellery?'

'There's less call for that. It's expensive.'

'Did you ever make anything for Susannah?'

'Not specifically. A ring, once.'

'Does anybody ever ask you to copy a particular design?'

'They sometimes do that, yes.'

'You just do the setting, do you?'

'Usually. They provide the stones, if it's a copy. With the modern pieces, I find my own, design round them.'

'Anybody want you to do something like in the past year or so?'

'Uh – yeah. I guess so.'

'Who?'

'I don't know.'

'How come?'

'Some guy showed up here one day. Didn't tell me his name.'

'Keep shovelling it, Josh.'

'You think I'm lying?'

'You seriously expect me to believe you accepted a commission from some guy forgets to introduce himself?'

128

'Sure. What's there to get antsy about? He gave me some drawings. Asked me to reproduce them. Put a deposit down on the table. Even brought the stones with him.'

'What were they?'

'Diamonds. Some pearls. Naturally I'm not going to turn down a commission like that.' He sounded defensive.

'Did Susannah Alphonse see them?'

'Yes. Matter of fact, she wanted to borrow them for some play she was in. She said they were the right period.'

'Did you let her?'

'Certainly not. If she'd lost them I'd have been up shit creek. The stones alone were worth thousands. I can tell you I was pretty mad when I discovered she'd worn them anyway.'

'You saw her wearing them, presumably.'

'That's right. I took Mrs Fontaine — that's the lady runs the gallery where my show is right now — to see Susannah in that Russian thing where she played some old Countess covered in jewels. I can tell you, Mrs Fontaine just about died.'

'Why?'

For a moment he seemed disconcerted. Then he said: 'She's commissioned things from me. Knows what it costs. Seeing Soos sitting there, draped in my stuff . . . she said if anyone had cottoned on to the fact that they were the real McCoy, rather than dummies, they'd —'

'Except they couldn't be, could they? I mean, you'd made copies, hadn't you?'

'Sure. But I was using real stones. Even if they were copied from a Fabergé design, those pieces were hell's valuable, as Susannah very well knew.' Darn it. Another theory with its teeth in the dust. She ought to be glad, though. If Susannah merely borrowed the pseudo-Fabergé jewellery for her play, the link between her death and Barnaby, and therefore Barnaby and Benjamin's abduction didn't exist. Or did it? The connections might be tenuous, but they were there. The steel threads which went to make a hawser were surprisingly fine. She thought of Susannah in her Grand Duchess outfit. Of the Contessa's pearl-and-diamond sunburst. Of Josh Peters working with Cartier's. Of Barnaby palming a chamois leather full of expensive history. Even of Monsieur Fabergé beavering away in his workshop to produce expensive knick-knacks for an effete suzerainty.

Which still left the question of who had caused Josh to make the pseudo-Fabergé parure. And whether it was a copy of the diamonds that had been stolen in Paris earlier in the year. And if they had any bearing at all on Benjamin's disappearance. It seemed unlikely. The more she dug into it, the more that seemed to have a political basis. On the other hand . . .

Josh smoothed out the back page of his paper. Penny caught a glimpse of the less important news. Missing heiress found in Mexico. Schools closed because of landslides further down the coast. Road accident figures on the increase. Whales disrupting the single-handed transatlantic yacht race. She hoped Lady H. hadn't been swallowed by one.

She tried a spot of stone-turning. 'Ever head of someone called Georgie Lambton?' she said.

'Lambton? No. Should I have?'

'Don't think so.' She wondered if Kimbell had got himself out of bed yet and was on the ball, calling up his contacts, getting something done. If she could just get back to Eve, ask her a few more questions, she would be a whole lot nearer finding where her father was. But the paramedics had rushed Eve into hospital to have her stomach pumped out and last time Penny'd rung to check on her, she'd been told Miz Alphonse was still in intensive care. She'd try again on Josh's phone. Meantime, she was banking on the fact that wherever Benjamin might be, it was this side of the North American continent. Partly because Nkasa was still here. Tomorrow the President arrived from Senanga and there would probably be some action. She just *had* to find Benjamin first. If he'd been kidnapped with some political end in view, once the President got here, all hell might break loose.

Josh had turned his paper to the front page. She took in the headlines. Earthquake tremors further south. Corruption at City Hall. Again? Another woman's body dumped on the freeway. And at the bottom a photograph.

She snatched the paper away from Josh. There it was. A bunch of non-Americans standing at the top of a flight of steps, smiling at the camera. And some way behind them, as though he had emerged unexpectedly and found himself in the middle of a group to which he didn't belong, was a face she recognised.

Delegates were gathering in Boston today for the start of tomorrow's International Conference on World Peace to be hosted by Harvard University, ran the caption. It gave a top-level name or two: the English Foreign Secretary, couple of French ministers, a member of the Praesidium, an East German.

Penny scarcely noticed them. She concentrated on the face at the back of the crowd. Even in a newspaper photograph, the coldness in the eyes came across, and the ruthlessness of the mouth.

'Ever seen this guy before?' she said.

Josh shook his head. Then he looked closer. 'Matter of fact . . .' He looked at Penny and the grief in his face expanded to fill his whole body. 'Matter of fact, I painted him once, about a year or so ago.'

'How come?'

'Susannah brought him in. Like I told you before, I took my friends to see her plays, buy the magazines when she was in them. Even write fan letters under different names. And she'd bring me people who wanted to buy things I made.'

'Who was he?'

'Someone at Berkeley. Tell the truth, I wasn't too keen on doing him.'

'Why not?'

'I kind of got the feeling that he and Soos, that they were, like, an item. You know what I mean?'

'Yeah. What was his name?'

'Leo's all I remember. Leo something. Why're you asking? You seen him before too?'

'Yeah.'

Just a couple of days ago, when he'd been waving a gun at her father.

Preppy, by God.

14

The place they'd taken Eve Alphonse to looked like every other hospital in the world. Same smells. Same staff. Same patients. Only the dressings were changed.

Eve lay in a high bed, both arms outside the covers. Without the exotic silver decorations and the dramatic clothes, she seemed reduced. When Penny came in, she turned her head. Her expression didn't alter. Had she been white, she'd have been pale and drained. She looked like she felt it.

'How are you?' Penny said. She was bad at sickrooms. They made her health seem even ruder than usual.

Eve turned her head negatively on the pillows.

'Not good, huh?' Penny said. She tried not to sound sympathetic. Rule One of the Amateur Dicks' Book said you had to lay off the sympathy if you wanted to solve the case. Especially if you weren't too sure who the good guys were.

'I wish they'd let me die.' The voice was weak. Difficult to imagine that only a few hours ago it had produced those full-blooded jungle sounds. Today it marched to a different drum, one that must have kept pounding out the stark fact that her child was dead.

Penny said nothing. There was nothing to say. When someone feels like dying, not much folks can do except hang until they don't. She laid the pink carnations she'd brought down on the covers.

'Why're you here?' Eve said.

Good question. 'I need some help,' Penny said, sitting down on the side of the bed. There was a faint smell of vomit. She took Josh Peters's newspaper out of her bag. It was time for a spot of windmill-tilting. Pointing to Preppy's picture, she said: 'Ever seen this guy before?'

'Yes,' said Eve. She made a crumpled sound, like a dying paper bag.

'You *have*?'

'Yes. Many times. Far too many.'

'Where?'

'Around town.' Eve cranked herself up a couple of inches and squinted at the photograph. 'Where's that taken?'

'Harvard.'

'That figures. He's a graduate student there.'

'How come you know him?'

Eve glanced at her and then lay back on the pillows, closing her eyes. She lifted one of her arms and placed it across her chest. 'He's Susannah's lover,' she said. There was a plastic identity bracelet on her wrist. Small circles of black flesh bulged through the perforations. 'And Pilot Whitman's son.'

'*Whaaaat?*' The five honest servingmen were working overtime today.

'Yes.'

Penny looked down at the picture again. Even though it was a lousy reproduction, Preppy's undeniable good looks came over loud and clear. Also his ethnic origins. 'The guy's black,' she said.

'Right.'

'Is Whitman?'

'No. He's big and he's rich and he's a son of a bitch, but I couldn't call him black.' Eve's eyes shot open. 'Unless we're talking about the colour of his heart.'

'I wasn't.' Nonetheless, it was an item of information Penny'd bear in mind.

'I thought not,' Eve said. She quirked her mouth in a dismal facsimile of a grin.

'So how come his son's blood?'

'Pilot married a local woman,' Eve said, 'while he was out in Senanga.'

'Guess I could have worked that one out,' said Penny.

'Not many whites did in those days. Slept with them, yes. Used them. But marriage wasn't even thought about. I guess it's a point in his favour.'

An old man in a red towelling bathrobe shuffled past, pausing to peer in through the glass pane set into the door. The air-conditioning gave a small harsh cough. 'Where's the wife now?'

'She died.' Eve turned away. 'Long time ago now.'

'Why did you call him a son of a bitch?'

'What else do you call a man who runs out on his family, leaves his wife with a young one to raise and never even says goodbye?'

133

'Son of a bitch'll do, I guess,' said Penny. 'Does he have any other family?' She was still trying to absorb the idea that Preppy was Whitman's son.

'Just a girl,' Eve said, staring at the wall behind Penny's head.

'There was a daughter too?'

'Yes.'

Penny took a deeper breath. Out of the window she could see a stretch of white wall with other windows set into it. Also, the top of a date palm. It fidgeted around, as though there was a stiffish breeze blowing outside. Inside, things were falling together. Sort of. 'I've been kind of slow here,' she said. 'The girl was Susannah, right?'

Eve sighed deeply. Her chest lifted the covers a couple of visible inches. 'That's right.'

'Which makes you – what?'

'One of the used ones.'

Penny waited a heartbeat or three. That explained why Pilot had a portait of Eve in his private collection. A remembrance of things past. The girl she had seen lying in the sea-mist was nothing to do with Benjamin. So she was no blood of hers. Momentarily she mourned the sister she had never had. 'But if Preppy —'

'His name's Leo.'

'— if Leo was also Pilot's son, then he and Susannah were half-brother and sister.'

'I know.'

'As well as lovers?'

'Yes.'

Penny tried not to look at the fragile skin around Eve's mouth. 'Did they know?'

'Not from me. I couldn't have borne to destroy them.'

Incest. The most ancient of taboos. It ought not to matter, but it did. Perhaps more than any other except murder. Yet when you considered it, between consenting adults, ignorant of their blood-tie, could anyone condemn? They were not to blame, any more than Oedipus had been, though their fate at society's hands would be no less implacable than his.

'You were never Pilot's wife?' she said.

'My Lord, no.'

'Why do you say that?'

'Pilot is the kind of man I wouldn't trust further than I could spit. I never saw a man with more charm, but if he handed me a drink of water, I'd want to know what was in it for him. Women melt like wax candles whenever he looks at them, even now. But trust him? I wouldn't trust him with my wash-cloth.'

'I guess you must have done some melting, if Susannah is his daughter.'

Eve stared at Penny sombrely. 'I did a lot, child. And always hated myself for it, afterwards. Especially that last time.' Her mouth twisted.

'What last time?'

'I can't tell you. It's not my secret to share. Pilot once asked me to do something for him which I should never have agreed to.' She grabbed her top lip between her teeth and bit down hard. The pain of it distorted her face. 'And now Susannah's dead.'

'You think the two are related?'

'Yeah.'

'And that has to do with Georgie Lambton?' Penny said.

'It sure does.'

There was a long silence. Penny shifted about a bit. She went and stood by the window, looking out. In the angle of the building she could see the sun lounge at the end of Eve's corridor, balconied, trailing with plants. Below, two nursing auxiliaries in mint-green dresses walked along the concrete paths which bisected the shrubs between the hospital buildings. They were giggling together, the force of their own laughter bending them as though they were walking into a gale. What had Eve done for Pilot Whitman all those years ago that filled her with such self-disgust now?

'I didn't tell them,' Eve said. 'I didn't want Susannah to know anything about her father still being alive. When she sent me that article . . .' She shook her head from side to side, closing her eyes.

'Article?' Penny said. She felt as if she were a milkmaid, perched uneasily on a three-legged stool, trying to coax milk from the udders of a recalcitrant cow.

'In her magazine.' Eve caught Penny's look. 'Did you know that she worked for one of these gourmet magazines?'

'Kind of.'

'She came out here after she finished up her journalism course. That's really what started it all, I suppose.'

Penny nodded vigorously. 'Yes,' she said. Coax, coax.

'She wrote an article. One of these Where-to-Eat-in-San-Francisco-type features. She sent me a copy. I was still living back in Boston then.' She laughed, painfully. 'Naturally I read every word. It was her first byline so I was very much the proud mama. And there it was – Pilot's name. Him and his restaurants. His own daughter had

interviewed him, without either of them having the faintest idea.'
Was that why Susannah had been up in Santalina? Picking up the
background information on the man she hadn't known was her
father?

'I think Mr Whitman might have,' she said. 'He has two pictures
of Susannah up at his house.'

'It was a shock to read about him,' Eve said. 'I hadn't seen or
heard of him for over twenty years, ever since I was forced to leave
Senanga.'

'Forced?'

'By the Nkasas. Ralph's family. They were very powerful in those
days. Still are, I guess. After the – after it all happened, it seemed
best to get out while I could. I took Susannah to Boston, where I
knew some people. That's where she grew up.'

'What did you do when you realised Whitman was in San
Francisco?'

'I came out here.'

'Why?'

Eve hoicked herself further up in the bed and leaned against the
pillows. Her skin was greyish, the colour of grape-bloom. There
were dark pits beneath her eyes. 'I wanted to protect her, if I could.
Didn't want her to discover who he was. Or if she did, I wanted her
to hear about it from me. That was a while ago now.'

The date palm was suddenly frenzied. The white wall outside
darkened momentarily as though thin cloud had smeared the sun.
The fog must be rising, banking in again from the Pacific.

'Was he surprised to see you again?'

Eve grimaced. 'Very.'

'Pleased?'

'No.'

'But he made you a partner in his business.'

'He had no choice, child.' For a moment, the Eve Penny had
glimpsed the other night at the African Queen squatted behind the
outer shell of the sick woman in the bed.

'The thing I haven't quite followed,' Penny said, 'was your
interest in all this. Whitman was Susannah's father, but you can't
have been too worried about that if you didn't try to find him
before now.'

'My interest,' Eve clasped her big hands together on the coverlet
as though she were about to pray, 'my interest was his wife,' she
said softly. 'Rebekah was my closest friend. He left Senanga
without even bothering to tell her he was going. She was seven

months pregnant. Six months after he went, she killed herself. Doused the house with petrol and set light to it, then sat there while the fire took hold. She just let herself burn to death.'

'How horrible,' Penny said, appalled.

'They found her with the new baby on her knee. That was my interest. I wanted him to know about that.'

'But not about Susannah?'

'No.'

'What happened to the other child?'

'Leo? The Nkasas took Leo in, brought him up. I always wanted to know whether Whitman had heard about Rebekah. Whether he cared.'

'I see.' Penny left a long pause. It was the only explanation of why Susannah was up in Napa, asking about Whitman, wasn't it? But it still didn't explain what she was doing down at the beach house. Penny asked the questions aloud.

'I wouldn't know,' said Eve bleakly. 'She called me to say she was going, but not why.'

'Did she tell you *how*?'

'She was driving.'

'But her car was in the garage for repairs.'

'Yeah, that's right. She was driving down with someone, some actor friend, and then at the last minute she got a better offer.'

'Who from?'

'She didn't say. Leo Nkasa, I guess. She said they were going to make a vacation out of it. Do some swimming, some surfing, have some fun.'

'You don't think Leo could have killed her, do you?'

'I doubt it. I've seen the two of them together. He loved her too much.' She moved her head so she was staring from a few inches away at the side of the metal cabinet next to her bed. 'I guess we all have our turn. But it's a long time since anyone loved me like that.' All the strong emotions that had filled her before were seeping away. She looked sad, as though she were about to put up the shutters and call it a day.

'Are you sure it was Leo?'

'Of course I'm sure.' The big woman shifted in the bed again. She half sat up, clutching at her throat as though the movement made her nauseous. She spoke slowly, looking away out of the window. 'You have kids, you bring them up, you love them the best you know how. And then they get to be big and they're gone. They're people. You love them just the same but they're people, like anyone

137

else walking down the street. You got no more control over them than you have over anybody else. Sometimes you don't even like them, what they've become. But they're your kids and you go on loving them. Even when they hurt you more than you ever believed anyone could. And there's not a damn thing you can do about it because although you're still their mother, they aren't any longer your children.'

She paused to take in another heavy lungful of breath. Penny nodded.

'Tell the truth, child, I haven't talked to Susannah about anything serious in weeks. Not since I discovered about her and Leo. Just couldn't face telling her, couldn't face seeing them together, knowing what I knew. So I don't really know what shit she'd got herself into.'

Penny felt awash with information. Revelations may have made St John divine. They only made her confused. Did any of this have anything to do with Benjamin? Would any of it help to find him?

'You said you thought this Georgie Lambton person was the one who – uh – was responsible for killing your daughter, out of some kind of revenge.'

Eve hesitated. One of her hands slowly tapped at the thigh which lay alongside it under the sheets. 'I still think it's possible,' she said.

'Does Georgie Lambton have anything to do with the person whose death you said you were involved in, back in Senanga? Or with whatever it was you did for Pilot?'

'Everything, child,' Eve said heavily.

A nurse came in, candy-striped and white-shoed. They like to poke the finger at cops, but there's nothing flatter-footed than a nurse. This one brought pills with her in doll-size plastic cups. An electronic-type thermometer hung from her waist. The ancient art of healing allied to modern progress. It had to be a winner.

'You ready for these, Miss Alphonse?' she said.

'No,' Eve said.

'Don't be that way, hon.' The woman squinched her face up at Penny, inviting her to join some kind of conspiracy Penny was fairly certain she'd prefer to be left out of.

'I told you I wanted to be let die,' said Eve.

'Now you just hush up, you hear?' said the nurse. Smiling, she picked up the carnations. 'Why don't I put these in water?'

'Why don't you put them up your ass?' Eve said.

'Oh now, hon. That's no way to talk,' the woman said. If she cared about the reasons why Eve was there, she was keeping it buttoned up inside her. Perhaps distance from human emotion was another characteristic nurses shared with cops. 'Now, when your visitor's gone, we'll have you up, shall we?'

'No,' Eve said, 'I don't want to see people.'

'You can go into the lounge. Sit out in the sun for a while. Nobody'll bother you in there, hon.' Squinching once more in Penny's direction, she clopped out of the room, white rubber soles squeaking on the shiny composition floor.

'I should have thought a powerful lady like you would find it more satisfying to nail this Lambton character, instead of opting out,' Penny said suddenly, Gauleiter-brutal. Kicking them while they were down often got results, even if you ended up feeling like all kinds of jerk. Eve looked about as down as a person could get. On the other hand, if she was sweet-talking the help like that, she couldn't be right on the bottom. Stood to reason.

'What's the point of living?' said Eve. 'I've concentrated my whole life on my daugher. Now she's dead. I haven't got anything worthwhile left. Anyway, I deserve to die. It's my punishment for what I did. What we did, Pilot and me.'

'You don't really believe that,' Penny said.

There was another long silence.

'No. I suppose I don't. Maybe I just think I ought to feel that way,' Eve said. 'Funny. Ralph Nkasa was in earlier to see me. Suggested I should think about going back to Senanga. Said he'd be glad to help if he could.'

'Good idea. The country could use some people with a knowledge of the outside world. From what my father says, it's a very insular place.'

'Yes. You could be right. I been thinking I might take Ralph up on it.'

'Right,' said Penny. 'No use in your dying, is there? It won't help Susannah any.'

'No. No, you're right. It won't.'

Silence fell again. Penny broke it. 'If you know the Nkasa family, you must be pretty clued up on this Nkasa-for-Prez campaign.'

Eve smiled tiredly. 'Just isn't one little itty-bitty pie Ralph doesn't have those sticky black fingers of his in. Up to the elbow.'

'Was Susannah involved in it somehow? Or Prep – Leo?'

Eve shook her head. The long bare lobes of her ears each had a small black hole in them. 'I don't know.'

'What about Nkasa himself?' Penny asked. 'What kind of a person is he?'

'Depends what you want. Very upfront, very capable.'

'Ruthless?'

'Who isn't, given the right incentive?'

'You've known him a long time.'

'For ever. Which is why I also know that for all he's so big, he's real weak. Anybody can shove him around, make him do what they want.'

With a bulldozer and some heavy lifting gear, right? 'Okaaay,' Penny said. 'Another question: how did you know my father was in town, visiting Mr Whitman? How did you know who I was, that time at the restaurant? And don't bother giving me that crap about being in the front row of the audience when they dunked me in the font.'

'How do you think?'

Penny frowned. 'That doesn't answer my question.'

'Why is it you Western people think you're the only civilised folk on this earth? Senanga's still emerging from colonialism, still primitive in many ways. But we got ourselves a security system just as efficient as any old CIA or MI5.'

'Way I heard, that wouldn't be difficult.'

'Mossad, then. Or BOSS.'

'You trying to tell me you're some kind of a spy?'

'An observer. When I first came to the States, I had to find some way of making a living. Because I'd known people like your father, they took me on.'

'And one of the things you observed recently was your friend Dr Wanawake, right here in town.'

'Yes. Naturally I was already acquainted with his family. I'd seen photographs of you. I had . . . reasons for being interested. And then you have those Senangan looks, like Susannah. Anyone who didn't know you well would take you for each other. At first glance.'

'And you really don't know what Susannah was up to?'

'No.'

What else was there to do but leave? Penny left.

Walking towards the BART station, she kept two eyes peeled. Plus the one in the back of her head. Every sense was alert. Anyone approaching with an unpinned hand grenade, a cunningly disguised sword-stick, a Detective's Special aimed at her heart, and she'd have been a hundred per cent ready. So when the black car pulled up a couple of yards ahead, she didn't notice. Too busy working out how to avoid death by poisoned umbrella tip. Two guys got out. One leaned on the open door. The other walked briskly towards her. Both wore crotch-bulging jeans and short-sleeved striped shirts with buttoned-down collars. By the time she'd taken them in, the first guy had her hemmed between the car and himself. It was the classic interception, smooth as a gigolo's dancing pumps.

She'd seen it done a thousand times on any cop show you cared to mention. And always thought it stretched belief, the way no one took any notice when it happened. No one took any notice today, either. The street was almost empty. A young woman disappearing through her front door. A car rolling by with a Michael Jackson number leaking through the windows. And way down the hill, two senior citizens, bent as staples, every muscle tensed as they strove to lift half a dozen eggs and a jumbo pack of potato chips from the rear of a Pontiac. Even if they'd got their hearing aids adjusted, it'd take them till the end of the week to answer a cry for help.

'OK,' Penny said. She held her arms up and in front of her, hands like wooden paddles. 'I should warn you I'm armed.' The really scary thing about both guys was their stillness.

'Well, I just hope you have a current licence,' the first guy said. He was young and gymnasium-fit. Get any closer, and he could have used her lungs to breathe with. Penny didn't try resisting. He'd have had her in an arm-lock before she'd even begun. His pal on the door checked his watch. When he saw Penny noticing, he checked it again. If the action was designed to scare her stupid, it was fifty per cent successful.

The one on top of her grinned. She had a microsecond to decide whether it was the grin of a man who knew he had her totally at his mercy, or a different kind of grin altogether. If the latter, it would explain why he wasn't wearing the statutory black suit and shades. Also why he was saying 'FBI, ma'am,' out of the front of his mouth instead of the side. Showing her something cupped in his palm.

'Uh . . .' she quipped.

'Could we have a few words with you?' he said. He wore brown wingtips without socks. The buckle of his pants belt simulated the initials of a famous French designer. Trendy.

'What about?'

'Perhaps you'd care to step over to the car, ma'am. We'd attract less attention that way.'

141

From whom? Did he mean the male half of the geriatrics, now straining under the weight of a six-pack of Budweisers? Although she didn't care to, she stepped. He opened the rear door and she manoeuvred in. Inside the car was an odour of male sweat and Santini.

He sat on the back seat. He was wearing the same suit as he'd worn in Monterey. Three plastic ballpoints peeped over the edge of the patch pocket on the breast. 'Hi,' he said. He pulled a packet of Marlboros out and lit one.

Penny watched him. 'I hope you know what this is doing to my lungs,' she said.

'No. But I know what it's doing to mine,' Santini said, 'and it's great.' He inhaled heavily and breathed out smoke.

Penny fanned the carcinogens back towards him. 'What's going down, Santini?'

'We're ready to go along with the kidnap theory on your father,' Santini said.

'Theory, nothing. It's a fact,' said Penny.

'Not the way we heard.'

'You heard wrong. I was practically one on one with the jerks who nabbed him and Whitman. Anyway, what's it to you? Kidnapping's a federal offence and you're Homicide.'

'We're coming round to the belief that the death of Susannah Alphonse is more than a merely localised killing.' Santini sounded shifty. Looked it, too, his glance teetering off and on the two feds in front like a compass needle.

'How?' said Penny.

'Uh – we're working on it.'

'Why the fancy pick-up scene? Wouldn't it have been easier to call my hotel?'

'We preferred to wait until you finished visiting the sick,' said the guy with the wingtips. He sat twisted round in the front passenger seat so he could see what was going on in back.

'Comforting the afflicted,' said his partner, who was back behind the wheel, staring straight ahead through the windshield.

'Nice to know some of the old values still obtain, isn't it, Hank?' said the first guy.

'Heartwarming,' said Hank.

'Still what?' Penny said.

'Guess I'd feel better too,' said Wingtips, 'chick like you came to smooth my forehead, bring me pink carnations when I'd just OD'd on barbiturates. Wouldn't you, Hank?'

'Definitely,' said Hank.

'Have you guys been tailing me?' Penny said.

'I don't think I'd go that far,' said Wingtips.

'I would,' Hank said.

'I'll bet this is some kind of violation of my civil liberties. Harassment, or something,' said Penny. Her brain felt like it needed a booster shot. If she was being shadowed by the feds, she was in deeper waters than she wanted to be. Not only that. She was a mile from shore and the air was rapidly escaping from her buoyancy aid.

'Want to make an issue of it?' said Hank.

'I might.'

'We could always argue protection,' said Wingtips, bunching up his mouth as he pretended to think about it. 'What say, Hank?'

'Or national security,' said Hank. 'Dependant of a big name in the UN, guess we'd be entitled to keep a watch. Especially when there've been rumours of major trouble flying around.'

'What kind of trouble?' said Penny. But she already knew. If she needed it, this was merely confirmation of what Kimbell had told her.

'We're not at liberty to say.' Wingtips laced the fingers of both his hands together and flexed them. 'Way I see it, we're paid to prevent incidents within our own jurisdiction,' he said. 'Right, Hank?'

'Right.'

'So what exactly do you want me to tell you?' said Penny.

'First off, what did Miz Alphonse have to say?'

'I'd have thought you had the place bugged,' Penny said.

'We're still working on it.'

'Why should our conversation be of interest to your lot?'

'We'll be the judge of that,' said Wingtips. 'Just give us what she said, OK?'

'Forget the gist,' Hank said. 'The details will do fine.' He was still looking ahead.

Penny hesitated. Then asked herself why. She owed Eve Alphonse no loyalty. Didn't even like her much. And these were the best men to help recover her father and Pilot Whitman from wherever they'd been taken. She reran the conversation in her head. Nothing there they shouldn't know. So she told them.

Neither reacted worth a damn when she mentioned Georgie Lambton. The name of Nkasa, however, had a strong effect on Hank. He moved his head fractionally to one side and gave

143

Wingtips a dip of the head you had to be watching to recognise as a nod. It was when she brought up Leo that the chill of their eyes heated up from glacial to frigid.

'Look,' she said. She showed them his picture. 'He's one of the guys I saw out at Whitman's place.'

Hank was so moved that he removed one hand from the steering wheel and took hold of the newspaper. 'Leo Nkasa,' he said. 'Well, I'll be dipped.'

'We might've guessed he'd be involved,' Wingtips said.

'Should've,' said Hank.

'Did you know he was Mr Whitman's son, not Professor Nkasa's?' asked Penny.

The two men looked at each other without speaking.

'What's going on?' Penny said.

Wingtips gave her a glance that was pitying. It got her kind of steamed. 'Come now, Miss Wanawake,' he said, 'you surely don't expect us to tell you?'

'Or if we did, that we'd tell you the truth,' said Hank.

'I've read about guys like you,' Penny said.

'Playing both sides against the middle,' said Hank.

'Sell our own grandmothers down the river,' said Wingtips.

'Cute,' said Penny. 'Can I go now?'

'Of course.' Wingtips gave her a grin she wanted to push down his throat. 'Don't worry too much about your dad, Miss Wanawake. I expect we'll get to him in time.'

'In time for what?'

Hank shrugged. 'Whatever,' he said.

Penny grabbed Wingtips's arm. 'Do you have some idea where they are? He and Mr Whitman?'

'We're working on it,' he said again. He did something to his eyes that made them momentarily sincere. 'For the moment, he's OK. Believe me.'

Penny did. The President's plane didn't touch down at Kennedy until tomorrow morning. She turned to Santini. 'Did you ever find the car that Susannah Alphonse got to the beach house in?'

'We're getting there.'

'Which means there isn't one to find. Which means someone drove her down there and then drove back to wherever he – or she – had come from.'

'Check,' Santini said. 'By the way, we got a make on that body in the lake up at Whitman's place. An actor. Had some kind of a fancy name.' His eyes were languid behind the smoke.

Penny wasn't fooled by that. He wanted to see if she knew about Courtney Collins. She wasn't going to tell. Nobody could say she was withholding information. She tapped the newspaper. 'If it's any help,' she said, 'Susannah Alphonse is this Leo guy's half-sister. And the daughter of Pilot Whitman.'

'Is that a fact?' Already reaching for another cigarette, Santini sat forward. 'Come on, guys,' he said, 'why don't you run Miss Wanawake back to her hotel? She can update me on the way.'

He smiled at Penny. She didn't buy it. Someone wasn't being a hundred per cent open. And for once it wasn't her.

15

The lobby of the Sheraton-Regis was festive. Antique dealers milled around, all gussied up for the Gala Dinner which was laid on for them that evening. Some of them held champagne flutes in their hands. Penny saw Svante Svinhuvud lounging against a fake-marble pillar in a dinner jacket of navy-blue velvet, his curls glinting as though sprayed with gold. Close by stood Yawasata, neat as Pacman, chatting to a woman in strapless black worn under a *kosode* of white satin painted with cranes and bamboos. Penny might not know much about anything but she knew a *kosode* when she saw one. After five visits to the Great Japan Exhibition at the Royal Academy, so would anyone.

Hurrying across the marble floor she felt like the guest of honour at a Frumps Convention. It wasn't so much her jeans and collarless shirt as the dirty leather Reeboks on her feet. She didn't bother looking round for Barnaby. Even if he was there, he wouldn't be thrilled if she came over dressed that way. If you can't join 'em, beat it, she told herself. She checked at the desk. Nothing from Kimbell. Nothing from anybody. She caught the elevator upstairs.

Back in the hotel room, she could hear Barnaby in the shower. She took off her shoes and called Washington. Kimbell wasn't home. She used some bad language and punched out the numbers for a direct dial to her mother in London. Lady Helena answered almost immediately. Behind her, someone was having a ball.

'Hi,' Penny said. 'Did you have a whale of a time?'

'You're the fifth person to make that not-very-funny joke in the past hour,' said her mother.

'Thank God you got back safely.'

'Don't thank God, darling. Thank the Navy.'

'A British tar is a soaring soul.'

'I was the soaring one. Have you ever been winched aboard a naval helicopter in a Force Nine?'

'Never,' Penny said. 'I'm glad I wasn't along.'

'No, well, you wouldn't have been, would you? It was a single-handed race.'

'Mother, I want to throw a few names at you.'

'Throw away then.'

'Pilot Whitman.'

'Why the hell are you ringing me?' Lady Helena's voice sharpened. 'Is something wrong with your father?'

'No,' lied Penny.

'He's right there in California with Pilot. Why can't you ask him? Or Pilot himself?'

Penny wasn't about to reveal that Benjamin Wanawake was currently unavailable for questioning. 'Because the two of them've gone off on a little trip,' she said, 'out to the desert or somewhere.'

'Why hasn't he called me?'

'The phones're probably full of sand. Or maybe he doesn't realise you've abandoned ship. Tell me about Pilot's wife.'

'What do you want to know?'

'Almost anything.'

'She was a beautiful little thing. Absolutely ravishing. I could quite understand why he married her. Not that he had a lot of choice, with those fearsome male relatives keeping such a close eye on her. Your father disapproved strongly.'

'Why?'

'Mixed marriages weren't at all the done thing in those days.'

'But he married you.'

'He disapproved strongly of me too, darling. Still does, sometimes.'

'Try to concentrate, Helena. We're talking about Pilot's wife, if you remember.'

'Yes. A timid child. Terribly in love with him, too. Which is why it was all so tragic, later. I mean, the revelations about his mistress, and then him going off like that, without a word. We all watched her just wasting away and there wasn't a thing any of us could do.'

'Do you remember the mistress's name?'

'Um . . . it was one of those basic biblical names. Miriam, or something like that. I can't remember.' In the background, a voice began richly reciting bits of *Paradise Lost*. It sounded like Peter Corax, well-known novelist and even better-known drunk.

'How about Eve?'

'Eve,' said Lady Helena slowly. 'As a matter of fact, I think it was. It's biblical enough.'

'So is Abishag.'

'She definitely wasn't called that. I'd have remembered.'

'Did Pilot and this basic biblical lady have any kids?'

'Possibly.'

'Name?'

'Really, Penelope. This isn't the Senangan branch of Debrett's. And besides, in those days everyone was incessantly having babies.'

'Except you.'

'I do hope you're not about to reproach me for not providing you with a little brother or sister.'

'Since you bring it up . . .'

'I've told you before: I took one look at you and decided I'd better stop while I was ahead.'

Penny said nothing. She thought of Susannah, lying on a refrigerated tray in some Californian morgue. Dead, dead, and never called me sister.

'Has something happened?' her mother said. 'Why do you want to know all this?'

Penny wasn't sure. She'd certainly believed Eve Alphonse's story. Yet there was still the feeling that some vital fact had been omitted which would make sense of the whole thing. Looked like she wasn't going to get it from her mother.

'Anything more about Whitman?' she said. 'Like, what was he into out there?'

'Into?'

'Mother, if you can't cope with the vocabulary of the 1980s, it's time you started thinking about a geriatric ward.'

'Pilot was involved with the military in some way, if that is what you mean.'

'I know. Did he have any scams going down? Anything that he could be blackmailed for? Anything that might make him skip the country before it got known?'

'We-e-ell . . .'

'Yes?'

'There was a rumour once that he was gun-running. I know my father, as the British Ambassador, had to look into it.'

'What did he come up with?'

'Very little. Not that that surprised anyone. You could buy anything, if you paid enough. Even silence. And of course, we were all aware that he used the diplomatic pouch to get bits and pieces out that he had no right to.'

'Artistic-type things?'

'Yes.'

'Here's another name: Ralph Nkasa.'

'A very dangerous man,' said Lady Helena.

'Why?'

'Mainly because he was weak. He let that fearful old father of his push him around exactly as he pleased. And poor little Rebekah, the sister, didn't have an ounce of spirit left in her by the time she married Whitman. Naturally Ralph was dead keen on the marriage: Whitman was in a position to help the Nkasas in all sorts of ways, in spite of not having two pennies to bless himself with. Yes, a dangerous man. And an unscrupulous one, was Ralph.'

'You didn't like him much.'

'No. Though I wouldn't have dared say so. The Nkasas were a very powerful family.'

'So Ralph Nkasa was Whitman's brother-in-law.'

'Yes.'

The transatlantic wires whispered softly as Penny took this in. There wasn't time to digest it. That'd have to come later.

'. . . when Lambton was killed,' her mother was saying.

Penny felt as though she had been working on a jigsaw and found the key piece at last. 'Lambton,' she said. 'Georgie Lambton?'

'Yes. I mean it was common knowledge that the two of them were having an affair —'

'Pilot and Mrs Lambton?'

'. . . yes. And we were all convinced that he had something to do with the murder. But of course, he had the alibi from Whatever-she-was-called . . .'

'Eve?'

'. . . yes, from her, so there wasn't anything anyone could do about it.'

'Just a minute, Mother. Are you telling me that Pilot Whitman and Mrs Lambton were screwing around and that when Georgie found out about it, Pilot wasted him?'

'I'm not saying anything of the sort,' Lady Helena said. She drank crossly from some container she was holding close to the telephone. 'Honestly, Penelope, couldn't you have given me prior notice of all this? It's a bit much to ring up a person who's just been winched off the deck of a sinking yacht with the sea absolutely solid with whales and a howling gale blowing and start demanding intimate details of people she hasn't heard of for twenty years. You may not have realised it, but all I want to do is put my feet up with a good book and a mug of cocoa, not ferret around in the recesses of

149

my brain trying to dredge up details of a lot of ex-pats I'd rather forget.'

'Mother, if you're drinking cocoa, I'm Snow White.'

'I would be, if some friends hadn't dropped round to check that I was all right after my ordeal.'

'Who *was* Pilot supposed to have knocked off? Mr Lambton?'

'Yes.'

'Georgie.'

'Not Georgie, darling. Henry.'

'Who's Henry?'

'Her husband.'

'Georgie is a *woman*?'

'As far as I know.'

'Well, hush ma mouf.' A woman. Did that change anything? She was trying to decide when Barnaby came out of the shower. He snapped his watch on to his wrist then looked at her and tapped its face, indicating that she should hurry. It was all he wore, apart from a sprinkle of water drops across his shoulders. Staring at him, Penny felt weak at the knees. She had two choices. She could go and start licking them off, one by one, and take the consequences. Or she could stay where she was. She'd have opted for the consequences, if her mother hadn't still been talking.

'There were a lot of women like Georgie out in Africa, before everyone went independent,' she said across the airwaves. 'Hard-drinking, hard-shooting, hard-living.'

Eyes on Barnaby, Penny said, 'What did Henry Lambton do?'

'He was a coffee-farmer. Fabulously rich, of course.'

'And how did he die?'

'Someone shot him one evening while Georgie was out.'

'And they never managed to pin it on someone, even though the buzz was that Whitman did it?'

'No. Especially after that enormous woman insisted that he'd spent the whole night with her. Some people thought Georgie herself was involved. The servants had heard Henry and her quarrelling a couple of hours earlier, though God knows that was nothing new. There'd been plenty of scenes at various parties, when one or other of them got drunk and abusive to the other. Henry was a gent, of course, which you couldn't have said about Georgie. But the authorities didn't have any proof. To save face all round, it was decided in the end that it must have done by a disgruntled hand who'd then run away.'

'Uh-oh. Watch out for those hands when they get disgruntled.'

'Better them, dear, than one of us. Much more convenient for everyone. And anyway, they didn't think any of us would have rifled the place.'

'You didn't say the place was rifled.'

'Well, it was. Georgie was distraught. All her diamonds gone. She minded more about them than about poor Henry, I think.'

'She had a lot, did she?'

'Masses. Henry was always buying them for her. It was probably an investment on his part, but she always said they showed how much he loved her. When she wasn't quarrelling with him, that is.'

'What happened after that?'

'Pilot got out as soon as he decently could after the verdict. I think he made it to the airport about a step ahead of the Nkasas. The little wife had been absolutely shattered, you see, by the news that he was sleeping with her best friend, this Eve woman. Who by then had made herself scarce too.'

'What about Georgie? What was she like?'

'Those widows were all the same, darling. Thin, rich, and very very merry. Had affairs with just about everyone: black, white or in between. Even women, sometimes. As a matter of fact, as far as Georgie was concerned, I was never quite sure whether or not she and your father . . .'

Not another one. 'Benjamin?' Penny said. 'Surely not?'

'Actually, I quite liked her. I always think there's something rather endearing about naked greed.'

Penny looked at Barnaby. He was very close to her. She stuck out her tongue and swiped off two of the drops on his arms. He wore no clothes. Very naked. Very endearing. 'I'll go along with you on the first bit,' she said into the phone.

'I remember poor Georgie coming to the Embassy once, decked out in the most outrageously unsuitable diamond necklace her husband had just brought back for her from Paris.'

'When are diamonds unsuitable?'

'At an Embassy tea in Africa,' Lady Helena said firmly. 'Not that Georgie ever gave a damn what people thought of her. She had a diamond necklace so she wore it.'

'What happened to her?'

'It turned out that Henry had put absolutely all his money into the diamonds, which of course she no longer had. The poor girl was left more or less destitute. We had a whip-round for her, and my father saw to it that she had what she needed. But in the end she left Senanga.'

151

'Just like that?'

'Not quite. First she burst uninvited into Whitman's house during a dinner party and made the most frightful scene, screaming that we were all a bunch of snobs who'd been against her from the first. She said we'd ruined her life and she'd get even with us one day. She accused Pilot of killing her husband, which we were all sure he had done so that wasn't much of a surprise. Then she started ranting on about her diamonds, and how we were all trying to kick her back into the gutter where she knew we all thought she'd come from.'

'What was she saying about the diamonds?'

'Some nonsense about Pilot stealing them as well as shooting Henry. Rebekah was terrified, I do remember that. She had these huge beautiful eyes, like demitasse coffee. The sort you feel you could drown in quite happily. I don't think she'd ever seen a woman drunk before.'

'What did you do?'

'We must have appeared awfully hard-hearted but to tell the truth, we didn't take much notice. We'd all heard it before, or something very similar. You know the dramatic sort of nonsense people talk when they've had too much to drink.'

'Not really.'

'Well, there was a lot of it out in Senanga. Perhaps it was because we didn't have the telly. We had to provide our own entertainment in those days and most of it came out of a bottle. In the end Georgie picked up an axe from somewhere and in the middle of the screaming, she started laying about her with it, chopping at the verandah rails and totally annihilating the cane furniture. Madly exciting. We all cowered like anything.'

'What happened?'

'Whitman took the axe away from her and drove her home to sleep it off. A couple of days after that, she was gone.'

'Where to?'

'The States, I should think. That's where she came from originally.'

'It's a big country, Mother.'

'I have absolutely no idea which bit of it she was from. Atlanta faintly rings a bell, but that could have been someone else entirely. Now listen, Penelope, I want you to tell me precisely where your father is and why you're ringing me.'

'He's tucked up safely in bed,' Penny said, hoping, 'and I'm ringing you for the reasons stated above. One last question: why did Benjamin come out here to see Whitman? What were they going to discuss?'

'I don't know,' Lady Helena said. 'Can't you ask him in the morning?'

The drunken voice had switched to Tennyson. ' "Ruin seize thee, ruthless king . . ." ' it throbbed.

'You too, you boring old fart,' someone else said in a House-of-Lords accent. 'I had enough of that sort of thing when I was at Winchester.'

'More than enough,' said another voice. There was a sharp cry from a female throat and the thump of 'Chopsticks' being played very fast on her mother's Steinway.

'You better get back to your cocoa,' Penny said. She rang off quickly, before Lady Helena could ask again about Benjamin.

'Learn anything?' Barnaby said.

'Something. I'm not quite sure what it means, though. If anything.' Penny turned over on the bed. She lay on her stomach with her chin cupped in her hands. 'Hey, Barnaby.'

'Yo.'

'Suppose you were a young widow . . .'

'I know the feeling well.'

'. . . alone in a strange country, not much cash, in an ex-pat community that despised you, or at least cold-shouldered you.'

'Swine.'

'Suppose eventually they ganged together – or you thought they had – and got you more or less kicked out of the country. What would you feel?'

'If I hated them all that much, relieved, I should think.'

'Not vengeful?'

'OK, a little vengeful.'

'So vengeful that when many years later you saw an opportunity to get even, you took it?'

'Not that vengeful,' Barnaby said. 'Anyway, what opportunity?'

'Like three of the people who you felt had done you down all being in California at the same time.'

'California being where I'd ended up, huh?'

'Yup.'

'I guess as theories go, it's a theory.'

'Thing is, there seems to be a definite Senangan Connection involved with Susannah's death and my papa's abduction, wouldn't you say?'

'Possibly. Are you suggesting that I, the former Merry Widow, am finally wreaking my vengeance?'

'Yes.'

'Ralph Nkasa doesn't seem to be having vengeance wreaked on him.'

'Not yet. Though I kind of like him for the perp rather than a potential victim.'

'His being here is probably purely coincidental. If it wasn't for the Antique Fair, he'd be back in Senanga.'

'The Fair gave him a marvellous excuse to be out here if he needed one. From what my mother's just said, he'd be glad to do something fairly major to Pilot Whitman on account of what happened to his kid sister. And there's also a murder Whitman's supposed to have committed. No statute of limitations on murder – it could be a coup for Nkasa to get him back to Senanga and have justice done. And if not that, there's always Whitman's secret art collection.'

'What's this got to do with the Merry Widow's revenge?'

'I'm just talking possibilities at the moment,' Penny said. 'One should keep one's mind flexible as one gets older.' She jammed her teeth together and clenched a fist. 'Darn it. I just wish I had some idea what Whitman wanted to talk about to my father.'

The phone bleeped suddenly. Penny picked up. 'Yes?'

'Penelope.'

She couldn't grasp what she was hearing. 'Hello?' she said, her voice thick with incredulity.

'Penny, it's me.'

'My *Gaahd*,' she said. 'Pop. At last. Where the hell are you?' Relief flooded her, making her legs shake. He was safe. She could scarcely believe it was really him. Adrenalin surged hotly through her body. She felt as though she had just been kick-started. Her heart thumped. She covered the receiver with her hand. 'It's Benjamin,' she said urgently.

'I don't know precisely,' her father said. His voice was slower than usual, bordered with an uncertainty she'd never heard in it before. She very much hoped she'd never hear it again. 'I don't know.'

'But are you OK? How did you get away from those jerks?'

'He's wit' me, doll.' The voice that took over was trying hard for Mickey Spillane. For all the good it did, it might just as well have opted for Mickey Mouse. Penny would have recognised those East Coast vowels through six layers of concrete. Preppy again. A.k.a.

Leo Nkasa stroke Whitman. You might be able to fool all of the people some of the time. You sure couldn't fool Penny Wanawake for much of it.

'Just a minute, you turd,' she began. 'If you —'

'Shut up and listen good, sister. I got your dad. You want him back in nice shape, you do like I say, OK?'

'Depends what you say, buster.' Penny hoped she sounded cool, laid-back, in control. The opposite of what she felt. She licked her dry lips and motioned at Barnaby to hand her the glass beside his bed.

'I wanna see you,' Preppy snarled.

'What about?'

'You'll see when you get here.'

'When's that?'

'Let's say tonight.'

'You say. I'll be there. What time?' She could scarcely concentrate for the relief of knowing that Benjamin was alive and unharmed.

'Lessee. There's that Gala Dinner you're supposed to show for. Howsabout after that, like, say, midnight.'

'Fine. Where?'

'Never you mind where, doll. Here's what you do.'

Listening, she guessed Leo's youth had been the misspent kind. Only a non-stop diet of cheap thrillers and gangster movies could have produced the kind of instructions he gave. They involved so many car-changes, waits in lay-bys, flashes from headlights, even blindfolds, that her kneecaps itched. 'Got that?' he said finally.

Penny knew she ought to feel scared. Instead, she felt high. Invincible. Benjamin was safe. And if anyone was going to rescue him and Whitman, she was the man for the job. 'Got it,' she said. 'But don't like it.'

'You're not here to like nothing, sister. Just do what you're told.'

'Don't you want me to bring any ransom money or anything? An airline bag full of unmarked bills of low denomination? Crap like that?'

He laughed. 'There isn't enough money in the world to buy this particular baby,' he said.

'What exactly is the baby?'

'You'll see.'

'Suppose I contact the police?'

'Then the doctor dies.'

'Very Grade B.'

'Grade B, Grade friggin' Z: who gives a shit?'

155

Penny drew in a long breath. If he could do it, so could she. 'Touch the doc,' she growled, 'and you're history. Do I make myself clear?'

'Abundantly.'

'Don't think I'm kidding, Leo.'

Time passed, silently. During it, Penny began to wish she hadn't spoken. Perhaps she'd played the joker too soon; put the safety of her father and Pilot Whitman in jeopardy. Oh God.

Finally Preppy spoke. The cheap hood had left his voice. She was glad to notice that the smoothness had gone ragged along the edge. 'You're in way over your head, Miss Wanawake,' he said.

Too right. She forgave him for being patronising. Standard male technique. There were other things he could have been which were worse. 'Can I speak to my father again?' she asked. She tried to act humble but her knowledge of his name still hung there on the wire which stretched between them.

'Why not?' Hands shifted. Her father spoke once more.

'Penelope.'

'You OK, Pop?'

'For the moment.'

'And Mr Whitman?'

Dr Wanawake's voice broke. 'Oh Lord, I hope so. They've been keeping us apart, so I can't be sure. Penelope, I'm seriously perturbed about your mother.'

'She's just fine, Pop.'

'They had the wireless on. I heard something about whales sinking some of the boats sailing the Atlantic.'

'I just spoke to her. The Navy stepped in and baled her out. I said you were out of town, in the desert. Hey, Benj: are you really all right?'

'For the moment I don't believe I'm in any danger.'

'Exactly what Trotsky was saying when they brought out the ice-pick.'

'These people are misguided rather than evil. Also, too stupid to realise how little can be achieved by brute force.'

There was some kind of commotion. A clatter. A thud. She heard her father draw in his breath sharply. She knew he would be too proud to cry out. The dull rage that violence always induced in her started to ember.

'Listen, you bastards,' she shouted, 'you touch my father and you'll be really sorry.'

Preppy came back on the line. 'I already am,' he said smoothly.

He could have been about to begin an upmarket sales pitch. 'My —
uh — assistant is a little cruder in his working methods than I am.'

'You mean that moron, Dezzy?'

There was another silence. Then a cough of the sort that indicates
that the frog in the throat is not even a minor tadpole. 'I was, of
course, aware that you had investigated one or two minor cases in
the past,' Preppy said softly. 'Perhaps I've underestimated you,
Miss Wanawake.'

'You better believe it, boy.'

'If I have done so, that only increases the danger to your father. I
very much hope you are aware of that.'

'Suck eggs, creep.'

'Be careful, Miss Wanawake. And of course I don't need to say
that you won't tell anyone. The police. Or Midas. See you tonight.'
The line disconnected.

Barnaby put his arms round her. 'What was all that about?' She
told him.

'We're going,' he said.

'Of course. After your antique dinner. At least, I am.'

'Me too.'

'No.' She looked at him. 'If you do, it could endanger my father.'

'If I don't, it could endanger you.'

'No, Barnaby. Please.'

'That's just stup—'

'And we aren't going to contact the police.'

'They're there to protect you, honey.'

'In the normal course of events. But this isn't normal. And I just
can't risk anything happening to Benj. It'd kill my mother.'

He screwed his face up. He could tell she wasn't going to change
her mind. 'So no cops,' he said slowly.

'No Midas. No cops. Not that I have anything against Santini —
except his dress sense — but if we told him, he'd want to be in on the
act. And that could mean trouble.'

Barnaby shook his head. 'Where will it all end, one asks oneself?'

'Almost certainly in tears. The question is,' Penny said, 'whose
will they be?'

16

If the banqueting room of the Sheraton-Regis had featured rafters, they would undoubtedly have been ringing. The acoustic ceiling panels did their best. It wasn't the same. The roar of five hundred antique-dealing throats rose and was deflected, growing in direct proportion to the amount of Californian Cabernet poured down them. Penny had already done her·bit to increase wine sales in the area. She wished she hadn't.

She finally gave up on her *filet de boeuf*. She pushed it to one side of her plate and closed her knife and fork. Half the world was starving while the other half chewed themselves into high-number cholesterol levels. She tried for fine indignation. Didn't make it. The reason she couldn't eat had nothing to do with inequality and everything to do with the fact that midnight burned ahead of her like the light over a bordello's front door. All too soon, she'd be keeping her date with destiny. Or with Leo Nkasa. It came to much the same thing.

Up and down the room, waiters in mess jackets of blue cotton began removing plates. Others slapped down fresh ones. A troop of waitresses brought in a series of *bombes*, each one big enough to house an Eskimo. Penny wished she was better armed. If she was up against Leo Nkasa, then she was into politics – unless she'd misread the situation entirely. So should she tell the feds or not? They were the guys to handle sensitive issues like that. But if she did, what might Leo do to Benjamin? She thought of Susannah, brains spilling out across the corn-row braids like snail trails in the mist, of Courtney Collins with half his handsome face pecked away, then decided not to.

Was Leo responsible? He hadn't seemed the sort to soil his fingers with violence. Easier to see him as the man who operated Dezzy's switches. And killing his sister/lover was stretching sibling rivalry to extremes.

Across the heads of the diners, she could see Nkasa at a distant table, shiny as a beetle in a silk dinner suit. He was talking to a woman in green, using his hands, laughing. She turned to speak to a man on her other side and the smile eased from his face like peeling sunburn. His large head pivoted towards the woman on his left and, catching Penny's eye, stopped in mid-turn. He stared at her, unsmiling, unwinking. *Have you got him?* she wanted to scream. *Do you know where Benjamin is? And if you have, how's it going to benefit your political ambitions if he publicises what you've done?* And with that thought came the realisation that those who held him – Nkasa and his surrogate son? – weren't going to release him. Not alive.

She looked down at her own lap. The sleeveless gown of white satin, its high neck elaborately embroidered with seed pearls, made her look tall and, if Barnaby was right, brutal.

Sitting betwen Barnaby and Yawasata, feeling fresh out of brutality, possibilities churned her brain to mush so that she couldn't think straight. If Leo Nkasa was holding her father, what about this Georgie Lambton? Even if she'd killed Susannah, did she have anything to do with Benjamin? Across from her sat the Contessa, broad as a supermarket with her henchmen behind her on hard bentwood chairs. She had the kind of air that is usually called baleful. Every now and then her eyes manoeuvred from between the flesh-folds towards Penny. Unlike Penny, she was having no problem eating. Penny stared at her. Nothing made any sense. She remembered Carlo Bonami and his remarks about Whitman's financial situation. A desperate man can be driven to desperate measures. Could Whitman have engineered this whole thing? Leo Nkasa was his own son, after all. But Leo had said money was not what they were after. Could Whitman have struck a bargain with the Nkasas: my collection for your money, and Benjamin Wanawake's endorsement thrown in for good measure? If so, where did Susannah fit into it? She was a journalist. Had she stumbled across the plot and been silenced, been cast up on the deck of the Big Sur house like a piece of flotsam recovered from the beach?

Beside her, Yawasata uttered some incomprehensible syllables. So far, she had only understood one word he'd said and she'd probably got that wrong, judging by his bewilderment when she passed the melba toast. She nodded at him. Fifty million pounds he'd paid, for a picture of some irises or something. What would she pay for a Fabergé parure? What would the Contessa pay? Who had asked Josh Peters to duplicate the original? Where did Barnaby come into all this?

159

For days she'd been chasing up and down the state talking to people, asking questions, and all she'd done was uncover a whole heap of shit, none of which was any help.

A bellboy of some decrepitude appeared at the door of the vast dining room. He spoke into the ear of a dignified gentleman in white gloves who carried a napkin in one arm and looked like he could take over the running of the country without even blinking. A telephone message. It had to be for her. Penny half-rose. Benjamin's body, found halfway between here and New York, hideously mutilated. A ransom note asking for sums impossible to obtain before the deadline expired. Political demands made with hideous consequences to her father if the terms weren't met.

But the message was for Nkasa. She watched him push back his chair and hurry out, a frown the size of a cattle grid across his brow. Should she follow? It might have been his nephew, Leo. Beside her, Barnaby talked with animation to a woman whose mammary glands appeared to suffer from a wasting disease.

A few minutes later, the bellboy reappeared. Again he conferred with the napkined gentleman. Their heads turned towards the top table. This time the call *was* for her. Urgent. Long-distance. She hurried along the polished flooring behind the dining chairs, her heels slipping on the parquet.

She took in a lungful of air before she lifted the receiver. 'Hello?' she said cautiously.

'Hi, doll.' It was Kimbell. 'Hope I'm not interrupting anything. You said to call no matter what.'

'Right.'

'So I'm calling.'

'Way to go, boy. What'd you find out?'

'Whitman. Want the potted version?'

'OK.'

'He's English, originally. Born in Nettlebed, sent off to school in Rugby, followed by Sandhurst. Went out to Senanga when he was just twenty, stayed there for the next fifteen years. Married a lady called Rebekah Nkasa, had one son. Second child born two years later but died shortly after birth, along with mother, in a house-fire. How'm I doing so far?'

'Great. Do your notes let on that the house-fire was in fact a suicide?'

'Is that right?' Kimbell considered it. 'She must have been pretty desperate. That's a helluva way to go.'

'What else about Whitman?'

160

'He seems to have raised all kinds of hell while he was out there. Not drugs, but just about everything else, from girls to guns.'

'Girls?'

'A couple, they told me. Plus these guns he was running across the border. It was a capital offence in those days, so I guess he was kind of lucky to get out.'

'When he did, where'd —'

'Back up a minute here. I haven't even mentioned the murder.'

'Henry Lambton's, you mean?'

'You're no fun, you know that? I waste hours on this and you already got the answers.'

'Tell me about the murder, Kimbell.' Through the glass door of the cubicle, Penny saw Nkasa. He stood uncertainly in the middle of the lobby, as though trying to decide which way to go.

'Yeah, well, there's this guy, see, whose wife Whitman's having it off with. He comes home one night, finds Whitman in between the percales, the wife doing the dance of the seven veils with a rose between her teeth, only it's not her teeth it's between, if you follow.'

'Perfectly.'

'Naturally, the guy isn't too happy. Not only does he kick Whitman out, he says he intends to hand him over to the authorities, says he's got proof of what Whitman's been up to. And the very next night, somebody breaks in, kills the guy, steals the guy's wife's jewellery and gets out. Nobody knows who did it, except the wife, and she only guesses because among the loot he took was a very special necklace or something which she'd hidden in a spot only she knew the whereabouts of.'

'She and Whitman.'

'Right. If the bedbugs don't get you then the pillowtalk will. Anyway, she's fingering him to the cops before he's got back home, only turns out she was wrong. Wanna know why?'

'He had an alibi.'

'Listen, will you tell me why I been busting a gut to get this stuff for you?'

'I'm guessing, honeybun. Just guessing's all.'

'Well . . .' huffed Kimbell. 'Anyway, the girl who gives him the alibi is the wife's best friend. So the in-laws squeeze her out for a start. Then they get on Whitman's case. He's out of there and back to Beanrow —'

'Nettlebed.'

'— before you can say liquid fertiliser. After a few years selling insurance and double glazing, stuff like that, he lights out for the US

161

where we lose his track for a while. He surfaces again about five years ago in California, respectable businessman, all the trimmings – the suits, the Mercedes, the fistful of plastic, the subscription to the *New Yorker*.'

'What about the woman?'

'Which woman?'

'That no respectable businessman should be without?'

'Nope,' said Kimbell. Penny heard pages riffle. 'Got no mention of no women down here. Anyway, he starts up in the catering trade, moves on to the estate in Napa, does well, buys a second restaurant. Mr Squeaky-Clean, far as I can see.'

'What about Georgie Lambton?'

'Quite a bit. For starters, the Georgie Lambton guy you asked me to check out isn't a guy at all.'

'I know that,' Penny said impatiently.

'Why'd you ask me to bone up on him?'

'Because I didn't know then. Anything else?'

'She was darn difficult to trace but I did it . . .'

'Clever Kimbell.'

'. . . thanks to my perseverance and the way I gave the dame in the records office the eye. Boy, that was some eye. You should have been there.'

'I think I already was. Once is enough.'

'In the end she worked overtime on it for me.'

'Did she come across?'

'That's no question for one lady to ask about another.'

'With the goods, Kimbell. What she does in private's no concern of mine.'

'She sure did. And the goods are, not only is Georgie Lambton not a guy, she's a foreign non-guy. Once she arrived back in the US, she dropped out of sight. Then she surfaced in Europe. London, first, then Paris, and finally Milan. Where she got hitched to some Italian bozo who was quietly going bankrupt south of Florence.'

'Get to the point, Kimbell. There's a lot riding on this.'

'Just hold your horses. The Italian died after losing an argument with a transporter on the autostrada, leaving the lady with a lot of debts and some family heirlooms. She said the hell with the debts and took off with the heirlooms, which I might have done myself in similar circumstances.'

'Can't imagine a bankrupt Italian wanting to make an honest woman out of you, Kimbell.'

'To see me is to love me.'

162

'Natch. Where'd Georgie light out to?'

'Paris. The dead guy's family tried to recover the goods, or at least get their hands on some of the moolah, but she produced papers to prove he'd handed them all over to her before his death. There were some paintings . . . just a minute, I've got a list . . .'

'I'm not really inter —'

'A Veronese *Madonna and Child*. An undistinguished, it says here, Botticelli of Ackis and Galatea, whoever the hell they are.'

'Ackis?'

' 'S what they've got down here. Ackis and —'

'It's like oasis without the "O".'

'Whatever. There's a preliminary drawing for a *Trinity* by Masaccio. A small —'

'Was it all paintings?'

'There was quite a few items of jewellery too. Want me to read them out?'

'Not necessary,' said Penny. 'If this non-guy's not American, what is she?'

'Some years back she set up a commercial artistic venture, it says here. I *think*. My French is on the lousy side. Then she applied to become a French citizen. Application granted four years ago, after she'd completed residency. I've got the name right here for you. Ready?'

'Don't tell me. Let me guess,' Penny said. Everything was at last making some kind of sense. You had to look for the parallel lines, not the links in a chain. It looked as though for Pilot, a whole lot of chickens had come home to roost, all at the same time. Whitman had stolen Georgie's diamonds all those years ago. Eve had covered for him. Now he was going to have to pay for them. And Eve's debts had been recovered in full. An eye for an eye, a death for a death. Nkasa's sister had killed herself on Whitman's account. Now Nkasa wanted recompense. Leo Nkasa, né Whitman, had never known his father. Now he was getting acquainted in the closest possible way. Vengeance is supposed to be sweet but you'd think that twenty years on, it would have lost some of its savour.

'Hey, Pen. You still there?'

'Yeah.'

'I mean this call's costing bucks. You know?'

'I'll pay you back, Kimbell.'

'Long as it's understood it's not money I'm after.'

'Right.' Penny roused herself.

'You still guessing who she is?'

'I don't need to. I know,' Penny said. She felt exhausted. She stared out at a party of tourists without really seeing them. Behind them, Nkasa sat on a seat, head hanging down.

If only she could get a handle on the motive behind her father's kidnap. But she couldn't. However much she fastened down the ends, they kept coming loose again. Why take Whitman, who was non-political, along with her father? Why take her father, if Whitman was the target? Benjamin might have been no more than an innocent outsider, but that didn't lessen his ordeal. Though in that case, why not dump one or other of them after the pick-up?

'Bet you don't,' Kimbell said.

'I do.'

'Who, then?'

'The Contessa di Sforzini.'

'Wrong.'

'You're kidding.'

'I'm not.'

'Not the Contessa?'

'No siree.'

'Who, then?'

'Uh.' She heard Kimbell riffle through his notes again. 'Uh – just a second, doll. I can't find it now.'

'Get your ass in gear, Kimbell.'

'Here we are. The former Georgie Lambton, presently residing in Napa County, California, goes by the name of – ta-dah! —'

'Kimbell.'

'Mrs Georgina Fontaine.'

17

Lisa Druckner picked up before the first beep had ended, as though she'd been sitting with her hand on the receiver. 'Yes?' she said suspiciously.

'Hi, this is Penelope Wanawake,' Penny said.

'Who?'

'Penny Wanawake.'

'I thought you were my ex-husband,' said Lisa.

'He's black and sexy too, is he?'

'Huh?'

'You gave me Josh Peters's address the other day,' said Penny.

'Oh sure. I remember now.' The incorporate voice brightened. 'How was he?'

'Just fine.'

'What a hunk,' sighed Lisa. 'Now that is one guy I could really —'

'I need Mrs Fontaine's address this time,' Penny said, crisp as lettuce. 'But she's not listed, either.'

'You're the lady from La Jolla, right? With the art gallery?'

'Right.'

'Gonna do a deal?' said Lisa. 'We charge ten per cent commission, straight up, but that's between you and Miz Fontaine.'

'If and when I can get hold of her,' Penny said. 'Which I hope will be as soon as possible.'

'You gonna go up there *now*?'

'I don't have much choice,' Penny said, 'which is why I need that address. I've got a flight back tomorrow morning, first thing. If I don't clinch the deal now, it's off.'

'Oh, right, right.' Lisa skiffled through an address book. 'Hang on while I find the address for you. It's kind of a shame you can't wait until you get back and can call her from there.'

Penny thought herself back into the part of art-gallery-owner in up-scale La Jolla. 'That's not the way I do business.'

'Here we go,' Lisa said. 'It's 1786 Catalina Drive. It's a big old house about five miles off the main road. You can't miss it.'

'Thanks,' said Penny. 'Hey, I think I met Mrs Fontaine once before somewhere. Least, I thought it was her. Only she seemed to be called something else then. Kind of an Italian name, like . . . uh . . .'

'Fontana,' said Lisa. 'She changed it. Used to be Fontana, on acccount of her being married to an Italian, but then she moved to France before she came here. Fontaine, see. It's French for fountain. And Fontana is —'

'Quite,' Penny said. 'Well, guess I'd better be on my way. Thanks for all your help.' She put the receiver down.

In the lobby, Ralph Nkasa was sitting with his head between his hands. Despite her hurry, Penny stopped.

'Are you all right?' she said.

Nkasa lifted his head. She'd never seen a shark with its teeth removed but she knew it would have the same look. Lethal yet powerless. Until it found a dentist to come up with a false set. The points of his stiff collar stuck into the soft black flesh under his chin. The royal-blue bow tie had slipped sideways. Each time he breathed, it quivered beneath his ear like a rakish butterfly. 'Eve Alphonse is dead,' he said.

'What?'

'Eve. She killed herself. The hospital just called.'

'That's terrible,' said Penny. With a bigger brain, she might have been able to compute the various effects this could cause. As it was, she could only take hold of the fact.

Nkasa seemed shattered. She wondered how many other deaths there had been in his life. How many more there would be if he succeeded in his takeover plans. How many fanatics would be eliminated as Susannah had been eliminated.

'She threw herself off the balcony outside the hospital's sun lounge.' His voice was bewildered. 'Why would anyone do such a thing?'

It was the question they always asked, the ones left abandoned by suicide. After it came the guilt for not seeing, not helping, the intolerable burden bestowed by such radical opting out. 'She must have felt she hadn't got anything left to live for,' Penny said.

But that wasn't right. When she'd left the hospital, Eve had seemed almost reconciled to a life beyond Susannah. Had even spoken of returning to Senangaland.

She sat beside Nkasa, holding on to one of his big hands. She tried not to imagine it round her own neck. Suicide took the ethos of the throwaway society to its logical conclusion, she thought. Waste disposal carried to extremes.

'I told her last time I saw her that I knew she wasn't to blame for my sister's death,' Nkasa said. 'I've thought since that it would have happened anyway, some time. Rebekah was always nervous, always frightened of everything.' He stared at her, talking to himself rather than an audience. He was close enough for her to take in the bloodshot lines which streaked his eyeballs, the cloudy yellow edge to their whites. 'She'd tried to kill herself once before.'

'Your sister?'

'Yes.'

'Why did the hospital call you?'

'Because Eve left a letter addressed to me, saying she was sorry.' He snorted unhappily, shaking his head. 'My God. Sorry.'

For the lips of a strange woman drop as an honeycomb and her mouth is smoother than oil; but her end is bitter as wormwood, sharp as a two-edged sword, Penny thought. Eve Alphonse had been a strange woman. Now she was a dead one, come to her bitter end.

She disengaged herself gently from his grasp. 'Look, Professor Nkasa, I'm afraid I must' – she'd been going to say 'get going.' She changed it – 'get back to my table.' Stricken he might be about Eve's death and almost certainly nothing at all to do with Susannah's. That didn't rule out the possibility of his involvement in her father's kidnap. If she had a lead at last to where he was being held, Nkasa mustn't know. She reminded herself that it was only a lead, not a certainty. And that she had better shift ass if she was going to check it out before midnight. If she found Benjamin, OK. She'd wing it from there. If she didn't, Barnaby would have to cover for her until she was back. She tried not to let Nkasa see her surreptitious glance at her watch. It was 8.45. Three and a quarter hours. She'd have to drive some, and start like *now*, if she was going to make it in time.

The roads were surprisingly full. Vehicles streaked along the freeways, jockeying for a space here, a clear run there, endlessly changing, sliding back and forth across the hard-top, in and out of the traffic lanes, each driver isolated from the others yet all of them united in a common desire. I.e, to get where they were going as quick as they damn well could. She honked sharply at some jerk who cut in front of her with a half-centimetre to spare. Hey, creep. Tell me about it. Quick doesn't have to mean dangerous. She killed

167

the thought as soon as it appeared. If there was one thing she hated, it was a person behind a steering wheel who bad-mouthed everyone else on the road.

It wasn't until she had turned on to Highway 29 that she was able to start breaking the fifty-five m.p.h. speed limit. She did it thoroughly. Scenery shifted backwards past her, looming out of the orange darkness ahead and receding in to the night she was leaving behind. Not exactly a blur, but fast. Fast enough that she ought to concentrate on holding the wheel steady, rather than worrying about her father. Or Eve and Susannah. Or even about the fact that someone had already attacked her once.

She tried to fit the facts together, make sense of the timings. The arrival in San Francisco of aspiring journalist Susannah Alphonse had not necessarily been the catalyst that started a whole chain of reactions. Whether Georgie Lambton Fontaine had come out to the West Coast in search of Whitman and her diamonds was difficult to say. It would seem unlikely. The Italian husband had been dead for years, Lambton for even longer. The diamonds would have been sold on aeons ago. More likely, she had arrived here because of the climate. Plus the fact that San Francisco was a place people came to. She probably hadn't had any idea that Leo Nkasa, Whitman's son, Nkasa's nephew, was in his last year at Berkeley. If she'd read Susannah's article, Alphonse was a name she would have recognised. So was Whitman.

Or perhaps she'd met up with Josh Peters through the gallery, gone to the theatre with him, seen Susannah, recognised the name, learned about Whitman.

Or maybe Susannah was nothing to do with it. Maybe Georgie'd seen Whitman while eating at one of Whitman's restaurants, heard Eve sing, recognised them both, realised how badly she still wanted revenge.

Maybe she just – Penny swerved across the road to avoid a truck parked without lights – *nerd!* – just plain bumped into Whitman in the street. Or met him via Josh Peters.

Whichever, the how of it didn't matter. Any more than the connection between her and Leo. It was enough that it existed.

With the publicity given to the arrival of Ralph Nkasa and Benjamin Wanawake, it would have seemed as though all the main figures in the landscape of Georgie's past had suddenly come back to life. She must have realised that this was her chance to get even. Unlike the Senangan days, she was now rich and powerful enough to punish them all for the injuries that, singly or collectively, they

168

had once caused her. Obsessive. Briefly, Penny lifted her foot from the accelerator. Was she rushing into something she couldn't handle? If she was right about where her father was being held, the answer had to be yes. Barnaby was quite wrong to say that obsessive people were harmless. Her only weapon was the fact that Georgie couldn't possibly know anyone was on to her real identity. With any luck, she'd be off her guard for long enough for Benjamin to get away. Once again Penny cursed herself for letting Leo know she knew who he was.

Darn it. How did they all connect up? She found herself driving past the entrance to Bonami's Winery. Should she stop? Get help? But help in this case would most likely mean Ed Lutz. If she was wrong about Mrs Fontaine, she could end up worse off than if she went in on her own.

The street lights began to peter out. The road led into thick blackness. No lines along the road for her headlights to pick out. She could have been driving through space for all the signs of humankind there were. A few miles further on, she pulled up to the side of the road. She turned the car round so it was facing back the way she'd come and got out. She was parked tight up against a tall hedge of beech. She unzipped her dress. Tossed it into the back of the car. Got into the black warm-up suit which was lying on the back seat.

She walked towards the entrance gates set in the hedge. Through the whispery brown leaves, she could see lights on in the house. She hoped it wasn't a burglar-repellant. She hoped somebody really was home. The windows of the house were uncurtained. She held her watch close to her face. Just after 10.30. She'd made good time getting here. They wouldn't be expecting her. The two wooden gates were open, folded back against the inside of the hedge. She walked up the drive, keeping close to cover where she could. The Chevvy was parked out front, and close by it, the yellow compact. A rectangular spill of light from a latticed ground-floor window to the left of the front door showed the edge of a lawn, and a tumble of gravel in need of raking. Walking across gravel without advertising your presence was one of those things that only ghosts did well. Keeping well back, she stood on tiptoe. She guessed it to be the main living room though she couldn't see much. The padded backs of some upholstered seating. The upper half of a glazed break-front. An ornately carved cupboard in dark wood. And the tops of two heads. One black. One grey. Even as she watched, the grey one rose so that she could see the face that went with it, and came towards the window. A woman. She stared out into the night. There was a restlessness about her that spoke of frazzled nerves. She held some kind of small dog in her arms, stroking its fur with a sort of fierce intensity that shouted louder than oaths. Was this the dog she had threatened Penny with on her earlier visit?

Penny stood absolutely still, a black shadow in the night. For a while neither of them moved, then the woman who was once Georgie Lambton moved away, out of sight.

Penny stepped carefully round the side of the house, keeping to the soil bed in which the hedge was planted. Its sharp little twigs wrenched at her hair and bit her bare hands and face. Beyond the hedge which bounded the road, a fast-driven car rushed by. Its lights swept across the house, momentarily brightening the black shingles which decorated the front elevation. Before its noise had been soaked up again by the silence from which it had come, Penny was at the back, on a moss-riddled patio made of herring-boned brick. Above her head, much too high for her to reach it, a wide balcony spread from one edge of the house to the other. She stood directly in front of a long glass door overlooking a half-acre of wild grass and untamed shrubs. Buried somewhere among them she could just make out the outline of what had once been a pool. Further off, was the shape of hills. She realised she'd seen them before, from the far side.

She should have been more on the ball. Should have realised earlier that this place backed on to the Whitman property. That was undoubtedly the reason why Georgie had so recently purchased it in the first place. Georgie Lambton and Leo Nkasa. He the scabbard, she the blade. At the moment there was no proof of anything, but personal and political motives united in the pair of them to form the perfect instrument of revenge.

Easy, therefore, to imagine their consternation as Dezzy returned to the pink castle to report slugging some black bimbo on the head and dumping her in the lake. Had they trooped out to look at her unconscious body, recognised who she was, assumed she'd tracked them down, hurriedly crammed the two captives back into the Cadillac? She imagined the late-night drive across some back road linking the two properties, and the rising tension as they wondered whether the black bimbo was alone, how much she knew, whether she'd told anyone where she was going.

She eased apart the two sections of the patio door. Behind them was a darkened room. A line of light at floor-level indicated a door leading to the rest of the house. She listened. Nothing, except the

170

steady murmur of a television somewhere. If the black head she'd seen belonged, as she was sure it must, to Leo Nkasa, then he wasn't putting any polish on his cheap hood accent, even though it could do with some. She folded her hand round the doorhandle. Barnaby had taught her that doorhandles were like nettles: they needed to be grasped firmly. She turned this one. Outside was a wide hall, a slab of newly sanded floor, the risers of an old-fashioned curving banister. She listened some more. The doors of this turn-of-the-century house were old and thick, built to strain out noise. If someone was about to appear, she'd have no prior warning. Quickly she made for the foot of the stairs. She could see a neo-Sheraton table with a maroon telephone on it. She'd already sussed that the story about the phone not being connected was a lie, the best excuse Mrs Fontaine could come up with on the spur of the moment. The last thing she'd wanted was Penny Wanawake coming into the house where her kidnapped father was imprisoned.

Poor Georgie. What a lot of trouble she must have gone to, trying to implicate Benjamin in scandal by leaving a dead body on his patio. Poor Susannah, that the dead body should be hers for no other reason than that she was the daughter of Eve. Talk yourself out of that one, Benj. And when you've realised you can't, endorse Ralph Nkasa for President; it's the only way you'll get yourself off the hook. Because as sure as shooting, there had to be a way off. Georgie would have seen to that. She was a patient woman. She'd waited years for a chance to revenge herself. She wasn't going to spoil things at this stage by inattention to detail.

Penny started up the stairs. She knew that if she was going to find what she came for, it would be on the first floor. No one giving houseroom to a couple of kidnap victims was going to keep them downstairs. You never knew who was outside, peering in. Especially when there were no drapes.

A long landing. Several doors. Any one of them might be the right one. Common sense told Penny that the furthest from the escape route of the stairs would be the best place to start. She tiptoed down the carpet runner. Up here, the sound of the TV was louder. For a moment she contemplated getting out on to the balcony and using that route, but realised it was bound to have been blocked. Would the prisoners be guarded? It seemed unlikely. Her father had said he and Whitman were being kept apart. If Dezzy had already started the drive into San Francisco to guide her back here through the maze of blindfolds and lay-bys that Leo considered appropriate, then at least two more guys had to be involved. That was more manpower than she thought there was. Which meant her father and his friend would be tied up. She felt for the Swiss Army knife she'd brought and reminded herself that, so far, she had no proof either Pilot or Benjamin was actually in the house. Nor, for that matter, that the black head downstairs belonged to Leo.

She began to wish she hadn't been so trite in her treatment of Barnaby. Insisting on going alone to meet the baddies was what they always did in books. If there'd been two of them, Barnaby could have created a disturbance downstairs while she checked out which rooms they were holding her father and Whitman in. As it was, she had an awful lot to do.

She was about to start doing it when downstairs, someone created a disturbance. They rapped loudly at the front door. For a moment nothing happened. It was as if everyone in the house listened to the sound, weighing up what it meant, wondering how to respond. Then someone came out into the hall. Penny shrank back against the landing wall. Once the front door was opened, she'd be in the direct line of vision of anyone standing on the porch. Quiet as a cockroach, she moved towards the end of the passage where a graceful arched window looked out over the side of the house. Below, she heard Mrs Fontaine's voice raised in greeting, an answering voice explaining that it had just been passing, seen the lights on, decided to drop in although it realised how late it was. The voices moved together into the living room.

She had recognised the new arrival. *Quel* relief. If she needed it, at least there was an ally in the house. Quickly she opened the door of the furthest room. She met darkness. She felt for a switch and snapped it on. The room was mainly occupied by a dozen packing-cases full of articles wrapped in newspaper. The rest of the space was taken up by a temporary cardboard wardrobe stuffed with hangered clothes, a stripped pine box pushed up against a chest of drawers with white china handles and several rolls of carpet lying along the skirting board. Nothing that looked remotely like a missing diplomat or a former military adviser.

Penny backed out and tried the next door. It was locked. She hunkered down to peer through the keyhole. Inane television chat punctuated by synthetic roars of laughter rolled through it. The view was impeded by a key. Quietly she turned it, then the handle. Inside, lying on a bed, was her father. His hands and ankles were bound with parcel tape. At the foot of the bed, set on a chest, was a miniature television set, tuned to an overloud rerun of *I Married A Witch*.

Relief hit her like a kick in the stomach. She whooshed out her

172

breath. So she'd been right, after all. Georgie was at the bottom of all this. Georgie and the art gallery lady were one and the same. For a while there, she was afraid she was leaping to hunch-like conclusions. And every amateur gumshoe knew you shouldn't back hunches, only certainties. Not that knowing it stopped them, usually.

'Hi,' she said. 'How's things?' She kept her voice low, despite the TV. The sight of him lying there, helpless as a side of beef, stirred feelings in her that made her heart tumble about in her chest. *The child is mother to the man.* She wanted to hold him close, tell him it would be all right, soothe him. Irrationally, tears sparked at the back of her throat. He'd asked her to sound out Svinhuvud about the snuffbox he wanted, and she'd done nothing about it. Suppose he'd been killed. What would she have felt like then, not having bothered to comply with her own father's last request? An absolute jerk, is what.

As she came in, her father turned his head. He was not a man given to loud demonstration. Surprise registered briefly then gave way to dark despair.

'Penelope,' he said.

It was one way to greet the cavalry when they'd galloped to the rescue. She guessed that in his own understated way, he was being heroic. Don't make a fuss. It was the credo of his generation.

'Father, dear Father, come home with me now,' she said. She kept it syllabub-light. Was it really going to be this easy?

'I'd be delighted to,' he said. 'If I have to watch that woman twitch her nose once more, I shall go insane. No wonder her husband behaves as though he's a registered lunatic.'

She moved the set so he could no longer see the screen. She wanted to ask some serious questions about the collective IQ of a nation that produced such drivel. Were they capable of rational thought? Should they be trusted with the B-1 bomber or nuclear power? But the same questions could be asked of any Western nation. TV, the great leveller. 'I can't turn it off,' she said. 'They'd hear downstairs.'

She pulled out her knife and cut her father free. The whole thing was as remote as though she had stepped into a movie. Later, she would relive the whole episode and feel then the emotions she did not dare give way to now. Fear. Anger. A frantic sense of haste. For now, she had to find his friend and get them both out of the house before someone came up to check on the prisoners. 'Where's Mr Whitman?' she said.

'I don't know. They blindfolded us,' her father said. He rubbed

173

his ankles with hands that trembled. He had the same look of vulnerability she'd found so disturbing last time she'd seen him, through the windows of Whitman's pink palace.

'We'll check the rooms as we go. Come on.' Penny stepped back into the corridor. Again she listened. No sound but Glendora being cutesy-poo on the TV and a faint rumble of voices from the living room below. She ushered Benjamin out into the corridor and tried the door of the next room along.

It was a spare guest room entirely empty of spare guests. Or anything else except three cabin trunks and an unmade four-poster bed hung with green-sprigged curtains. The room next to it was clearly Mrs Fontaine's. It too held no sign of Whitman. Nor did its *en suite* bathroom. Nor the one attached to the next and last room on the floor.

Penny and her father stared at each other. Benjamin frowned. 'He was all right this morning,' he said. 'I heard him calling out, asking for something, though with that damn television set on twenty-four hours a day, I couldn't hear what he wanted.'

'Maybe he wanted them to let him go, and they agreed,' Penny said. OK. So she was overreacting, being flip when the situation called for smart thinking and tough acting. The hell with that. Flip helped relieve tension. And boy, did she ever feel tense. What had happened to Whitman? Where did they look for him now? Surely they hadn't already – gulp – eliminated him.

'Let's at least get out of the house,' she said, whispering now as they crept down the stairs.

'I can't leave Pil —'

'Then we can work out what to do next,' Penny said. 'Call the police might be the best thing. With one of you free, they won't dare harm the other one.'

Dr Wanawake didn't look convinced but he followed her out of the patio door and round the side of the house. Penny was less concerned about noise this time. Her car was parked just down the road and once the two of them had reached it, only a submachine gun was going to stop her taking off like a bat out of hell.

As they passed the windows of the living room, a shadow darkened the lit panes. Oh my God. Had they been seen? A man stared out at them. He was vaguely familiar though she couldn't at first remember where from. She hissed at her father to freeze. He stood still. 'What's going on?' he said.

'What's going on is that someone's standing there watching us,' Penny whispered.

'I can see that,' her father said, 'but I don't understand.' He raised a hand to his glasses, as though he thought his vision must be faulty. The movement caught the eye of the man inside the room. His mouth opened. He turned fast and disappeared.

'Come on, for chrissake,' said Penny. She grabbed his arm and ran.

His footsteps pounded after her. 'Penny,' he said behind her. 'There's something wrong.'

'Tell me about it later.'

They passed the Chevvy and the convertible. The two had been joined by a third, a dirty white pick-up truck with tyres that seemed to be as high as the cab roof.

'Penny.' Her father stopped. 'We can't just run off like that.' He glanced over his shoulder at the house. At the same time, she heard the front door thrown open and voices calling.

'I can.'

'No.'

'Why not?'

'Because that man who saw us . . . the man looking out of the window . . .'

'Yes?'

'That was Pilot.'

'What?'

'That was Pilot Whitman,' her father said.

The jigsaw puzzle was almost complete. Behind them, footsteps crunched across the gravel. Someone demanded to know what was going on. The voice belonged to the person Penny had hoped would help them, if it came down to it. Now, she dared not stop. An innocent passer-by, dropper-in, would not have come prepared for violence, would probably be no use to them. She wasn't about to put it to the test.

She grabbed her father's arm. 'Which is precisely why we can run off like this,' she said. 'Now, move.'

18

She felt as if she'd been driving up and down this road for days. Centuries, even. The car seemed to be bogged down in the quicksands of nightmare, rushing through the night at over eighty miles an hour, yet standing still. She pressed her foot down harder on the accelerator.

'You worked it out perfectly correctly,' Dr Wanawake said. 'Though as far as I can tell, poor Ralph Nkasa knew nothing about it. He never did have much brain-power, even in the old days. What he had then seems to have evaporated since.'

'The idea was for Ralph to take over from the present incumbent, was it?'

'Yes. From which position Leo Nkasa would operate, sheltering behind his uncle's substantial shadow.' Dr Wanawake shook his head. 'The thirst for power. I've never really understood it.'

'And by calling me here tonight, they were going to blackmail you into an endorsement for him by doing something mean to me?'

'That seems to have been the general idea.'

'Would it have worked?'

Benjamin Wanawake didn't answer.

'Would it?' Penny said.

Her father sighed. 'I can't possibly say. I'd like to think that it wouldn't. But I couldn't be sure. All that high-sounding talk of the greater happiness for the greater number vanishes when the individual whose rights are being eroded happens to be someone you care about.'

'Where does Georgie Lambton fit into this?'

'She wanted Pilot to suffer the same kind of loss as she had once sustained when he stole her diamonds,' Benjamin said. 'It was quite appalling to see the anger and outrage that she still felt, even after all these years. Taking his art collection – or helping Leo Nkasa to – seemed a fitting revenge to her. Though perhaps not as fitting as she might have hoped. Pilot seems considerably less attached to material possessions than she does.'

'Why would she be party to forcing you to endorse Nkasa? I thought he was responsible for making her quit Senanga.'

'He was. But she had absolutely no interest in the political side. I don't think I've ever seen someone in the grip of an obsession before. She seemed to be eaten up with the desire to revenge herself on Whitman.'

'Why did he go in on the scheme in the first place?' Far away in front of her was a faint multi-coloured glow. Bonami's Winery, she guessed it to be. If they could reach it, they would be safe.

'Did you know he was financially embarrassed?' her father said.

'Did you know that you're probably the only person in the entire world who speaks like other people write? Financially embarrassed. Yes, I did know that. Or I heard hints.' From Carlo Bonami, from Earl, even from the wiseacre kid at the filling-station, the first time she'd ridden this road.

'Ralph was prepared to pay substantially for his art collection. It was Leo who decided that on its own, its restoration to Senanga wouldn't be enough to ensure his uncle's election. Particularly since the whole scheme could have gone sour if they weren't very careful.'

'How?'

'Because apparently Ralph Nkasa was largely instrumental in helping Pilot get it illegally out of the country in the first place. If anyone had gotten wind of that . . .'

'Goodbye President Nkasa.'

'Exactly. So in order to get the money, Pilot agreed to help him further. Otherwise they'd have ruined him.'

'By conniving at your kidnapping?'

'Yes.'

'Agreeing to be a victim too, so you wouldn't smell a rat?'

'Yes. Not that I realised that until just now.'

'So that Ralph could heroically rescue the pair of you?'

'Added to the kudos he'd get from bringing back the Whitman Collection, it should have been enough to swing his election as President.'

Penny could see that her father was upset. Betrayal, even by those from whom it might be expected, was always hard to take. 'Are they really planning to bump off the President?' she said.

'Not directly. But they knew of a group who was, and weren't going to do much to stop it.' Dr Wanawake sounded exhausted. He turned to her. 'Oh, Penelope, does no one have ideals any more?

177

Sometimes I think I should get out of politics altogether. The way people behave towards each other is so appalling.'

Using different words, Santini had said much the same thing. 'Yes,' she said. Or maybe she meant no. She glanced at the mirror. Headlights were coming up fast behind them. Friend or foe? She wasn't going to take any chances. She floored the car and felt the sudden surge of power. The coloured bulbs marking out Bonami's were closer now. She calculated they were about two miles away.

If her father was right, not-so-gentle persuasion was all the conspirators had in mind. Not death. Not murder. So how did Susannah fit into all this? Who had fired those shots at Eve Alphonse? Who, for that matter, had clonked her on the head and dumped her in Whitman's lake? While the answer to that one was probably Dezzy, it left the others hanging. She eyed the mirror again. The lights of the car behind were definitely closer now. So much closer that they were going to reach her well before she got to Bonami's.

'I don't suppose you carry a gun, do you?' she said. It was one of those hopes that gets bracketed with forlorn.

'Yes,' her father said.

'What?'

'It's standard practice.'

'Do you know how to use it?'

'Yes. Except —'

'Get ready to use it, Benj.'

'I can't. Unfortunately, Leo Nkasa removed it from me shortly after he'd picked Pilot and myself up.' He smacked his fist against his forehead. 'God, I've been naive. I should have realised long ago that Pilot was involved with this. That girl more or less told me so, but I refused to listen. She said she'd been snooping around up at Santalina and found out that Pilot was desperate for money and was seeing a lot of Nkasa. I'd assumed it was because they were old acquaintances.'

Penny was pointing like a retriever.

'Which girl?'

'The one that came down to interview me for her newspaper. Magazine. I don't remember which. She looked amazingly like you.'

'*Whaaat?* You mean you actually talked to Susannah?'

'That's right. Susannah Alphonse. Eve's girl.'

'Yes.'

'And Whitman's, of course. Not, apparently, that she was aware of that. Not at first. When she rang up and fixed an interview, she didn't tell me her name, just the magazine she worked for. Or newspaper. She said she wanted to talk about Senangaland, since it was very much in the news at the moment. Naturally, I agreed, though I told her it was pointless for her to come to the beach house since I was going back to San Francisco that same evening and could see her there.'

'Why didn't she buy that?'

'She said she was seeing someone in Carmel the following day so it would all dovetail very neatly.'

'Did she drive down?'

'Yes. At least, she came down by car. I don't know who did the driving, her or her friend.'

'Which friend?'

'She said something about a friend coming along for the ride. Waiting for her on the beach.'

Leo Nkasa. Killing a brace of birds. Enjoying a couple of days' vacation with his girl. And checking up that his intended snatch victim was going back to San Francisco as planned, ready to be set up by Whitman. 'What was she wearing for this interview?' she asked.

'A natural linen jacket and skirt over a striped shirt,' Dr Wanawake said. One of his most endearing traits was his interest in women's fashions.

'Not the bottom half of a bikini?'

'She may well have had that on as well. If so, she didn't offer to show me,' said Benjamin.

'What did she ask you about?'

'She was obviously a good journalist. She'd done a lot of background work on modern-day Senanga and my work at the UN. She had a great many intelligent questions to ask. And then somehow, we got on to the past. The colonial era. She seemed to know several people I'd known: the Nkasas and Whitman, for instance. I suppose that's natural, since she was Eve's daughter. She seemed particularly interested in a whole lot of gossip and scandal that we were once involved with. I'm not frightfully good at that sort of thing. I said she should have been talking to your mother, not me. But I told her about Whitman's wife dying, and Georgie Lambton being expelled from the country, and Eve and . . . oh dear.'

'What's the matter?'

179

'I even dredged up that old scandal about Henry Lambton's murder. How Eve and Pilot Whitman were implicated. If I'd realised she didn't know Whitman and Eve were . . . I'd never have . . .'

'How did she react?'

'Badly. She went a most curious colour. I hadn't appreciated that she wasn't already aware of her relationship to Pilot. She seemed absolutely dumbstruck. "You mean Whitman's *my* father as well?" she said. Of course I had to say that he was, as far as we all knew. And she said: "But that means . . ." Then she was suddenly taken ill like that and was forced to terminate the interview. She kept saying it was just like *White Mischief*, whatever that means.'

'It's the name of a film, Pa.'

But it was black mischief that killed her. With her quick journalist's brain, she must have instantly recognised not just the truth but its implications. That she'd been sleeping with her own brother. That they could never marry. That the shadow of that could dog her footsteps into the future. Susannah, the feminist. Susannah the ambitious, who was really going to make them sit up and take notice. Had she seen in those dreadful moments the death of all she had ever wanted, both politically and emotionally? No wonder she was taken ill. Had she stumbled down to the beach where he was waiting, told him what she'd just learned?

No. More likely she'd gone to the car she'd been driven down in, had changed into her bikini, gone running past him where he waited on the beach, gone splashing into the sea to swim away some of the self-disgust she must have felt. And then later when she told him, he'd tried to put his arms around her, to say it didn't matter, that they'd work it out somehow, and she'd backed away in horror, angering him so that he'd struck her on the head and . . . what then? Had he sat down there on the beach with her? Had he pretended she was sunbathing or asleep, waiting until darkness came and the other beach people left? Waiting until Dr Wanawake had come out of his house and gone up to the parking area and driven away? Had he dragged her up across the sand and dumped her on the deck, arranged her in that seductive pose, gone back to San Francisco, carried on with his own plans, waiting for someone to find her?

Plausible, Miss Wanawake. Very plausible. Neatly covering most of the facts. But *all* of them? She tried to recap, tried to sort theory from fact. From here, now, the diamonds seemed little more than an irrelevancy, nothing to do with Susannah at all. They had to do with Georgie, were only one of the strands which wove together into this complicated plaiting of events.

She glanced into the rear-view mirror again. The car was filled with distracting light from the following vehicle. It seemed so near it might have been touching theirs. The driver had his headlamps full on, dazzling her. Why was he so close? What was he trying to do? Ahead she could see the coloured bulbs which marked the edge of the Bonami Winery. She realised with a thrill of fear that she wasn't going to make them in time.

The car behind suddenly swerved out into the road. It drove parallel with hers for a while. She glanced sideways. It was the white pick-up truck. Thank God. Against all the odds, it had been friend after all, not foe. She lifted her foot from the throttle and pulled the car to a stop.

'Wait here,' she said to her father. She got out and ran down the road towards the truck which had overtaken her and come to a stop against the grass verge. As she approached, the door opened and a man jumped down. He wore a black Chicago Bears T-shirt. Over it, white dungarees.

'Josh,' said Penny, 'am I glad to see you.'

'Are you?' he said.

That was when she took in the gun. He was no more than a yard away from her yet it was almost invisible in his hand. It pointed straight at the middle of her forehead.

If he fired, she was dead meat.

Slow, she thought. That's what I've been. Slow and stupid. She should have seen it all long ago. From the minute he'd thrown that casual 'Hi, Soos', at her over his shoulder. They were alike, she and Susannah, sure. But no one who loved either of them could possibly have mistaken one for the other.

Parallel lines, she thought. She'd been looking for links in a chain, not a set of parallel lines. It was the natural tendency to think that one event followed on from another. That wasn't always how it worked. Just because Susannah had been killed on Benjamin's deck didn't mean that the murder was related to the subsequent kidnap. Even though the principal players in the various dramas were all interconnected, it didn't mean that they were working towards the same end. Georgie Lambton, the Nkasas, Whitman, Susannah: they'd all wanted different things.

'Oh, Josh,' she said sadly. Love's old sweet song causing trouble once again. 'What a mess you've got yourself into.'

'Not me, baby,' he said. 'You.'

'What good's it gonna do, Josh?' she said. 'It won't bring her back. Nor Courtney Collins.'

The chunky body jerked. 'How'd you know about him?'

'It's obvious. She was supposed to be driving down to Monterey with him; I suppose he'd have dropped her off and gone on to see his family, then picked her up again on the way back. The poor guy could have led the cops straight to you.'

'How?'

'By telling them that he didn't drive Susannah south after all. That her dear friend Josh Peters had suggested that they make a weekend of it. So you – I guess you had a picture or something to deliver to Whitman.' She remembered the flat rectangular package in the porch of the pink castle. 'You got hold of Courtney somehow – down at the Jumpin' Bean place, perhaps.'

'Is that right?' Peters said. He sounded real interested.

'Courtney must have met you before, he wouldn't have been suspicious. He'd have gone along if you suggested a beer or something, maybe across the road at the pizza parlour, some place like that.' She watched his eyes waver and knew she'd guessed right.

'And later you went somewhere less public where you could waste him. After which you drove out to Whitman's place, dumped him in the lake and came on home again. Could be . . .' She pictured Josh's kitchen, the first time she was there. 'Could be you stopped by Bonami's, picked up a crate of the Cabernet or the Zinfandel or whatever. Just in case anybody wondered why you were up there. Then I guessed you panicked. Drove back later, removed the body, dumped it out of the truck in Bonami's vineyards, just in case.'

'Ain't you the *cutest* mink?' Josh said. His voice was savage.

'Oh now. I hate that kind of talk,' Penny said. She scanned the road behind her. Black. Impenetrable. The little coloured lights of Bonami's, half a mile away, were the only lights she could see. No cars coming in either direction. No help.

'But that still left Eve Alphonse,' she said. 'You couldn't be sure she didn't know about the change in plan too – her and Susannah being so close and all. Which is why you fired at her from the roof across from her house. And why' – it came to Penny like a flashlight being switched on – 'why you threw her over the balcony at the hospital. What'd you do, Josh? Suggest the two of you walk down to the sun lounge and sit on the balcony for a spell, get some fresh air? Or was she already out there when you arrived with your grapes or your flowers or whatever?'

182

'Something like that.'

If only Benjamin still had his gun. Penny knew why intended victims tried to keep the man with the gun talking. They were buying time, wanting the last few seconds of their lives to last for ever. She knew she hadn't a prayer. This man had already killed three times. Two more murders would not add substantially to his sentence if the law ever caught up with him, and they might just save his skin if it didn't.

She smelled the scent of some flowering plant, heavy in the darkness. Felt the roughness of the road under her feet. Life was sweet. What a cliché. What a substantial overriding truth.

'You don't understand,' he said suddenly. 'You've never known the kind of squalor I grew up in. I was never going to go back to that. And with my reputation growing every year, I'd never have had to. If Susannah hadn't died.' He made it sound as if she'd done it deliberately. 'I didn't mean to kill her, you must see that.'

'Why must I?' Was that the click of a car door behind her? Penny prayed that her father would stay where he was. Maybe, just maybe, Josh hadn't realised he was in the passenger seat.

'I loved her,' Josh said, 'and she loved me. She always came back to me. Always.'

'Except this time, you realised she wasn't going to, right?'

'She came running out of the sea,' Josh said. 'She threw herself on me. She was all wet and salty. She said it was so awful, so awful that two people like us could love each other and yet it wasn't a marrying kind of love.'

'What did you do, Josh?'

'I said, far's I was concerned it was. Always had been. She was right there on top of me, you know? All scrunched up in my arms. Warm and soft and . . . and naturally I started to get kind of horny. So I undid her bikini top, just to, like, you know, like we had lots of times before.'

'And she pulled away.'

'Yeah. Like I was Count Dracula or something. Said she just didn't feel like that about me any more. That we were like brother and sister. And then she started screaming and sobbing, saying, oh *Josh*-yew-ah, what'm I going to do? You can't marry your brother.'

'And?'

'I said the hell with that. I said, I'm not your brother, no way. Said, come on, Soos, let's do it. Come on, baby. So she tried to get away from me, her face all disgusted. Said if I would listen to what she was saying I'd understand. And she got up and ran off, so I ran

183

after her. I was kind of mad by then, so I hit her.' He looked at her beseechingly. The slaughterer begging the lamb for forgiveness before he slit its throat. 'I sure as hell didn't mean to kill her.'

'What did you hit her with, Josh?' Penny said. All around was darkness and silence. Death was imminent. She could see that in the way his muscles were tensing, his mouth was firming up.

'My hammer. My geological hammer. Never go anywhere without it. I swear I didn't even realise it was in my hand. And she just kind of fell down there in the sand.'

He frowned. The lines were still forming when Penny kicked out. Half of the body's length is in the leg. On a person six feet tall, that meant three feet of snapping flesh and bone. For once she got it right. Her foot connected with his hand, knocking the gun into the back of the truck behind him. Together they listened as it clattered into a metal corner. Then he turned, lunging for it, plunging across the raised panel to scrabble desperately towards it.

She hadn't a hope of getting there first. She didn't even try. Instead, she thought herself into his mind. It didn't help. Confusion. Panic. The need to cover his tracks. He'd clawed his way up out of the Chicago slums where he'd been raised, built himself an international reputation, achieved all the things he'd wanted. Then a moment's rage, or disgust, or whatever else it was that had swept over him as Susannah told him she didn't want to make love with him, and the whole edifice had crumbled like a sandcastle. If only he'd listened to her. She would have told him about Leo being her brother. He'd have realised that once again she would have come back to him, when the first rush of grief was over. Instead, out of anger, out of a momentary sexual frustration, he'd killed her.

And gone on killing. Courtney. Eve. Then been afraid that Eve had passed on to the nosey black girl the information about the change in drivers that he thought she possessed. Penny realised he must have followed her here from the hotel that evening. He obviously still thought that if he wiped her out and then her father, sitting behind her in Barnaby's car, he could get away with it.

She started to speak. To say to that frantic back: 'After me, and my father, there's Mrs Fontaine, and Mr Whitman, and Leo Nkasa. And then to be safe, you'd have to get rid of Professor Ralph Nkasa. And probably Lisa Druckner, too. And there'd be others.' She'd only managed half a sentence when from behind her there was a shot. Peters collapsed across the tailgate. In the glare of the headlights she saw how the blood spread across the back of his dungarees, and his legs went suddenly limp, as though the spring which worked them had broken. He grunted, his head working up and down as he tried to straighten and found he couldn't.

Behind her, Dr Wanawake called. He sounded cool. 'Did I get him?'

She turned. He was standing against the open car door, both hands on the top rim. She couldn't see the gun. It had to be there somewhere in the dark. She might have known Barnaby kept one. In the glove compartment, perhaps, or taped to the bottom of the driver's seat. Some damnfool James Bond place like that. Clever of Benjamin to have realised. 'My God,' she said. 'I didn't know you were a crack shot.' Tears came into her eyes.

'Neither did I,' her father said modestly. 'Last time I went for target practice, I didn't score a single point.'

'It's a good thing your eye was in tonight.'

Her father came towards her. He took her in his arms and stroked her hair the way he had done when she was a child. 'That's right, sweetheart,' he said. 'But then it would have been. It's called the eye of love.'

19

'I'm glad I didn't kill him,' Dr Wanawake said. 'I would have found that hard to live with.' Through the wide windows of the airport's VIP lounge he watched a woman on a stretcher being carried aboard a United Airlines carrier. Behind her came three nuns, each carrying a black zippered flight bag. Penny wondered if the plane was flying south; whether Santini was already aboard, discreetly handcuffed to his prisoner.

'I feel sorry for him,' rumbled Professor Nkasa. 'He didn't mean to kill Susannah Alphonse.'

'But he did mean to kill Eve.' Penny held her glass out for more champagne. Barnaby filled it. 'He tried to shoot her in cold blood, and when that didn't work, he went to the hospital and shoved her off the balcony.'

'Ironic, really, that if he'd done nothing, she might have died from the effects of the pills she'd taken,' said Barnaby.

'Even more ironic that he killed her to prevent her passing on information she didn't even have.' Outside, a man with crutches hobbled to the foot of the aeroplane steps and looked helplessly about him. 'It would have been almost impossible to pin Susannah's murder on him.'

'And even if they had, he could have pleaded involuntary manslaughter,' said Barnaby. 'Juries tend to look sympathetically on crimes of passion, don't they?'

Which is what this one had turned out to be. Susannah coming down on to the beach to tell him, her best friend who'd driven her down the coast when her own car conked out, that she'd planned to marry Leo Nkasa – and before she could get out the terrible 'but . . .', before she could scream out her despair at the incestuous veto that would now make it impossible, Josh, frustrated love raging inside him, had brought the lethal hammer down on her skull.

Tangled webs, thought Penny. However hard they tried, the deceivers couldn't avoid them. Gossamer-thin to start with but, before they realised, grown into ropes strong enough to hang a man. She thought of Susannah, laid out on Benjamin's wooden deck among the camellias and gaudy birds-of-paradise plants. Josh's last sight of her, posed as he had painted her once, with the eye of love. She'd never gone along with Oscar on the idea that each man kills the thing he loves. Oscar loved a good line, but this one meant little, if anything. And said nothing at all about the shattering effect of accidentally, hot-bloodedly, doing just that.

'Hey, Barnaby,' she said. Kept her voice easy, idle, uncaring. 'Ever meet Joshua Peters?'

Barnaby put his glass down carefully. The guy had red hair, right? That didn't mean his face was red, too. Not usually. Not like it was now, the blood pushing up under his skin until it reached way into his hair. 'What're you saying, hon?' he said. Man hadn't got a care in the world.

'Just asking a simple question. Requiring a simply yes or no.' Yet she knew whatever answer he made, it wouldn't be simple. Not that she needed any further answer. That giveaway flush told her everything she wanted to know. She wondered what he would say when he discovered that the Fabergé brooch he'd stolen from the Contessa had gone. For that matter, what the Contessa would say when she discovered that the Fabergé parure she now owned was the fake Barnaby had commissioned from the gifted Mr Peters, and not the real one she had lifted back from Barnaby at the Sheraton-Regis. It takes a thief to catch a thief. It takes Penny Wanawake to catch them both.

After all this time, Georgie Fontaine, formerly Lambton, deserved the set more than either. How lucky Penny had been that, usually inept, for once her attempts at breaking and entering had worked like a dream. The substitution of Barnaby's fakes for the Contessa's real had been easier than she could possibly have anticipated. She was gone again from the Contessa's suite before the low-level loo had finished flushing.

Over by the door, the two FBI men conversed together. Between them stood Leo. His face was cold. He avoided looking at his uncle. What would happen to Leo? Had he committed a crime? Her father was not pressing charges. They would all be flying back East together. Professor Nkasa and Dr Wanawake were to join the White House reception alongside the President of Senanga. After which, Professor Nkasa would be overseeing the removal of Whitman's collection back to Senanga. It was up to him what political hay he would subsequently make of it. If he had any sense at all, he would steer well clear of ambitious nephews. She watched as, for the dozenth time, he took a letter from his pocket and read it. 'I was going to ask her to marry me,' he'd said. 'I wanted so much for her to know I didn't blame her for Rebekah.' It was not a suicide note, as the hospital thought, but an apology for past wounds, now healed. 'I'm sorry,' Eve had written, and got no further before Peters had pushed her over the balcony's edge.

A tannoyed voice announced that the flight to Washington would shortly be boarding. Barnaby stood up. 'Good luck, sir,' he said. He tilted his glass at Dr Wanawake. 'I've got something for you.'

'Oh.' Dr Wanawake looked faintly apprehensive. 'What?'

'In case no one thanked you for saving Penny's life . . .'

'I did, actually,' Penny said.

'. . . I'd like to express my own personal appreciation.' He felt in his pocket and pulled out a small gift-wrapped box. 'I thought you might like this.'

'How very kind of you,' Benjamin said. 'What can it . . .' He pulled at the gold ribbon tied round the package. Inside was a snuffbox, the blue enamel bright against the diamonds which decorated it. He looked at his daughter. She raised her eyebrows at him. 'I don't know what to say,' he said.

'Svinhuvud's not as tough as he thinks,' said Barnaby. 'I haggled him down much further than he wanted to go.' Penny had the impression that he was smiling, though there was no hint of it on his face. She wondered how long Barnaby had known about the snuffbox collection at Hurley Court. Whether her father ought to see about removing it to somewhere more impregnable than the small windowless room where it was currently housed. Probably should, just to be on the safe side. If there was such a thing. After the last few days, she wasn't sure.

Benjamin closed the lid on the valuable little object and placed it carefully in the inside pocket of his suit. 'Thank you,' he said.

'In case you hadn't realised just how much your daughter means to me,' began Barnaby, 'perhaps I could take the opportunity to say that I —'

Benjamin held up his hand. 'Please,' he said. 'Snuff said.'

Penny assumed it was meant to be a joke.